aug 2010

STRANGER

STRANGER

A Death Valley Mystery

Melissa M. Garcia

iUniverse, Inc.
New York   Bloomington

Stranger
A Death Valley Mystery

iUniverse books may be ordered through booksellers or by contacting:

iUniverse
1663 Liberty Drive
Bloomington, IN 47403
www.iuniverse.com
1-800-Authors (1-800-288-4677)

Because of the dynamic nature of the Internet, any Web addresses or links contained in this book may have changed since publication and may no longer be valid. The views expressed in this work are solely those of the author and do not necessarily reflect the views of the publisher, and the publisher hereby disclaims any responsibility for them.

ISBN: 978-1-4502-3691-1 (sc)
ISBN: 978-1-4502-3692-8 (dj)
ISBN: 978-1-4502-3693-5 (ebk)

Library of Congress Control Number: 2010908431

Printed in the United States of America

iUniverse rev. date: 07/21/2010

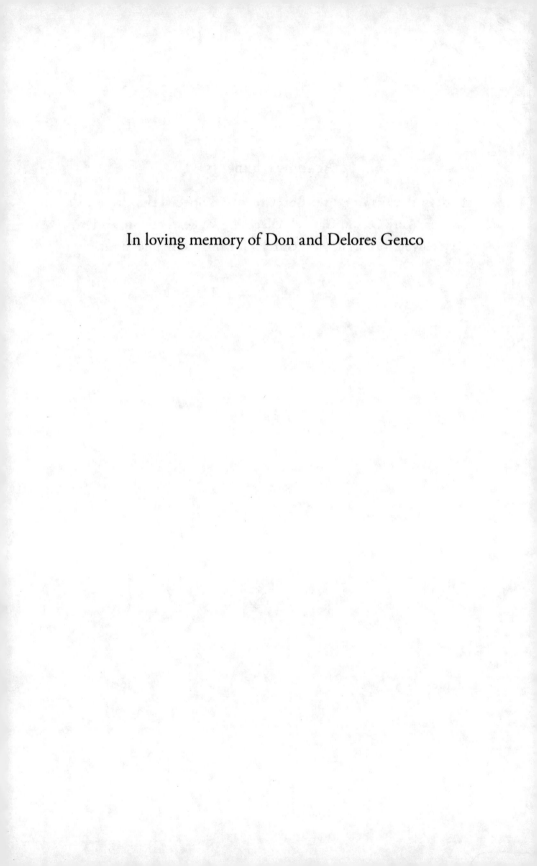

In loving memory of Don and Delores Genco

Acknowledgments

My deep thanks to Editor Bob Greenleaf. Special thanks to Lisa Collins, Amy Olson, Garrick Olson, Mike Featherston, and my beloved husband, Neri Garcia, for their valuable input.

Chapter 1

What happened to Tuesday?

She stared at the desk calendar and tried to remember the past twenty-four hours. *Could she have forgotten an entire day?*

Alex Delgado remembered every day she had been in prison. She could recall every minute of the ten years, two months, and seven days she had spent behind bars. There were days, early on, when she would have encouraged the blackouts. There were nights she would have loved to erase from her mind.

She had thought the memory lapses were in her past. She hadn't had a blackout since the night she'd been arrested.

"Did you hear me?"

She looked up at her brother, Ric, standing in the doorway of the office.

"I said the guy's dead in room 110."

"I heard you," she said, ignoring the sick feeling in her stomach.

1

Staring out the window at the brown desert, she wiped the perspiration from the back of her neck. She tried to keep the fear from rising in her gut. She didn't want to go back to prison. She rubbed her head, which was starting to pound at the temples—a side effect of the memory lapses.

Their guest had arrived on Saturday. Saturday she remembered. She even remembered Sunday and Monday, despite the fact that every day in this small, boring desert town was exactly the same as the day before.

She couldn't forget him because he was the only person staying in the motel other than herself and her brother. He hadn't looked sick. Nor had he looked suicidal.

"Please tell me he was older than he looked."

"Age wasn't an issue."

She turned to her brother. He was wearing a white wife-beater and black shorts. His arms were covered in tattoos, the largest a fading crucifix on his right forearm. There were also black stripes lining his left shoulder. His left arm was covered in Aztec art—a fading yellow sun, a pyramid, and a black snake with red eyes that slithered toward the black stripes. She had no idea how many more he had. The tattoos and his dark eyes gave him a menacing look.

"Alex, I gotta ask …" He didn't finish. He didn't need to. He was pacing now. That worried her more than the dead body in room 110.

"I didn't do it," she told him, but a sick feeling in her stomach made her wonder if she did have something to do with this man's death. *Why couldn't she remember yesterday?*

"What's the scene look like?"

He stopped pacing and looked at her now. She waited for an answer despite the annoyed look on his face. He sighed.

"Door was closed, but no deadbolt. He was dressed. Looks like one shot to the side of the head. Dropped by the bed. Thirty-eight revolver at his feet. Blood and brain matter on the dresser."

"Revolver?"

He nodded and then rubbed his hand over his face.

She clicked on the fan and laid her head on her hand and closed her eyes to think. As her head continued to pound, her fear turned to nausea. The fan cooled the back of her neck as the sun warmed her face. She pushed away the fear. She needed to think.

She shouldn't have complained about the boring quiet life in Lake City, Nevada. It was better than prison.

She had gone to bed Monday night. As always she had trouble sleeping. *Then what?* The fog had crept into her brain. She remembered coming down the stairs to the office just before seven and relieving her brother at the front desk. He'd gone off to clean the rooms.

But the calendar showed Wednesday.

She hadn't heard a gunshot. Her room, 200, was close enough to room 110; she would have heard it. All she remembered was blackness. She tried to will her memory back, but knew the missing hours wouldn't return. They never had before.

"I need to see it."

She pulled her long black hair back in a ponytail. She felt Ric's eyes on her but she ignored him. She grabbed a lint brush from the drawer and rolled it across her chest and shoulders. She grabbed a pair of cleaning gloves for good measure.

"Not a good idea."

"Give me the card."

He handed her the card. "Don't do anything stupid."

She walked out of the office into the parking lot of the Death Valley Motel. Scanning the parking lot, the street, and the other rooms, she approached the door to room 110. She waited for a pickup truck to drive past, and when everything was quiet again she swiped the card, saw the green light flash, and slipped in.

Standing in the crime scene, her lungs expanded as if filling with air for the first time. She felt her heartbeat in every inch of her body as her eyes searched the room. She felt awake and alert. The fear of returning to prison faded, replaced by her childhood memories of wanting to be a cop.

She scanned the edges of the room first, taking in the scene. There was no forced entry. No sign of struggle. The back of the door was clean. A plaque hanging just under the peephole listed the checkout time. The window was closed, the shades drawn, the bedside lamp lit. It looked like a normal motel room, except for the smell.

The air wasn't on, making the room stuffy. That bothered her more than the stench of blood and the early stages of decomposition permeating the room. She could see no blood splatter on the window or drapes. She looked across the room, ignoring the body on the floor. The room seemed bare, even for a motel room, with no personal belongings visible. It reminded her of her own room upstairs.

The bathroom door was wide open. No blood on this door, either, but as her eyes traveled around the room, back to where she stood, she saw the deep red splatter on the television stand and the wall behind. More dried blood covered the dresser.

And gray brain matter, still wet.

A shot to the head. Their guest was tall. If he had been standing, the splatter was too low. *Maybe he was kneeling or sitting on the floor*, she thought. She felt her headache worsen.

She walked to the closet and edged it open. The rod was empty. A small suitcase sat on the floor. Moving aside the L.A. Dodgers cap on top, she flipped open the top and inventoried the clothes. Two shirts, tee shirts, two pairs of shorts, underwear, and socks. The guy didn't need much, and he hadn't bothered to unpack. She closed the bag.

Slipping off her flip-flops, she tiptoed carefully around the blood on the floor. The bed was empty, the pale blue bedspread pulled back to reveal the white sheet underneath, also splattered with blood.

She found a condom wrapper, torn open on the floor. She opened the nightstand drawer and found it empty. No wallet or cell phone anywhere.

She looked at the mass on the floor beside the bed. The skin was gray. She didn't check for rigor; she didn't need to touch the body to know he'd been dead for hours. His mouth was open slightly, as if he were about to whisper a secret. She didn't look at his eyes, but she was positive it was the same man she had seen check in on Saturday. She was sure of that even though a portion of his head was gone and the rest was covered in dark blood.

In his late thirties, he had arrived alone. She had noticed a bad vibe as soon as he walked in the office. His intense, cold stare told her he was tougher than his small build suggested.

She had been concerned about the limp. He was too young for back problems. She presumed he was a gangbanger, but he was older than the guys she knew in Los Angeles. She guessed he'd been caught in a gun battle before and had escaped with just the limp.

This time he hadn't been so lucky.

He was dressed in jeans, a white tank top, and socks that had started out white but were now black from drying blood. His shoes were kicked aside, the shoelaces missing. She found the laces lying under the chair.

Tattoos covered his arm. On his left breast, above his heart, was penned the number *18*. She found the *666* tattooed on his right hand.

A silver chain hung around his neck. She recognized the martyr on the metal: St. Jude. *Patron saint of lost causes.* She wasn't sure why she did it, but she pulled the necklace from him, wiped the blood off, and slipped it in her pocket.

As she started to back up, she spotted the gun on the floor—a revolver. It looked old. Well used or not well kept.

She looked down at the man's half-obliterated face. The gore didn't bother her. She'd seen worse.

She looked back at the condom wrapper and then the gun.

She was capable of finding a revolver. She was capable of pulling the trigger. She had access to the rooms. In the darkness of her brain where she couldn't remember, she could have come down the stairs to his room, opened the door with a keycard, and shot this man in the head. *But why?*

She glanced back at the television and the spray of blood. From where he had fallen, it was easy to explain it away as a suicide. A stranger in a lonesome desert town. But as Alex looked at the bed, she stopped. The fitted sheet that normally hugged the mattress was missing. The remaining sheet was pulled loose from the mattress and lay limply over the bed. Alex backtracked and checked the trash. She noticed a fast food bag, but no sheet. She slipped on her shoes and reviewed the room again, making sure she left no evidence that she had been there.

Why was he in Lake City? Why was the blood splatter so low? The shoe laces, the missing sheet? There were no answers in this room, only more questions.

She glanced through the peephole before walking from the room. She closed the door behind her and followed the hallway straight to the dumpsters behind the motel. She peered over. A sheet lay right on top of the trash, marred by several black stains. Blood.

Her head pounded as she stared at the bloody sheet. She looked back at the door of room 110. She had no reason to kill this man, but she knew she would be the perfect suspect.

Chapter 2

Ric was watching a movie when Alex returned to the office. Two extremely uncomfortable folding chairs provided the only seating in the room. Ric sat in one of the chairs in front of his so-called entertainment center: a 20-inch television, a DVD player, and a printer. His feet were propped up on Alex's desk.

He had pulled on a long-sleeve shirt to cover the tattoos, or to cover his past. His eyes were no longer red. He looked respectable now, respectable enough so he wouldn't draw interest from the cops that would be swarming soon.

He would seem relaxed to most people, but Alex saw his interest wasn't in the movie. He often put his feet up when he was heavy in thought. She also recognized the worry on his face.

She threw him the keycard and took off her gloves. He caught the card one-handed without taking his eyes from the screen.

Cheerful music spilled from the speakers. Confused, she peered over

7

her brother's shoulder and recognized the movie. Mr. Blonde was pulling a shaving blade out of his boot. Alex watched as he danced around to the music. The camera panned to the left, and the playful music increased. Then shrieks of pain filled in the blanks that the image refused to show.

Alex knocked Ric's dirty boots from the desk and turned away from the screaming. "Call it in," she said.

Behind Ric was her makeshift kitchen, a sink and a coffeemaker. She poured out the stale coffee and made a fresh pot.

"Already did," he said. "Patrol's on the way. You need to leave."

She shook her head. It would be the smart thing to do, but she couldn't leave now. Her blood was moving. "I think it's time to meet the local pigs."

He grunted at the term, but looked at her. "I wasn't asking."

She could see the concern in his eyes. "We both know talking isn't your specialty. Neither is being friendly to police. I'm staying."

He jabbed a finger at her. "*You* talking is dangerous. I can keep up a basic conversation about a dead body without drawing suspicion or shooting someone."

"Fine. I'll stay quiet if you promise to be good. Either way, I'm staying."

He said nothing.

She opened the refrigerator. Only she and Ric knew it never held food, but rather the surveillance system they had installed less than a month earlier.

The red light glowed. As always, Ric had thought ahead and turned the cameras off before she walked into room 110. She pulled the disc from the recorder and took her time inserting a blank disc and setting it to record again. The green light lit up. She expected Ric to say something, but he remained silent.

"What was his name?" she asked.

"Eddie Chavez, from Henderson, Nevada, just outside Las Vegas."

He was still watching her, watching her hands. The concern on his face had changed to worry. He was thinking, and that made her uneasy.

She returned the stare until he turned back to the movie. He pushed up the volume on the remote.

She turned to the computer on her desk and glanced through the record he had pulled up on their guest. It was basic information Ric had received from the customer's driver's license. It would tell her nothing about why her guest had appeared in Lake City four days ago.

"Where's his car?" she asked.

He shrugged. "Missing. I didn't see it at all last night. I figured he was out when I went to clean the room."

No other guests were booked in any of the rooms. That meant the cops would be left with only Ric and herself to question as witnesses. This was going to be a problem. They would need to give the cops a suspect, or the cops might turn on their only witnesses.

She noticed there was a note on room 105 for cleaning. "Did we get someone else in last night?"

There was a pause. Alex looked back at her brother.

"Ric?"

"We had one check in last night. She stayed for a few hours, then checked out. Paid cash. It's already in the safe."

"Stop renting our rooms out to prostitutes. This isn't a brothel."

He didn't take his eyes off the movie. "Hey, hookers have to sleep somewhere, too. Last I checked, it's not a crime to check into a motel. I can't turn them away. They'll just find another place to do business. Besides, we could use the money."

She didn't bother to comment that he had given her five excuses. She had recently noticed he did that when he was uncomfortable with the conversation. Spending all this time in the hot desert alone was making her more conscious of his habits and his changing attitude.

"They're committing crimes inside our rooms," Alex rebutted, "and we have the cops on their way. She's now a witness." She recalled the scene. "Or a suspect."

He shook his head. "She wasn't here but a couple of hours. My guess, he bought the farm after she left."

Alex started to protest, but he held his hands up. "I'll find out for sure," he offered.

"Try not to mention her to the cops, or they'll have something else to hang me on."

She pulled her old sweater over her tank top. She didn't have any tattoos like her brother, but the scar on her right shoulder could bring unneeded attention. The sweater was old and ratty beyond anything her old pit bull had ever destroyed. It had once been red, and now couldn't even be called pink, but it was her favorite. It smelled of home, so she refused to throw it away. She would endure the heat for the comfort it now brought. The sweater was also a size too big. Not that she had meant to lose the weight. She had no desire to be 110 pounds. The weight loss had left her gangly and awkward. That's what happened when you sat in a prison cell for ten years, she supposed. If she continued to push herself, she would gain it back in muscle before New Year's.

Alex said, "I think he raped someone."

Ric looked at her. "How do you know?"

"There's a bloody sheet in the dumpster," she said.

"Maybe it's his blood on the sheet."

"Yeah, he walked over to the trash and dumped it in after he shot himself."

He shrugged. "Maybe the killer did."

"Why dispose of the bloody sheet? There's plenty more blood on the floor and walls," she said.

"Maybe the killer got cut and it's his blood."

"The dumpster would be part of the crime scene; the police will find it. If you're trying to prevent yourself from getting caught for murder, you hide the sheet better than that. The blood is completely dried. I think whatever caused that blood happened earlier. He had a gun. Condom wrapper and bloody sheet points to rape."

"You're stretching. Or projecting."

She started to argue, but he stood and stared out the window.

"Put the gloves back on. Your friends are pulling up now."

Alex obeyed her brother and put on the gloves. She slipped the disc into her sweater pocket.

"Last chance to take off," Ric said.

"Not a chance."

Chapter 3

Two patrol cars pulled into the lot. Two officers stepped from one cruiser. Alex watched as one pulled a box from his trunk and scanned the lot. The second stood waiting for instructions. Out of the second patrol car a third officer emerged, pulled on his jacket, and walked toward the office.

She quickly evaluated the three men and determined she could take any of them with no problem.

As the officer pushed open the door, Ric stepped forward and introduced himself first. Alex knew it was his way to assert his control in the room.

"My name is Patrol Sergeant Jeff Morgan with the Lake City Police Department."

The man's jacket covered his name badge. His pants were a dull green. His boots could have used some polish. His hair could have used a comb. His appearance didn't invoke a lot of confidence.

"You called dispatch about a deceased male?" The sergeant glanced at Alex and then back to Ric.

"He's in room 110." Ric handed him the keycard. "It's all yours. We'll be here when you're done."

At least he had kept it simple, Alex thought.

"My men will work the scene. What can you tell me about the victim?" he asked.

Alex watched Sergeant Morgan. He shifted his weight, but continued to slouch. She noticed his gun holster was unlatched. On his left side was his Taser. She stared at it until her focus was broken by the man's voice.

"Like I mentioned to dispatch," Ric continued, "we have a dead guest. Male, mid-thirties. Checked in four days ago. Gunshot wound to the head."

"Can you turn the television off for a minute?" the sergeant asked.

Ric flipped off the television and glanced at the sergeant. "Do you get distracted easily?"

"You said the dead body was in room 101. Who was registered to the room?"

Ric clenched his fists and then released with a sigh. "Room 110. If you're going to interview me, then do it right. I talk, you write. There's no excuse for lousy police work."

Alex prayed her brother wouldn't blow up. She didn't want to play referee.

"I'm just doing my job, Mr. Delgado. If you let me, I can be out of your hair quickly. Otherwise, we'll do the interview at the station."

Ric's eyebrows rose. "Are you going to arrest me, Sergeant?"

He didn't answer, but he did glance at Alex again. Maybe he had hoped she would help him out. She decided to keep her mouth shut.

"Who was registered to room 110?" Sergeant Morgan asked.

"He said his name was Eddie Chavez."

"How did he pay?"

"Cash."

Morgan shifted his feet, wrote a note and then asked, "When was the last time you saw him?"

"I didn't see him yesterday and he refused housekeeping. I did see him Monday afternoon. He was leaving. I didn't notice him return."

"How did—"

"He seemed normal to me," Ric interrupted, expecting the question. "He didn't seem antsy or troubled. He didn't look angry or frightened. He didn't look suicidal either. He just drove out. I didn't ask where he was going."

"You have access to all the rooms?"

Ric didn't answer.

Alex turned at the sound of another car. A burgundy Escalade pulled to a stop behind the patrol cars. Clean and shiny, even in the desert dust. She wondered how a small town police department could afford such a vehicle.

A man stepped from the Escalade's driver's seat. He walked as if he owned the town, Alex thought. He wore jeans, tennis shoes, and an olive green polo shirt. Athletic build. Tall. Shades covered his eyes, but he had a stern look on his face.

A badge and a gun were at his right hip, but she could have pegged him as a detective without them. His walk was fast, determined, maybe even a little impatient, as he approached the officer stringing police tape around the parking lot. He pointed toward room 110, then toward the office. As the detective turned, she turned her head back toward her brother and the sergeant.

"Where were you yesterday?" the sergeant asked.

"I slept from noon to about six. I spent the remaining evening sitting right here. All night. I didn't hear anything. I checked his room this morning and found him dead on the floor. Called you guys right away."

"What else do you know about the victim?"

"He drove foreign wheels, but his car is gone."

"Foreign wheels? Mexican plates?"

"I'm done," Ric said, looking at Alex, obviously frustrated.

"Sergeant Morgan, I believe your detective just arrived," Alex said, pointing out the window.

Morgan turned to look. "Excuse me a minute."

After he left, Ric joined her at the desk.

"Your thoughts?" she asked.

"I'm wondering who Sergeant Moron slept with to get his stripes."

"Why the jacket? It's hot out there," Alex said.

"Either he forgot his badge or his name plate. He doesn't want to get caught so he covers his uniform with the jacket. What about the other cops?" Ric asked.

"They broadened the crime scene to include the parking lot and dumpsters. The taller one waited for the detective before he started taking pictures."

The sergeant spoke briefly to the detective before heading toward room 110. The detective headed toward the office.

"How are we playing this?" she asked her brother.

"Straight," Ric said. "Let me start. This guy isn't going to miss anything, so he's going to turn to you at some point to talk. Keep it simple," he said as the door opened.

"Mr. Delgado, I'm Detective Will Stellar." He offered his hand. "You found the body?"

Ric shook the man's hand. "Yes, sir. Ricardo Delgado. I'm the manager."

The detective turned his attention to Alex. He removed the sunglasses and dropped them on the counter. Ray-Bans. Expensive frames for a cop.

He reached his hand out to her. "And you are?"

"Alex," Ric answered for her. "Alex Delgado, my sister."

She didn't offer her hand.

Detective Stellar dropped his hand but continued to stare at her. His intense blue eyes seemed to look through her. She didn't look away. She should have, but her interest overpowered her reasoning. Strong jawbone.

Chin cleft. Just enough stubble to know he was a usual shaver, but recently he was neglecting his face. It gave him the rugged look, or the hungover look. His eyes looked alert and clear. Strong but observant.

He returned his focus to Ric and pulled out a notebook and pen.

"Fairly new in town?"

"Been here four months. Lived in Los Angeles before that."

Detective Stellar looked confused, as if he had never heard of Los Angeles before. As he wrote, Alex noticed the watch on his wrist. A Rolex, solid and expensive. She spotted a tattoo sneaking out from under the shirt, possibly a name, but she couldn't identify it.

"Tell me how you found the body?"

Ric folded his arms over his chest. "I thought he was already gone. I didn't see his vehicle. I went in to clean, but the blood on the walls was a little too much for me."

"And you're sure he was dead?"

Ric nodded. "Doesn't take a doctor. Half his skull is gone. It looked like an old .38 revolver on the floor."

"Are you familiar with guns?"

Ric smirked. "A bit."

He waited to see if Ric would elaborate. He didn't. Ric's shoulders relaxed, his face slackened. Stellar glanced at his notes. Alex reminded herself to breathe.

"Do you remember the make of the car?"

"Best guess from what I remember, it was probably a Benz. Newer model. Gray or black. Two-door. It's not in the lot."

Stellar wrote it down. "Did he provide identification when he checked in?"

"ID said his name was Eddie Chavez." Ric spelled it for him.

"Make a copy?" Stellar asked. Ric shook his head. "How many other guests do you have right now?"

"None. We're in a dry spell."

"Summer in the desert will do that. Was there anyone else with him?"

"He checked in alone," said Ric. "I never saw him with anyone. In fact, I don't think he knew anyone from town."

"You didn't clean the room yesterday?"

"No. He was in the room when we normally clean. I waited until noon, but he hadn't left. I knocked, but he said he was okay on towels."

"Did he open the door?"

"No."

The detective looked up. "Did you think that was odd?"

"Not at the time. I figured he was nursing a hangover or something. Drinking too much is a popular thing to do around here, right, cowboy?"

Ignoring the comment, Detective Stellar asked, "Did anyone else go in the room this morning?"

Alex held her breath. Ric had a thing about lying to cops. He never did it. Ever.

"I didn't see anyone go in."

The detective nodded and glanced up at Alex, as if to make sure she was still there. He turned back to Ric. "Did you hear anything last night? Maybe a gunshot?"

"Lots of 'em. Watched *Scarface* around eight. Then did a *Godfather* marathon right after. I never left the office."

Stellar grunted. "Good flicks." He looked at Alex. "Were you here last night?"

She nodded.

"She lives in room 200," Ric answered for her. "But she has the evenings off. She stays away from the guests."

Stellar kept his eyes on Alex. "Did you hear anything last night?"

She shook her head. Stellar seemed to consider this. Alex knew what he was thinking. A revolver is loud. She wished for her memory to return.

"Any visitors or phone calls in or out of his room?"

Ric shook his head. "He kept to himself. I never saw anyone with him and I checked the phone system. No calls, although I did see him with a cell phone when he checked in."

"Lonely man in a lonely town. If you think of anything else, let me know. Sergeant Morgan will be back later to have you complete an interview card. We'll get this cleaned up as soon as we can, but suicides can be a little messy."

He turned toward the door, but Alex couldn't let him leave.

"It wasn't a suicide."

Both men turned toward her. Her brother's eyes narrowed on her. She ignored his annoyance. The detective's eyebrows rose in interest.

"You don't know the man, but you don't think he's capable of suicide? Are you some sort of expert?"

She shook her head. "He has tattoos. I saw them when he checked in. He had '666' tattooed on his hand."

"So you think the devil came for him?"

"It's not devil worship."

He sighed. "I know. He's probably with the Eighteenth Street gang. This isn't my first encounter with Latino gangs, but even gangbangers have been known to commit suicide."

"He didn't commit suicide. The Eighteenth Street gang is known for auto theft, drugs, extortion—"

"Don't forget rape, assault, and murder. How do you know about Eighteenth Street?"

Ric coughed but didn't interrupt.

"And arms trafficking," Alex continued, ignoring the detective's question. "He would have had access to the very best automatic weapons. He wouldn't kill himself with a piece-of-shit revolver."

He was analyzing her again, as if his first estimate was incorrect. He wrote something down in his notebook. It made her uneasy, but she said nothing.

"Did you go into the room this morning?"

She shook her head. "I trust my brother when he tells me a guy's dead. Besides, I can't stand the sight of blood," she lied.

He continued to write, taking his time before looking back up at her.

Ric shifted, then moved between Alex and Stellar. "The room's yours, Detective. Let me know when you're done."

Stellar retrieved his glasses from the counter. At the door, he turned to Alex. "Thanks. I'm sure I'll be back later with more questions."

He smiled at her. It was the first crack in the stern demeanor, and Alex immediately felt uncomfortable. The stern look returned as he walked out into the sun, the shades already hiding his eyes again.

Alex watched the detective walk back to the Escalade. One of the men handed him a bag. She watched as Stellar scanned the parking lot. His head moved slowly. He spent a few minutes looking at the pool. Then his eyes moved to the motel room doors. Then the stairwell.

He's thorough, she thought.

"I don't like the cowboy," Ric said. "He's hung over."

"We all have our hang-ups."

Ric grunted. "He's arrogant and cocky."

"Have you ever met a good cop that wasn't?" She watched through the window as Stellar spouted orders to his officers.

"You know him?" she asked.

Ric didn't answer.

She looked at her brother. "You called him cowboy."

"I've seen him around. He rides horses. His family owns cows. I don't like the way he looked at you. I thought you were going to keep your mouth shut."

She turned back toward the window. "He's a small-town detective. He's not going to cause any problems for me."

Outside, Stellar took the camera Sergeant Morgan offered and walked slowly toward room 110, as if each step was more important than the last. Before he entered the room, he glanced back at the office.

"Too late," Ric said. "He's already decided we're suspects."

Chapter 4

Ric Delgado wasn't happy. He had known the second he'd walked into room 110 that he had screwed up. A man was dead. A stranger he didn't know, but the man was dead nonetheless.

The death had occurred much too close to his sister. She could handle it. If he'd had any doubt, he wouldn't have let her look at the scene, but blood and guts and gore had never bothered her. She had seen much worse, endured much worse. In that sense, she was stronger than he was.

The death brought back memories. It brought back emotions. It also brought the cops. He had sworn to keep all of that away from her. He had picked Lake City, Nevada, because it was far away from trouble. As far as he could be, at least.

Apparently, it wasn't far enough.

Walking into the office, Ric found Alex staring out the window. She was still wrapped in the homely sweater. He was surprised that her face held a light it hadn't a day earlier. Her eyes looked awake and alert. He was thankful she finally looked healthy again, but he knew the reason was a bad one.

"The ME and detective just left with the body," he said. "Sergeant Moron said they're bagging evidence and should be out of here within the hour."

Alex nodded, staring at the computer screen. "I want to review the discs."

Ric said nothing. He wouldn't stop her.

"I need to take a look at the guy's house first," she said. "I don't know how long we have until the detective confirms the identity and wants to take a look himself."

"No."

She stared back at him.

"I'm not a child."

"I didn't ask your age. You're not going to break into a dead guy's house," he stated. She wasn't going to shake him. Not this time.

"Eddie Chavez was in Lake City for a reason," she said. "His house may offer some clues. You know that."

"This may be true, but you're not going anywhere. You're not a cop."

"I can take care of myself, big brother," she mocked.

He didn't see the humor. "No. You got to see a dead guy with blood splattered everywhere. You had your fun this morning with the cops. Now we go back to being normal. Let the cops handle this and fade into the background."

"I'm not going to fade into any background. This guy died—"

"Lots of people died last night," he interrupted. "What makes this one special?"

He needed to hear her answer.

"I didn't kill him, Ric."

He said nothing.

"You don't even believe me. How the hell am I going to convince the cops I didn't do this? When they find out about me—and they will—I need to give them the real killer."

"You're staying here," he ordered. "You're not going to commit a B&E on my watch."

"Housebreaking. And I don't plan on stealing anything, so technically it's just trespassing."

He shook his head. "Semantics." He went over to the computer and printed out a copy of Eddie's address. "When the detective comes back, be nice and give him the discs. I won't be gone long."

He grabbed the paper from the printer.

"I'm coming with you."

"I work alone now. I'll handle the inspection of Eddie's home. You stay here."

She eyed him. "You sure? That's not exactly your specialty."

He looked at her, confused. "Searching a home?"

"Breaking and entering," she corrected. "Can you even pick a lock?"

"Don't be a smartass. You're lucky I'm doing this."

She sat down and slipped in a disc. Ric watched the image for a minute. Satisfied she would be safely occupied, he headed for his room. He wanted a nap, but he settled for a cold shower. He threw on black shorts and a white tee shirt. His arms were starting to lose their summer tan. He spent so many daylight hours sleeping that he wondered if he was becoming a hermit. His life consisted of hours upon hours of movies and periodic naps throughout the day.

He had once worked out regularly. At forty years of age, his body was still strong, but now it often reminded him of his age. In the past six months he found his energy was diminishing and the morning aches and pains were more pronounced. His stomach was also showing the signs of his lack of activity. He had always loved food and now with the loss of his metabolism, the effects of that love was evident. Soon the body he had worked so hard to make solid and threatening would become overweight and old. Alex had the pool to stay in shape, but Ric despised the water. Maybe he could convince Alex to turn one of the rooms into a gym.

He put on his watch and confirmed it was working properly. Stuffing an energy bar in his mouth, he walked out to his truck. The last of the Lake City Police were packing up to leave as well.

He sat in his truck and stared at the road. If he turned right he'd head West toward California and into Death Valley National Park. Turning left he'd head straight toward Las Vegas, the sin capitol of the world. He made the turn and followed the signs to U.S. 95 southeast toward Las Vegas.

Speed limits never concerned him, so he kept the car above ninety the entire trip. There was little traffic in the middle of the Nevada desert and he made the trip in less than two hours. Henderson, Nevada, had been one of the fastest growing cities in the nineties, south of casino land. The view remained the same as the freeway continued: patches of flat, empty dirt fields and groupings of houses under construction. The dirt surrounded signs of upcoming elections and *Coming Soon* banners. Ric found Eddie's address easily. His house was the first in a tract of un-gated homes on the border of Las Vegas. Henderson had its own police department. Similar to most police departments across the country, it was short-staffed. He didn't expect to see any patrols in this neighborhood.

Ric spotted two young boys playing in the yard next to Eddie's. He parked far enough away to not look like a pedophile, yet close enough to see the entire scene. He dug out his binoculars from the glove compartment and focused on the children. Toy cars. One kid chased the other. Maybe cops and robbers. Good guys and bad guys. The air conditioner blew cold air in his face, but the sun was beating too strongly for him to stay cool.

He felt the excitement slowly building in his system. The thrill of the chase. It'd been a long time since he had played cops and robbers, but he still knew how.

It was almost three o'clock. Plenty of hours left of sunshine. He hoped the kids would have to go inside for dinner soon. A man alone in his car would eventually draw attention. This wasn't his first stakeout.

He knew the routine. Wait. Be patient. Always stay alert. Be cautious. Don't fall asleep, and pay attention to every detail. Blend into the surroundings. He considered calling Alex, but he enjoyed the silence in the car. He enjoyed being alone. She would be stuck at the desk examining surveillance video.

He should have known Eddie Chavez was going to be a problem when he checked in. The man's hard eyes had said he'd grown up on the streets. His limp said he had struggled to survive. The oversized shirt indicated he carried a pistol, and his walk suggested it wasn't an odd feeling to have a gun within reach. The man was hard, cautious, smart, and dangerous, but Ric hadn't flinched. He considered himself smarter, and more dangerous—when necessary.

He looked up at Chavez's house. He didn't expect anyone to be home. Chavez didn't appear to be the type to shack up with any one woman, and he didn't think any woman would hate herself so much as to find herself under his thumb. But Ric settled in to watch the house anyway.

Chapter 5

Autopsies were not William Stellar's favorite way to spend a Wednesday. He despised the sight of blood and death. He didn't fear it like most people. He respected it.

Stellar had seen his share of autopsies. He had trained for two years at Las Vegas Metro, where death was a round-the-clock business. Autopsies were rare in Lake City, which averaged three deaths a year. Often, an autopsy wasn't needed or requested, but if it was, Stellar made sure he attended. He still had a lot to learn. He didn't want to forget why he did the job he did.

His last autopsy was only a few days old. An eleven-year-old boy, Cole Wesley, had wandered off in the middle of the night while at the local camp and fallen into the lake. Stellar had never met the child before seeing his body tangled in the brush along the lake, but the image was still burned into his head. The autopsy had confirmed the accidental drowning. Stellar had drunk himself to sleep that night. And the next.

He wouldn't apologize for it, even if it meant nursing a hangover at a fresh crime scene. The town had yet to bury this innocent child before another dead body lay on the cold metal. By day's end, the town would be engrossed in rumors of the murdered stranger, and looking to Stellar for answers.

Doctor Stephen Wagstaff, known to everyone simply as Wags, served as the city's medical examiner. He was a short, burly man with a balding head and droopy eyes. Overly cautious and thorough, he was a man of few words outside his morgue. Stellar knew little about him personally, as he never saw him without his lab coat.

Wags said little directly to Stellar. He rattled off medical jargon while his assistant stood in the corner writing down every word. He never seemed to notice the sound of bodily fluids flowing down the drain. Moving smoothly and efficiently from one body part to the next, he didn't doubt his movements or break his rhythm. The mask covered his mouth as he rambled, and his eyes flicked back and forth, catching everything.

Not that he could miss anything. The body of Stellar's victim was splayed out like the offering in a satanic sacrifice. Internal organs were removed, weighed, and labeled. It was too horrific for Stellar to watch, so he kept his eyes on the skin that was still intact, the arms and legs. He saw no recent bruising, no needle marks. A wound on one leg was surely an old gunshot wound.

Stellar had seen enough in the room to know this wasn't a suicide. It was just instinct, nothing he could prove. What he needed from Wags was his honest opinion. If Wags said it was a homicide, Stellar would be off and running. If he said it was a suicide, well, Stellar would probably look for another coroner to drive down to Lake City and give him the answer he needed.

Probing his victim's head, Wags forced his hand into a skull crevice, shoving his fingers into the flapping flesh. Stellar stretched his neck from side to side and tried to concentrate on the doctor's words.

Wags grunted and pulled back. "That's it."

Stellar watched as the doctor pulled his right glove down halfway. With his right hand, he carefully pulled off the left glove. With his clean left hand, he took hold of the inside part of the right glove and pulled it the rest of the way off.

Stellar yanked off his clean gloves. "What do you think?" he asked as he followed Wags out of the cold room.

"Well, it's no surprise. Cause of death is the gunshot wound to the head. I'd place time of death between three and seven this morning. Shot with a .38. Stippling on the skin indicates the gun was held very close to his temple when it discharged."

"Consistent with a suicide?" Stellar didn't want to ask, but knew he had to.

"To the standard observer, sure, but I have a few issues with that conclusion, so the manner of death will be listed as homicide."

Stellar held back his smile, even though he wanted to jump for joy. Not because a man had been killed or because Stellar himself would endure days without sleep. No, he was not happy about having a killer in his city.

"Tell me what makes you think that?" Stellar said.

"Well, you have GSR on his right hand and arm. The palms and fingertips."

"Consistent with suicide. He fired the gun with his right hand, leaving gunshot residue."

"The back of his hand lacked GSR."

"You think someone cleaned up after?"

Wags shook his head. "No, I suspect someone held his hand on the gun. Probably forced him to pull the trigger. The GSR would show up in the palm, but not so much on the back of his hand. Someone was smart enough to make him pull the trigger but just dumb enough not to think it through. Probably watched too many of those crime dramas on cable."

Stellar nodded and wrote this down. Whoever had helped pull the trigger would have to be big enough to overpower his victim. "Anything else?"

"The shot was angled downward. The bullet entered above the right ear and traveled down, exiting his left jaw. That means the handle of the gun was held slightly above and behind." Wags mimicked with his hand. "It's a strange angle. It can be done, but with most suicides, you see more of an upward angle. Some even lose control of the gun as it goes off, only grazing the head. It's not consistent. I'll run a basic drug screen and will have preliminary results for you in the morning. Complete toxicology report will take about eight weeks—if we're lucky."

Stellar hated hearing about the crime lab back log.

He shook the doctor's hand. "I appreciate you getting to this today."

"No problem. Since it's a homicide, everything else will go to Metro to be processed." Wags continued walking down the bright hallway toward his office. Then he stopped and turned. "Are you going to Cole's funeral?"

"It's today?" Stellar asked. "That seems fast."

Wags shrugged. "Lincoln is paying for everything. He knows how rough it is on the family, decided to get it over with quickly."

Stellar considered this. He had expected his brother Lincoln to pay the funeral bill, but actually planning the event was another matter altogether. He was a busy man.

"He's feeling guilty," Stellar said.

"Cole was at his camp. The child was his responsibility."

Stellar shook his head. "Lincoln couldn't have known the kid would wander off in the middle of the night and fall into the lake."

"You and your brother are more alike than you realize."

Stellar shook his head. "No, I'm not feeling guilty. I didn't even know the kid."

"And yet, you're punishing yourself anyway." Wags pointed at Stellar's eyes. "I'm a doctor. I know what a hangover looks like."

Stellar rubbed his hands over his face. "I'm fine. Just tired."

Stellar looked at his watch. He was running short on time. He had a murder to solve, but people would expect him at the funeral. He couldn't let the dead overrule the living.

Chapter 6

S tellar stayed in the back pew during the church service. He could hear the priest mumbling and Ann Wesley, Cole's mother, wailing. He could see the confused faces of the children Cole had called his friends.

He said nothing as he walked from the church. He left the shaking of hands and the hugs of sympathy to everyone else. He wasn't there to offer his condolences. He had already done that. He had done all he could for the Cole family.

He watched as the coffin was carried out. Ann Wesley followed, surrounded by women he didn't know. Stellar followed far behind the crowd to the cemetery. As they stepped onto the grass, he held back. He found his truck and watched from the street as the crowd gathered around the empty hole. His sunglasses blocked the sun and allowed him to watch the attendees without revealing his own red eyes.

He caught snippets of conversation from the people passing. *Father Webster performed a beautiful service. Ann is holding up well …*

Leaning against his truck, he watched as people gathered around the hole in the ground. Dirt was piled to one side. All eyes were on Cole's mother. No one wanted to look at the little coffin.

Sergeant Jeff Morgan walked alongside Will's brother Lincoln. Morgan was Lincoln's best friend. He had changed into a black suit, a stark contrast to his rumpled uniform. His demeanor had changed, too—he stood straighter, his chin up. Maybe it was his wealthy background, or maybe it was from standing next to Lincoln.

Morgan sat to the right of Erika Mack in the back row, where she had been saving a seat. She looked stunning in her black dress and large, dark sunglasses. Every blonde hair was in place, and her lips shimmered in the sun. Even at a funeral she could turn heads. Her father and Will's boss, Police Chief Mack, sat behind her next to Wags.

Stellar watched as Lincoln and another gentleman set up flowers at the site. Lincoln directed the man, gesturing his impatience with him. Stellar realized there were more flowers than guests—obviously Lincoln's doing.

A violinist arrived. She spoke briefly to Lincoln, and then to the priest, and finally set up behind the flowers to play a sad melody. Stellar could barely hear it as the guests quieted down for the priest.

Lincoln spotted Will just after the priest began talking. He leaned over to speak to the tall, lanky man he'd been ordering around. He pointed toward Will and shook the man's hand.

As Lincoln walked toward him, Stellar's eyes stayed with the tall stranger. He didn't know him. He didn't know everyone in town, but he knew most of Lincoln's friends, and this man didn't look familiar. Stellar would have remembered him.

The man looked almost seven feet tall, with big hands. His face looked like a golf ball. He looked like a boxer from the fifties who had been pummeled in the face one too many times, but he was much younger, maybe mid-twenties. His hair was buzzed close, and dark sunglasses hid his eyes. He wore a wrinkled short-sleeve shirt and black slacks that appeared to be a size too small.

Stellar was always leery of strangers in town, especially with a murder scene just a few miles away. Strangers sucking up to his powerful brother made him even more cautious.

As Lincoln approached, Stellar pulled his eyes from the stranger. Lincoln wore a black Armani suit. Although they came from the same family money, Lincoln always found a way to look the part. Will was comfortable in jeans and a police polo shirt and carrying a gun. They were as close as brothers could be, and Will considered Lincoln his best friend.

"Detective," Lincoln said, offering his hand. "I appreciate you coming."

Will shook his hand and smirked at the formality. Lincoln was older than Will by only three years, but being the firstborn put Lincoln in a different class. Lincoln had been named after their father and was in every aspect his father's son. When their father had been stricken with Alzheimer's five years earlier, Lincoln had taken the family reins. He managed the family ranch, looked after their mother, and handled the family money.

Will wasn't jealous of his brother. He never cared about the money he had been born into or the burden it came with. At eighteen, he had moved out and defied his father to become a cop, leaving Lincoln to handle the family politics.

"You did a good thing here, Lincoln," Will said.

Lincoln tugged at his pocket and pulled out a pack of cigarettes. "I had no choice. If I left it to her, the boy would have been dumped in the desert somewhere with only a rock as a headstone. Damn vultures would be picking his bones right now."

Will looked at Lincoln. He was known for his crass edge, but it was a bit sharp today, even for him. Will knew it was a sign of hurt. They had been through their share of pain, but each handled it differently. Will's pounding headache rivaled Lincoln's bad attitude.

Lincoln lit a cigarette. "She's dirt poor. Just got kicked out of her apartment. I let her kid come to the camp as a favor. I couldn't have the kid living on the street, could I?"

He stood next to Will, leaning against the truck. He smoked as he watched the mourners gather around the hole. Despite his harsh edge, Lincoln had a heart of gold. He cared for the city and the people living there. He encouraged the homeless and destitute. He helped those who needed a helping hand, and he cried when he couldn't make a situation better for someone.

"Where is she staying?" Will asked.

"She's got another night at the apartment. I'm helping her pack it up tomorrow. I've got her a suite at the MGM in Vegas for a couple nights before her brother can come get her."

Will could see the despair in Lincoln's eyes as he stared at the tip of his cigarette. Nodding, Will watched as the priest released a white dove into the air. It jerked left, then spun right and took off into the cloudless blue sky. The bird soared into the distance, then veered back to fly above the mourners.

"It wasn't your fault, Lincoln."

Lincoln nodded and pulled his eyes from the cigarette. Will wasn't sure Lincoln believed him. The amount of money he had spent on the funeral showed that he still felt guilty. Will watched as the priest opened another box, and several more doves were released.

"What a moron," Lincoln muttered. "I told him to wait until she said a few words, and then release the birds. Is that so hard to get? This guy can't do anything right."

Will said nothing, just stared into the crystal blue sky. The single white bird was joined by the others as they flew up. He watched as the mass disappeared in the distance.

The priest made a motion, and the casket was lowered into the ground. They both remained silent as the casket disappeared. The man he had seen with Lincoln earlier walked over and said something to the priest.

"Who's the boxer?"

Lincoln's face lit up. "Ah, that's my new assistant, A. J. Met him on a business trip up north."

"Not your usual assistant."

Lincoln smiled. "Yeah, he doesn't look great in a miniskirt, but the guy is smart. He's a scientist, just got his PhD. He's brilliant."

"So what's he doing with you?"

"He likes my business ideas. We're trying to work on something together."

Will grunted. He disliked the look of A. J. He hoped his brother wasn't being scammed. "What about the camp?"

"I think this is the end of Camp Courage."

"It's not the end," Will said. "It's a hurdle, a big one, but you can move on from this. Everyone knows it wasn't your fault."

Lincoln shook his head. "Nah. The camp's had one foot in the grave for the past few years."

Will cringed at the metaphor but said nothing.

"Kids aren't interested in camps anymore. I'm hemorrhaging money every year to keep this thing going, to keep the staff trained and competent. This latest 'hurdle,' as you call it, is just a sign I was right. This was Dad's dream, and he did it well," Lincoln said with half a laugh. "We had a blast as kids, remember?"

Will remembered. His eyes turned to find Erika Mack in the black dress. She dabbed at her eyes. The seat next to her was still empty.

"So where do you go from here?" Will asked.

"I've got some things in the works."

Will sighed. "You were always a dreamer."

"I'm motivated by all the lurking possibilities. When I find something I want bad enough, I'll finish the final designs, see it through. You'll see." He blew out smoke and held the cigarette up to look at what was left.

Will was reminded of all the half-brained ideas his brother had attempted, and the financial ventures that had died before they had gotten off the ground. Lincoln had recently come up with the idea of delivering medicine to the elderly. He had purchased five delivery trucks before he discovered the bureaucratic red tape involved in carrying medical supplies. He had given up the idea and was still stuck with the trucks.

A nagging feeling in Will's gut had him watching A. J. again. He didn't look smart to Will. He looked dangerous.

"Well, before you lay down a load of money," Will said, keeping his voice neutral, "you may need someone to do some legwork and see if it's really a viable opportunity. You don't want to throw away family money on any more trucks."

Lincoln socked Will's shoulder. "I learned my lesson."

"Still, if you need someone to watch your back, you know I'd do it."

"You want in, huh?" He nodded, thinking. "I could always use another partner. Let me think about it, and I'll get back to you. A couple of us are getting together later. You interested in dropping the badge for a few beers and a deck of cards?"

Will shook his head. "I got a case."

Lincoln nodded. "Yeah, Jeff mentioned it."

"Try to keep Morgan sober tonight. I'm going to need him focused on this one."

"I'll do my best."

The mourners fanned out from the center, searching for their cars.

"How many cops you have here?" Will asked.

"Dunno. Maybe two dozen. Why?"

"Anyone mention to you that your tags are expired?"

Lincoln laughed. "They like me too much to mention that."

"You mean they're intimidated by you. I'm not. Get it taken care of."

"If they pull me over, I pull my money out of your department upgrade. I could throw in a helicopter."

"And what happens when you drive outside of Lake City?"

"Okay, fine. I'll take care of it."

Will turned back to look at the casket. Cole's mother stood with her hand on the casket.

"I placed some flowers on Sam's grave this morning," Lincoln said. "Did you stop by?"

At their younger brother's name, Will looked down at his feet, which were planted firmly on the sidewalk. He wouldn't walk on the grass.

Lincoln patted his back. "He's just over the hill if you change your mind." He dropped his cigarette on the curb. The smoke drifted upward. Lincoln made his way back to the grave to give his final instructions.

Will climbed in his truck and didn't look back.

Chapter 7

S itting in front of Eddie Chavez's house, Ric fought a mental battle
of morals. He didn't want to go inside. He'd been raised to respect
the law. His mother had been a highway patrol officer, his father an
LAPD detective. He respected the law because he respected them. It
was why he had joined the academy, and why he had been such a good
cop himself. But things had changed in the past few years. Since retiring
from the LAPD, he was constantly questioning what was right and
wrong. His whole life, he had concentrated on never, ever breaking the
law. He had seen partners tempted and pulled outside the lines, but he
had always remained loyal and honest. It had become a skill.

His parents were dead, but cop blood would always run through
him—that wasn't something he could change. He thought about
turning around and returning to Lake City. He could tell Alex he had
found nothing useful. He hated lying, even if it was to keep her safe.
He wondered if she would believe him.

Solving crimes wasn't her thing. It was his. He had been the successful detective. He could keep a step ahead of her and solve this thing while she was staring at useless video surveillance. He could get in and out and be done with all of this. He could get back to his quiet life, and Alex could forget all about the dead man in room 110. All he had to do was break the law.

When the kids were called inside at five o'clock, Ric opened the door and discarded the moral debate. He hadn't driven a hundred miles to return home with nothing. And the longer he had sat in the hot car, the more he realized he wanted answers for himself, not just for Alex.

He didn't know how much time he had, so he planned for a rush job. *Crash and dash, but keep it clean.* He moved quickly, slipping gloves on as he walked. He didn't run to the front door. He watched the street, the parked cars, the doorways, and the open windows. He listened to the noises a neighborhood makes: the creaking of doors, the barking of dogs, the sirens in the distance.

It took him longer than he wanted to pick the lock, but then again, he'd never picked one before. An alarm didn't bother him, either. A guy carrying a gun every day wouldn't rely on a security system. He could only hope there was no dog. He hated dogs.

He wasn't wrong. He opened the door to complete silence. There were no dogs waiting to attack him, so he slipped in and closed the door behind him.

Ric had made his assumptions about Eddie Chavez the second he had walked into the office at the motel. Walking into his house now, Ric threw all those assumptions out the window. The room he now entered—the living room—was airy and spacious. It was clean. Spotless, decorated. The furniture was modern and slick. Black leather couch, glass tables. On the walls hung Frida Kahlo prints, providing a contrast to the modern look. A cross hung over the door. Even in a professionally decorated house, Eddie Chavez had to express himself.

Then he saw it. An eighty-two-inch Mitsubishi projection television. His dream entertainment center was right in front of him. Speakers had been installed into the ceiling and walls. Shelves were lined with DVDs.

He wasn't just jealous; he was surprised. This wasn't a gangbanger's crib. Not a drug hole. This wasn't even a bachelor's pad. This was the home of a man who'd had a lot of money fall into his lap. Ric may not have respected the man, but he respected his tastes.

He didn't waste too much time drooling over the television. While sitting in the car, he had imagined the house layout. Now it was time to think like a cop and search like a cop. Down the hallway, he started with the bedroom on the right.

He had expected a master bedroom, but it was a child's room he walked into. Ric panicked. If there was a child, there was a family—a family that could come home. He took in the room quickly. It was too clean, just like the living room. Too clean for a kid. Not lived in. But there were toys, a bed. A Dodger pennant hung on the wall. Clothes hung neatly in the closet. Shoes were tucked neatly under the bed.

Maybe the room belonged to a boy who spent only weekends at the house.

As Ric walked from the room, he glanced into the bathroom across the hall, but he didn't waste time searching it. He moved down the hall to the other bedroom—another professionally decorated room.

The person living here had respect for the things he owned. Ric wondered if he had the wrong house, the wrong man. The king-sized bed was dressed up with a soft brown comforter and fluffy black pillows. Ric wondered how the sheets felt. He couldn't understand why a man would leave a comfy bed for a hard motel bed. Then he remembered he had done the same thing.

To his professional eye, this was a room made for a man. There was nothing here that belonged to a woman. The only personal belongings were a set of picture frames on the dresser. Examining them closer, Ric found a photograph of a young boy, around ten years old. The boy wore khaki shorts and a gray short-sleeve shirt with the words *Courage Builds Character* in bold red letters. Eddie Chavez stood behind him, smiling.

Another picture showed a much younger Eddie and an older woman standing outside a house. Based on the resemblance, Ric guessed the woman was Eddie's mother.

At least Ric had the right house.

The answering machine on the nightstand flashed two new messages. He ignored them, knowing Detective Stellar wouldn't be far behind. The messages needed to stay new.

He opened the drawer and began to search for anything that would explain why Eddie Chavez was lying in the Lake City morgue. In the bottom drawer, Ric found two full magazines for a Glock, the first sign of the Eddie Chavez he had met. Inspecting the magazines and finding them full, he returned them and continued his search. No gun. The gun found in the motel room wasn't a Glock. So there was a gun missing.

He didn't find the gun, but he did find an address book in the bottom drawer. He leafed through it, looking for anyone in Lake City, but came up empty. Only addresses in L.A. Stuck in one of the pages was an expired California driver's license. He memorized the number and then closed the book and buried it back in the bottom drawer.

He opened his cell phone and dialed the LAPD narcotics office. Detective Alan Becker, an old colleague from a past life, answered. It felt strange to hear the voice.

"Becker, it's Delgado."

There was silence on the other end and then music. Becker had put him on hold. Ric searched the closet with the phone to one ear. In a house so professionally decorated, he expected to find expensive clothes and well-tailored suits. Instead, he found the Eddie Chavez he expected to find—tee shirts, oversized sweatshirts, Lakers jersey. The top shelf was filled with hats for sports teams from L.A. to New York.

Finally, Becker came back on the line. "What's up, Delgado? Where are you?" His voice was cautious but friendly.

"I need you to run a name through the database for me."

"You're asking for a favor? Why would I help a civilian?"

"I wasn't asking."

Becker didn't ask for specifics. He wasn't one to waste time and Ric wasn't one to share information.

"What's the name?"

Ric gave him the name and driver's license number. Becker matched it within seconds.

"Tagged as the Eighteenth Street Gang, a.k.a. Big D. He's named as a suspect in two drive-by shootings back in the early nineties, but not enough evidence to arrest him. Most of his arrests are drug related—distribution, possession, and intent to sell. His last arrest was in March 1996 by CRASH. He did his time at Chino. He was cut loose in 1999 during the Rampart investigation."

CRASH was the Community Resources Against Street Hoodlums. Known for their ultra-aggressive tactics, the Los Angeles Police Department's anti-gang unit had been responsible for lowering the crime rate in the community surrounding the Rampart Division. Unfortunately, many of their tactics were questionable, and some of the officers were found to be downright dirty. Known as the Rampart Scandal, CRASH was investigated for planting evidence and violating civil rights. Most of those convicted on bad evidence were released—many of them with newfound criminal contacts and a greater distrust of law enforcement, making the Rampart area even more dangerous.

"Find out if he got a settlement," Ric said.

"That'll take time."

"What was his drug of choice?"

"Crack every time. It looks like he dealt only in the Rampart area. No hits since '96. Maybe he went clean."

"They never go clean. They die or get arrested. I need you to e-mail me the entire file including known associates."

"You know I can't do that."

Ric responded by giving his e-mail address. Becker would do it.

Becker sighed. "You want to talk to Dade? I'm sure he'd love to hear from you."

"No," Ric said. "And don't tell him you talked to me."

He closed the phone. He had little to go on. A crack dealer from Los Angeles living in a respectable suburban home in Nevada. Maybe a settlement had made him go straight. Ric doubted it, but he was having a hard time finding Eddie Chavez's past in the house.

Frustrated, he took another glance around the room, stopping at the photo of the young boy. Something familiar stared back at him. He grabbed the picture and walked back to his car. No one noticed him. He left everything as peaceful as he had found it.

Chapter 8

It was past seven when Ric drove up to the Death Valley Motel. The officers were gone and the crime scene tape had been removed. Everything looked as it had the day before. Alex sat in the same position he'd left her in, staring at the television screen. The room had grown cooler as the sun died.

"Go take your swim and go to bed," Ric said. He switched off the fan. "You need sleep."

"I'm not tired."

"I didn't ask if you were tired."

Alex smirked at him. "You're not going to ask what I found?"

"If I do, then you'll pressure me to tell you what I found out. I don't like to share."

"I could beat it out of you."

"Not with those scrawny arms, you couldn't. Gain some weight, and I'll consider sparring with you again."

She shrugged and pointed to the screen. "*Mira*. A woman arrived with our guest at ten o'clock." She pressed play, and Ric moved behind her.

He watched as the black Mercedes drove into the parking lot. Camera two showed Eddie Chavez parking next to the pool. He got out, moved to the passenger door, and opened it. A woman's face peeked out. He wasn't alone.

"How romantic."

"Not quite."

Ric watched the screen as Eddie helped the woman from the car. She was drunk—or half-baked. Her long black hair was wild around her shoulders and in her face. He couldn't make out facial features, as her head hung low to the camera angle. She wore a skirt and heels, but Ric was positive she wasn't a hooker.

They walked toward Eddie's room and then disappeared off-camera.

"Wait," Ric said. "Back it up."

He knew why Alex was grinning. She backed it up to the minute the woman stepped from the car and played it in slow motion.

Ric pushed Alex from the chair. "Move. Let me see."

"I thought you didn't want to know."

"Damn," he said, watching it again. "She can barely move. She's not drunk. He's practically carrying her across the lot." He rewound the disc and hit play again. "GHB."

"Date-rape drug?"

He got up to pace. He now thought the trip to Chavez's house had been a waste of time. A chance encounter had killed Eddie Chavez.

"They probably met at O'Sullivan's," he said.

"What's O'Sullivan's?"

"A bar just down the street." He looked at her. "You really should leave the property sometime." She rolled her eyes at him. "O'Sullivan's is close enough for him. Has to be a place he can slip something into her drink. A bar is the logical choice."

"And then he rapes her," Alex said. She grabbed the remote from Ric's hands. "Let's continue."

"You have more?"

She winked at him. "Our mystery guest leaves at about two in the morning. Alone."

The screen zipped through. Ric watched the time on the counter. At two-twenty, Alex hit play. The woman reappeared in camera two. Her hair was messier. She wiped her face and looked around. She was alone.

She fiddled with something in her hand. The Mercedes' lights flashed.

"She didn't know which car was his. The alarm helped identify it."

"She stole his car?" Ric asked.

"As she should have."

"He doesn't follow her out," Ric muttered to himself.

He watched the car drive away from the lot, wondering if this was Eddie Chavez's killer. She didn't look like a killer, but he knew firsthand you could never tell.

"Maybe he's already dead," Alex said.

"Any activity after?"

"Nothing caught on camera. Do you think you can get me a good still shot of her face?"

Ric shrugged, thinking. "Yeah. Are you going to canvass the neighborhood?"

It was a joke, but Alex didn't laugh. He needed to watch all of the surveillance tapes again, including the one he had hidden from Alex, but he couldn't have her watching over his shoulder.

"I'll start with O'Sullivan's."

"Alex, you can't start asking questions around here. If Detective Stellar gets wind of you doing your own investigation, he's going to get suspicious. He gets suspicious, he'll start digging on you."

"I'll risk it."

"Did you pull the other discs?" he asked.

She shook her head. "No need. It's not always how you live your life. It's about how it ends."

Ric considered Eddie's last day and knew Alex was off course. She wanted to know why Eddie had been killed. Ric only cared about who. He would let her go if it meant she was out of his way and out of danger. He could reel her back when he was ready. "I need to go see something. I'll get you your picture once you eat."

"Tell me what you found first."

He pointed to the picture he left on the counter.

"What's this?"

"Eddie Chavez and his son."

"He has a son?"

He heard the sympathy in her voice. "Apparently, but that's not the best part. Look at the photo." He turned to watch her. He wanted to see the moment she realized it. It took longer than he had expected.

"The motel. They're standing in front of the motel."

"Obviously before you decided to paint it, but yeah, that's the motel."

"He's been here before, with his son. Before we moved here."

"He's got a connection here in town. We just need to find it."

~~~

Twenty minutes later, Ric found Della standing in front of the mini-mart near the Schneider Computer store. He pulled into the parking lot and watched as she talked with another woman.

The other woman was thin and tall. Ric hadn't seen her before. Despite her obvious age, her skin was pulled tight around her cheekbones. Not from Botox. Her eyes were hollow and void of emotion. He couldn't help but wonder what horrible past had landed her on the streets.

He heard the old Ford Mustang before he saw it. He watched as the car pulled to a stop in the *No Parking* zone. The tall woman negotiated with the driver. Out of habit, Ric wrote down the license plate. Then he tossed it on the floor. He wasn't going to get involved.

As the driver drove off with his new passenger, Ric turned his attention back to Della. Her hair, pulled back in a ponytail, was in desperate need of a dye job. She wore too much makeup. He wondered if she piled it on in hopes that no one would see through it. She wore jeans and heels, and she tugged around an enormous purse that probably carried more than he currently owned.

He realized as he pulled the car up alongside her that he could be arrested for what he was about to do. First, breaking and entering. Now, solicitation of a prostitute. His life had changed so much since leaving Los Angeles, but he wasn't going to turn back now.

He opened his window, pulled out his wallet, and waited for her to walk up. When Della glanced inside, he held up a hundred-dollar bill. "It's not a sting. I promise." He hoped the money would relax her.

"What do you want?" she said, eyeing the money. Her fingers twitched but didn't touch the money. Her nails were painted black and bitten short. There were no rings on her fingers, no bracelets on her arms.

"To talk. Get in."

She shook her head. He watched as she stared at the money. After a minute, she finally looked up at him with bloodshot eyes.

"No one pays a hundred to talk. Tell me what you want."

"I want answers. Last night, when you were at the motel, did you hear anything?"

She laughed uneasily. "I heard a lot of moaning and grunts of pleasure, fo' sure."

"You heard about the dead guy?"

Silence. She fidgeted.

"You were two doors down," Ric said. "You had to hear something."

"I don't want to be dragged into this. I never even saw the guy."

"But you heard something, right? Just between the two of us. I'm not sharing with the cops. I just need to get an idea of when he was killed."

Ric waited. Della remained silent. He didn't want to push, but he needed the information. She tapped her fingers on the car.

"You left at two," he prompted.

"Damn, Ric, keep my name out of this. I got enough problems." She watched the street. He wanted her to look at him, but since he needed someone watching for cops, he let it go. He needed to keep his eyes on her.

"I can keep your name out of it, but you have to help me out. Did you hear anything?" he asked.

"No, I swear."

"You sure?"

She shrugged, tapped her fingers again. "I didn't hear anything, fo' sure."

She still wouldn't look at him. She didn't trust him yet, but he had yet to betray her. He made a judgment call to believe her.

"Good enough for me. How about your friend?"

She shook her head. He saw the fear rise in her eyes. "I can't tell you that."

He nodded. Maybe he was a regular. A good payer. She wouldn't risk putting him at jeopardy.

"You need to get out of here. I'm losing business."

"Okay. I understand. I'm not busting you. I just needed to ask." He stuffed the money in her hands. "You got a place to stay tonight?"

She didn't answer. She was shivering. Her fear interested him, but he didn't push it. If it became important, he knew where to find her.

"I got a proposition for you," he said. "I need someone."

"I'm not interested. You've already wasted too much of my time."

"We're looking to hire someone to help watch the desk. You can have a room and minimum wage. That's the best I can offer."

She folded her arms over her chest and stared at him. "Do you know how much I make a night?"

"This gives you a roof over your head and the cops off your ass. Only one condition."

"Fo' sure," she muttered.

"I can't have you hooking any more. No johns, no freebies, no dope. You gotta go clean."

"Why?"

He found he had no answer for her.

Chapter 9

Among the five detectives the Lake City Police Department employed, only Detective Stellar had scored an office. He had started as the other detectives had, at a small desk crammed outside the chief's office. He hadn't complained of the space, but as the only detective that worked death scenes, he received numerous complaints about the crime scene photos he posted behind his desk. Chief Mack caved to the complaints and offered Stellar an office. It was no bigger than a closet, but it had a window and provided him the privacy his cases often required.

Detective Stellar stared at the file for Cole Wesley. He wondered what had caused an eleven-year-old boy to wander out in the middle of the night. He wondered how his mother would go on after losing her only son.

He forced the thoughts away and closed the folder. He couldn't find the energy to get up and file it away, so he left it on his desk. He made a note to file it. Then he made a note to check into Lincoln's new assistant, A. J. He made a third note to call his mother.

Staring at the list, he knew he was stalling. He was getting nowhere with his case. He needed a suspect in the motel murder. He needed to know more about his victim. His frustration grew with his hunger. He opened a bag of almonds and threw a handful in his mouth. Dinner.

He heard the pecking on the window. His bird was back. Four months ago, the bird had first visited his office window. Every day it came back. From his desk, it looked red. Deep red, like drying blood. The sun shimmered on its feathers.

Stellar stood slowly, but the bird jumped from the windowsill to a nearby tree branch. It stared down at him. He moved even more slowly and inched the window open. When the bird tilted its head at him, Stellar dropped a few almonds on the sill. He leaned against his desk and watched as the bird considered the nuts. It still wouldn't eat anything Stellar offered. Upon closer inspection, the feathers looked more brown than red. He thought it might be a female mountain bluebird, but he couldn't be sure. His father had been the bird-watcher in the family, and despite his ramblings, Stellar had never been interested.

He was wasting time. Shrugging at the unmoved bird, he sat back down at his desk and opened the murder book Officer Florio had started. They had a name to start with: Eddie Chavez. The only other piece of evidence to help them was the body itself.

His tattoos told Stellar he was a gang member. The old bullet wound in the thigh told him he was probably pretty active in his day.

He reread his field notes. No cell phone. He was positive this man owned a cell phone. It would have been a great lead, but it wasn't in the room. Maybe he had left it in his car, which they had yet to find, along with a wallet.

He turned the page and flipped through the crime scene photos. The lamp was lit. The nightstand was bare. No forced entry. No sign of a struggle. The next picture showed the chair sitting next to the desk. The victim's shoelaces lay on the floor underneath. One was broken just below a knot. He flipped back to his notes. The chair had a broken arm. It didn't look broken in the picture. In fact, Stellar hadn't noticed it until he had gone to move it and felt the arm lift.

Sergeant Morgan and Officer Florio walked in.

"Do we have a positive ID?" Stellar asked.

Florio shook his head. "We ran a search with Eddie, Edward, Ed, and Eduardo Chavez. In the Las Vegas and Henderson areas, there are thirty-five hits. We found one in Henderson that has a similar tattoo listed, but Wags is hesitant to make a positive identification based on the fact that half his skull is gone. He's running the prints to confirm."

"As soon as Wags gets a positive, I want address and next of kin information on my desk."

Stellar looked at Morgan. He'd known Morgan since before he joined the force. Their families were close. He had never considered him a friend, but he was a friend of Lincoln's, which meant they saw a lot of each other even outside the job.

Morgan wasn't a big guy, but he was wide. Although strong and fast, he wasn't the smartest guy on the force. Unfortunately, he'd been there the longest, and with his connections, he would be next in line if the sheriff agreed to hire another detective. Stellar couldn't help wondering if he'd pass the detective test.

"Have you looked at the evidence retrieved at the scene?" Stellar asked.

Morgan nodded. "We found a McDonald's bag and a half-empty container of juice in the trash. A receipt also showed a purchase the day before at the market. I interviewed the employees at the restaurant and the grocery store."

Morgan read from his notes. "No one remembers him, but we still don't have a picture to show around."

Stellar wanted to see his eyes when he spoke, but didn't bother to stop him. Morgan wouldn't remember what he had learned without his notes.

Will rubbed his chin and remembered he had yet to shave. His cell phone vibrated on his belt. He glanced at the number then silenced it.

"You can follow up once we get an ID. And start a timeline. I want to know where he was from the minute he drove into town to when the manager found him. Florio, what about the trace evidence?"

Larry Florio was Stellar's right hand. He had stolen him from Las Vegas Metro a year earlier. He was never without a large smile on his face. After graduating from the University of Las Vegas, he had joined Las Vegas Metro and worked alongside Stellar until he moved back to Lake City. He had been there less than a year and had already gained a loyal following of friends. In Lake City he was well liked by everyone, even the ones he arrested.

"We've got prints all over the room, including the door inside and out, the broken chair, and the nightstand. It'll take a few days to get those reviewed," Florio said. He didn't need to read from his notes. "Unfortunately, the condom wrapper and the gun itself only consisted of smudges."

Stellar grunted and signaled to Florio to continue.

"The gun at the scene was a .38 Special revolver. Carlos was able to take a look at the fired bullet we retrieved at the scene. It's consistent with the .38, but Carlos said it was badly damaged, so he couldn't confirm it had been fired from the weapon we found."

"Did he run the gun's serial?"

"The gun was traced to a Wayne Corredor, a retired doctor in Reno. He reported it stolen from his home three months ago. A dead end. Carlos wants to send everything to a ballistics expert in Vegas Metro to see if they can get anything more from it."

"Tell him to go ahead. What else?"

"Blood samples were sent to the lab. We'll get blood screen back tomorrow, but it's going to take awhile for any other testing."

Stellar hated the delays. Working the evidence was slowing him down. He would have to interpret the evidence and see where it led him.

He looked down at his notes. The missing cell phone and wallet. Condom wrapper. A stolen gun and a stolen car, but no forced entry.

"A chance encounter leads to robbery and murder?" He thought out loud. "Talk to Detective Jonas. The girls on the street will talk to him. Let's see if any of our local girls happened to spend time with our vic."

Florio nodded. "You're thinking a hooker did him like that?"

Stellar shrugged. "Evidence could point to a sexual encounter gone wrong." Although he didn't believe it any more than the suicide angle.

"Going through your notes, I noticed you didn't give a description of Ms. Delgado," Florio said.

"Really?" Stellar pictured her immediately. The ugly sweater, her thin legs in the faded jeans and flip-flops. No makeup. No jewelry. He remembered how her innocent face revealed nothing.

"Why's it important?" Stellar asked.

"Well, we're looking at some of the hairs recovered from the room and found a black hair. Too long to be the vic's."

He pictured her long black hair pulled back in a ponytail. He imagined the hair falling down over her shoulders. He shook the image away.

Morgan answered for him. "She was the beautiful Latina in the office. She's hot."

Stellar grunted. He wouldn't call her hot. She was a bit on the thin side. She was an enigma. Her face was a mix of Spanish and Italian features. She had spoken in the slightest of Spanish accents, which told him she was fluent in her native tongue. Her older brother had no hint of an accent. Either they had been raised separately or she had held on to the accent as a point of pride, while he assimilated.

There were other differences between the siblings that intrigued him. Ric had spoken clearly and had chosen his words carefully. Alex had blurted out her thoughts without thinking about how it would make her look.

"How could you miss her?" Morgan asked Florio. "I couldn't keep my eyes off her."

Florio rolled his eyes. "I'm married with three kids at home. If I look at every hot Latina, you'd be scraping me off the floor."

Morgan laughed. "It's called observation in the police field. You'll never make a good detective."

Florio ignored Morgan and looked at Stellar. "So I can assume it's incidental. She probably cleaned the room."

"Wait. Where'd you find it?" Stellar asked.

"On the pillowcase."

"Any blood on it?"

"Yeah, a spot."

"Send the blood and the hair to the lab for DNA. She claimed she wasn't in the room."

"Why would she lie about that?" Morgan asked.

"People lie to keep secrets, Morgan."

Stellar stared at the photo of the crime scene, but didn't see it. He saw only Alex. He didn't like her. She had basically refused to answer his questions and had thrown him her opinion without him asking. He suspected she was hiding something. On a morning when he should have been enjoying a quiet breakfast at home and nursing a hangover, he was squinting in a dark motel room staged to look like a suicide.

A staged scene?

As if he was some amateur who wouldn't pick up on it. Someone had underestimated him. Someone with access to the room had staged it. He needed a suspect, and Alex had been standing there, pretending to be innocent. She had watched him from the second he walked into that cramped office, just as he had watched her. She had analyzed him as he had analyzed her.

He heard the scratching at the window and saw the bird pecking at it. The bird looked up at him, tilting its head again. Stellar turned to the field cards the Delgados had filled out. Ric's was completed, but Alex had only written her name and the phone number to the motel.

"We don't know anything about the Delgados."

The scratching grew louder. Stellar turned to the window. The bird hadn't flown away. In the sun, its feathers appeared more like copper or brass.

Stellar shook his head at the bird. He wanted to start with the witnesses. He wanted to dig into their pasts, but he had no real proof anything was out of the ordinary with them. He would have to start at the beginning, with the victim.

"Florio, put some pressure on Wags. We need a positive ID."

Chief Mack walked in and nodded at the silent officers. They took the cue and made a quick escape.

Stellar rarely saw the chief. He was a busy man. Doing what, he didn't know, but it wasn't his job to track his chief of police. Stellar's job was to solve crimes. Mack normally stayed out of his way, except for those times when he wielded an ax over the detective's head.

It was Mack's job to know more than Stellar did. If he knew something Stellar didn't, he would run to his office to shove it in his face. Stellar knew what this visit meant. He had missed something. Mack dropped into the chair across from him. Stellar still hoped it was purely a social call. He sat back down and waited for the ax to fall.

"I understand the incident at the motel was ruled a homicide."

Stellar nodded. "Looks that way. Erika bothering you already?"

Erika Mack was the owner of the *Lake City Times*. As a journalist, she had never held back on a story. Now, as the owner, she expected the same of her journalists. She was also Mack's daughter. Because of that, she was known to tell the news straight and honest. Even though some people looked down on her, she was trusted in the city. She was also Will's ex-girlfriend. Their on-and-off-again relationship caused problems on a normal day, let alone a day of murder.

"She hammered me with questions at the funeral," Mack said. "You?"

"She's left a few messages. I'll think about returning them tomorrow. I have more pressing matters than getting quoted in tomorrow's paper."

Mack nodded, knowing it was a jab at him. The chief had never been keen on the fact that Stellar had dated his daughter. Stellar wasn't sure how he felt that he had broken it off once again, but he would deal with it as he always did. He ignored it.

"What have you got so far?" Mack asked.

Stellar shrugged and pushed the murder book toward Mack. "Not much yet. The victim was apparently shot at close range with a .38, most likely the gun at his feet. He's a stranger in town. Ric and Alex Delgado, newbies to town, run the motel now. Brother and sister. They claim to have heard and seen nothing. No witnesses and no idea why he was in town."

"Identification?"

"Wags just pulled fingerprints. We should have confirmation soon."

Mack flipped to the next page of notes, reading thoroughly. Stellar had never seen him so interested in a case before. Frowning, Mack flipped to the final page. "What about the video cameras?"

Stellar flinched. He felt the ax before he could stop it. He looked out the window. The bird was gone.

"I didn't see any cameras at the motel," Stellar said.

"Erika thinks they were installed about a month ago."

Will cursed. Maybe he should have called Erika back.

"The Delgados didn't mention it?"

He stood up. "No. The Delgados failed to mention it. I'm going now."

Chapter 10

Stellar drove just under the speed limit with the stereo screaming Rascal Flatts. He sang along to try to calm himself. At a stoplight, a group of boys crossed the street. He recognized Jimmy but couldn't remember the kid's last name. At only twelve, Jimmy was a bit of a troublemaker, but he had a rough family life—his father was a drinker and his mother struggled to keep the family together—so Stellar always cut the kid some slack.

Justin Green carried his skateboard and waved. Stellar waved back. Friends of Cole. The boys should have been at camp enjoying sports and nighttime campfire stories. Instead, they were mourning their friend.

Lincoln had closed the camp due to Cole's death, but Will hoped he would reconsider. Camp Courage was situated on twenty-six acres of the family property. The remaining twenty acres was devoted to the Stellar Ranch, including an eight-bedroom main house and a two-bedroom guesthouse. The family made most of its money on the cattle ranch, for which Lincoln was now solely responsible.

Although Stellar had moved away the first chance he got, he had nothing but good memories of Camp Courage and the Stellar Ranch. At the lake, he had learned to swim and make a fire. His first fight had been at Camp Courage. As with every challenge since, Stellar had won. But he knew what it was like to lose, too.

His first kiss with Erika Mack had been at midnight at the lake's edge. The darkness had seemed romantic. The sound of the water lapping the edge always brought him back to that moment.

The sun was setting on Lake City. The temperature was finally starting to drop out of the triple digits. Stellar flipped off the air and opened the window. He enjoyed the desert at dusk. The setting sun's glow changed the sky from blue to orange.

He hoped the fresh air would calm his nerves, but his anger increased with every mile. Not only had he been embarrassed in front of his chief, but he had lost an entire day of investigation.

A staged scene and a damn video. He didn't know what it showed, but he sure wanted to see it. Why would two innocent people prevent him from seeing the video? What were they hiding?

Stellar didn't know someone new had moved into town and taken over the motel. He would have thought the people of Lake City would be talking incessantly about the strangers, but he had heard nothing—maybe because he had stopped listening to the gossip when the talk mostly consisted of rumors of his and Erika's on-and-off-again relationship.

Despite the questions that morning, he had been left with no distinct impression of either of them. Ric seemed reserved, but he had answered the questions. He'd been direct in some of his answers and vague in others. He seemed unconcerned with the dead body, but he was in a rush to push it on someone else. Alex had seemed concerned and hesitant to let anyone take over.

He pulled into the parking lot. Only one other vehicle sat in the lot, a white Ford pickup truck. The heat wafted from the hot pavement. He wiped away the sweat beading on his forehead.

Pulling out his gun, he locked it in the glove compartment. The handcuffs he stuffed in his back pocket were all he would need. He took his time walking to the door, examining his surroundings. He'd go for Ric first. He'd be harder to break, and Stellar enjoyed a challenge.

He saw Alex first, standing behind the counter. Her hair hung loose and curled at the tips, framing her face. She wore some sort of robe, white and soft. It confused him, and he felt his anger fading.

She watched him as he approached the office door, as she had earlier. When he felt he had the control, he yanked the door open. Ric sat watching a movie on the small television with his feet propped up on the table. A black short-sleeve shirt revealed numerous tattoos on his forearms. Ric didn't bother to look up at Stellar as he walked in, but he saw the twitch of someone unprepared.

Despite his composure, Stellar felt the rage return. He pulled out his notebook. Alex offered a friendly smile, and he saw the controlled emotion in her eyes. He decided then to ignore Ric and vent on Alex. He would force Ric to step up and cross the line.

"*Buenas tardes*, Detective," she said mildly.

"Ms. Delgado—"

"You can call me Alex."

She tucked her hair behind her ears. It made her eyes look warm. Her smile only annoyed him more. He didn't smile back. He wasn't going to be polite.

"I need to see your business license."

She didn't move to get it, but she continued to smile. She was trying to pull some of the power her way, but Stellar had the badge. He reminded himself to stay in control. "Did you apply for a business license when you came to town?" he asked.

She shrugged. "The city sent us several things. I don't know where all the paperwork went to."

"You'd better find it—now. It's supposed to be posted for your customers."

He saw Ric drop his feet to the floor and turn to look at him. Alex must have heard the movement as well. Her face flinched, but she moved to the desk and pulled out a folder.

When she returned to face him, her face was stern and daring. "The city's supposed to be sending us a new one."

"If you can't find it, I'll be forced to shut you down. I know you're both new in town, but there are laws that need to be followed."

Alex flipped through the papers, found something, and handed it to him. "This is what the city sent us."

He ripped it from her hands. She offered another smile. He could see the sarcastic gleam in her eye now. Then she winked at him. It almost worked to distract him. He tore his eyes from her. The Death Valley Motel was licensed under the name of Carson Realty, Inc.

"Make me a copy." He sounded rude. He was hoping for that. He glanced at Ric, but he had yet to get up. He was ignoring Stellar, watching his sister. Waiting. Stellar had mistakenly assumed Ric would take over, wanting the control.

"I'm sending an officer out here tomorrow morning to take your prints," Stellar said, pushing further.

She handed him the copy. Something in her eyes alerted him that he was stepping on dangerous ground. He wondered what would happen if the control she held on to was suddenly yanked away.

"Whatever I can do to help," she said, keeping her voice even. "The city and the police department have our full support." The smile was gone, replaced with a steady stare.

"That Ford truck outside yours?"

"Nope." She folded her arms over her chest.

Still no response from Ric. It was time to force him over the line. Stellar slapped his handcuffs on the counter.

"You really want to continue to stand in my way?"

Her eyes flickered to the handcuffs. She faltered, just long enough.

Ric stood. "It's mine, cowboy."

Stellar kept his eyes on Alex, but could hear the annoyance in Ric's voice. Stellar decided to push him harder. "I'll need to see the paperwork on that as well. License, registration, and proof of insurance. And since I'm not herding cows at the moment, you can call me 'Detective' or 'sir.'"

Alex stood motionless, as if frozen in Stellar's stare. Ric hesitated. Stellar finally turned to Ric and watched the man's gaze drop to his empty holster. Stellar pulled back a smile. He had Ric exactly where he wanted him. One more step.

"Do we have a problem?" Stellar asked. He took the moment to study the man's tattoos.

Ric grunted, then stomped past Stellar and threw open the door.

Stellar turned back to Alex. He was intrigued by the cold stare. For a full minute, he returned the stare, waiting for her to pull back, but she didn't. She was daring him to push her, as if she wanted the fight and was positive she would win. She looked dangerous, and Stellar was suddenly aware he may have made a mistake leaving his gun in the truck. He felt the sweat beading at his temples.

"I need a copy of your driver's license, too," he said.

"I don't drive."

"No license?" he asked.

"No."

Ric returned and spread the paperwork neatly on the desk. "Everything's in order," he said, having regained some composure.

"I've been more than patient with you, Detective," Alex said. "Are you going to tell me what this is about?"

Stellar took his time flipping through the papers. He wrote down the license information. This hadn't gone the way he had expected. Ric seemed like an arrogant hothead, but he had let his sister handle the heat. He seemed like he didn't like cops, but he hadn't crossed the line, even when his sister was being hassled.

"Neither of you mentioned the security cameras installed last month. Is there a reason for that?"

"What cameras?" Alex asked.

"Al—" Ric started.

"*Cállate!*" Alex interrupted.

Stellar slammed his hands on the counter. Neither flinched this time. "I don't like being deceived."

"And I don't like being harassed," Alex shouted back.

"I want the tapes for the past week."

Alex pulled her robe more tightly around her waist. "And I want to be left alone."

Stellar felt his blood pressure rise ever higher. "Do you have something against cops?"

Alex didn't answer. Stellar could hear Ric breathing. Alex hadn't moved, and her stare remained on Stellar. He was too tired, too annoyed to handle any more of her games.

"How about I drag you back to the station?" he said finally. "We can have a marathon interrogation. I hear the conference room is having problems with the air conditioner. It could be your own little sweat room. You want that, Ms. Delgado? You want me to drag all your secrets out in the open? That's what this is about, right, keeping secrets?"

Alex looked away. Finally, Ric stepped forward. Stellar matched it and waited for Ric to step over the line. Stellar had a pair of handcuffs waiting for him.

"That badge gives you a lot of power," Ric said, "but it doesn't always give you what you want, does it?"

Stellar didn't answer. Instead, he took another step forward and waited for Ric to make his move. Ric's muscles tensed, then relaxed, still holding the line.

"I manage this place," Ric said. "I don't own it. I gave you access to room 110 because it's a crime scene. Your officer released it a few hours ago, which means everything is off-limits to you without a warrant. Anything taped on these premises belongs to the owner. You want the tapes, bring a warrant."

"You're interfering with a murder investigation."

Ric folded his arms over his chest. "You're interfering with my movie. Show me a warrant, and I'll be happy to assist you. I'm sure you're familiar with the law. They don't hand out those badges to just anyone, right, cowboy?"

Stellar stared at Ric for another second, feeling the power shift. "I'll be back tomorrow to pick up the tapes."

"A bit of advice: next time you come in here, be nice," Ric said, glancing at Alex. "You might find it easier to get what you need."

Stellar turned and walked out the door. He stood for a long moment beside his car. He hadn't gotten the tapes, but he had learned more from Ric than he had expected. His composure was intriguing.

Hearing the office door open, he turned to watch Alex walk past him out to the pool. He pulled out his cell phone as he watched her drop the robe, revealing a blue swimsuit. She moved like a cat as she jumped into the pool.

He had learned just a bit about Alex. Nothing he could write down on a report, just an instinct. She was a dangerous woman. He would need to be careful when dealing with her.

He dialed Florio and was put on hold. When Florio picked up, Stellar asked him to run Ric's plate and driver's license number. Again he was put on hold.

"Ricardo Delgado, thirty-nine years of age, born in Los Angeles," said Florio. "No marriage certificate on record. No outstanding tickets on the vehicle, either."

"Rap sheet?"

"He has no record. No warrants, no arrests. The record looks pretty empty."

"That's impossible. The guy's covered in ink and has the attitude to match."

"Gangbanger?"

Stellar glanced at the office and found Ric standing in the doorway, staring back at him. His stance was confident and threatening yet relaxed. Stellar couldn't read him. He hadn't identified any specific gang tattoos, but Ric could easily scare anyone he passed on the street. He had the stance of a cop. Trained, maybe military. Someone who could blend in easily could be beneficial to a police department, or could be very deadly.

"Dig deeper. I want to know everything about him, from birth to present. He has to have a record somewhere. And start working on a warrant for the security tapes at the motel."

Closing his phone, Stellar glanced back at the pool and watched Alex wipe the water from her face.

A staged scene meant one thing: his victim wasn't killed because of hate or revenge. He was killed to keep a secret, and the Delgados obviously had something to hide.

Chapter 11

When Stellar returned to his office, Florio was busy putting notes in the murder book.

Stellar switched off the lights. Still angry, he grabbed the binder from Florio. "Go home, Officer. We can't do any more tonight."

Florio didn't leave, just watched Stellar with his dark brown eyes. "AFIS got a match on the prints. Your victim is Eddie Chavez, thirty-two years of age. Lived in Henderson, Nevada, for the past six years, but born and raised in South Los Angeles."

Stellar glanced at his watch. It was just past eight. It seemed later. He wondered if there was enough time to change his opinion of the day. He opened the binder and flipped through the rap sheet Florio had slipped into the binder.

"Not a nice guy."

He glanced at the last arrest photo of Eddie Chavez. Eddie's dark eyes glared at the camera, his brows tight and his jaw clenched, as if he were growling. He had been a dangerous man, but he was now Stellar's victim.

Chavez had been arrested in 1983 for possession, 1984 for trafficking, both as a minor. Did a stint in juvie, but obviously he was never reformed. Arrested again in 1993 for distribution of cocaine and again in 1995, and finally in 1996. He had received a life sentence on the three strikes law and was sent to Chino to serve his time. Three years later, he was released after the Rampart scandal revealed the evidence had probably been planted. Chavez had sued the department and received half a million dollars. Ten years later, he was living in Nevada without a blip on the radar.

To a start fresh, or to start a new clique?

"Did you find a vehicle registered to him?" Stellar asked.

"Yep, a Mercedes with Nevada plates."

"Put a BOLO out for the vehicle."

Florio nodded. "Your mother called while you were out. She said she'd try you at home later. And Erika Mack called three times."

Stellar didn't bother to look up. Erika enjoyed hounding him. She had called his cell phone ten times already, leaving three voicemails. Stellar listened to them, then deleted all of them.

"Tell her I'm trying to solve a homicide."

"She thought you would say that. She told me to tell you it's a purely social call. She wants to meet you for drinks at O'Sullivan's."

Stellar grunted. Nothing with Erika was purely social.

The calls would stop around midnight. Her deadline would be gone, and whatever she had from Chief Mack would be the only thing making it on the front page of tomorrow's newspaper. The calls would start again after she got her normal six hours of sleep. Six hours would be his quiet time. He needed the time to get somewhere on this investigation.

"Where was Eddie living?" Stellar asked.

"He has a Henderson address."

He looked back at Eddie's picture and wondered what had made him leave Los Angeles. Stellar didn't believe for a second that Chavez had changed in the past ten years. Las Vegas was becoming the new Los Angeles. Gangs were moving out in droves as money, drugs, and sex were practically advertised as part of the Las Vegas experience.

"Grab a black-and-white," Stellar said.

"Where are we going?"

"To see how a dead guy lives."

~~~

Stellar leaned against the patrol car and looked up at the dark house while he waited for Officer Florio to get off his phone.

He looked at Eddie's neighbor's house on the right. Lights were on. Florio hung up.

"The house is owned clean and clear by Eddie Chavez. It was his mother's before she died and was willed to him six years ago. He moved out from L.A. and immediately paid it off from the bank. Henderson Police will serve the search warrant first thing in the morning. Can't seem to find a next of kin listed anywhere. There's nothing we can do here now."

Stellar pointed to the neighbor's house. "Let's talk to them."

They approached the house, and Stellar held back as Florio knocked on the door.

"Don't tell them he was murdered," Stellar said before the door opened.

A woman appeared who could have passed for Florio's sister. Olive skin, dark eyes, and a huge, inviting smile.

Florio introduced himself and Stellar. Stellar watched the woman. She was relaxed, open, and friendly—an interesting reaction to cops at the door. She told Florio her name was Candy. Florio wrote it down. Stellar couldn't help wondering if she was a stripper in town.

"Is there anyone else home?" Florio asked.

She nodded. "My son, Christian."

Florio wrote this down, too.

Stellar grew impatient. "Do you know your neighbor, Eddie Chavez?"

There were two possible reactions to that question. When a cop asks, it means there's something wrong. He expected her to go with question number one: *What did he do?*

The smile disappeared. "Eddie?" She looked from Stellar to Florio. "Is he okay? What's happened?"

That was reaction number two: worry. Stellar hadn't expected that. "I'm sorry, ma'am, but he was found dead this morning. Did you know he was out of town?"

"Oh, my." She rubbed her forehead and leaned against the door jam. Stellar thought the woman might faint on him. Her worry made her look older. *Probably too old to be a stripper*, he thought.

"He said he would be gone a few days. I watch his house for him if he leaves."

Stellar straightened. "Can we come in for a minute? We just have a few questions."

She nodded. Stellar did a quick inventory of the tidy house as she showed them to the living room. He would never have guessed this woman was friendly with his victim. She waved a young boy up the stairs. She offered to make coffee, but Stellar and Florio both declined.

Candy settled in the chair, but she still didn't look at Stellar. "Our boys played together all the time. Poor Ollie. He loved his father. What happened?"

"Eddie had a son?" Stellar asked.

She looked up with tears in her eyes. "Yes. Ollie. He's only eight. He splits his time here. The rest of the time he stays with his mother, Joy."

"Where did Eddie travel?"

She looked confused. "I figured it was for work. I didn't ask."

"What type of work?"

"I'm not sure. I think he owned his own shipping company or something. I don't know much more than that. We didn't talk much about it. We were always talking about the boys."

"That's okay. So he was a good neighbor?"

"Oh, yes. I was worried when he first moved in. I knew his mother. Such a sweetheart. She always spoke of her son as a disappointment, so I was concerned, but he moved in with his girlfriend and son, and they were the perfect neighbors. He always comes by to help out. He pulls my trash cans up on trash days. The boys are best friends."

"When did his girlfriend move out?"

"Early last year. I think she was into drugs or something. Eddie tried to make it work. I know he was going to fight for custody of Ollie. He didn't need to be in that kind of atmosphere."

"Do you know how we can contact her?"

"Of course. I have her information in case of an emergency."

Ten minutes later, as Florio drove them into Las Vegas to find Joy Ochoa, Stellar stared out the window thinking of the child Eddie had left behind.

"I want you to serve the search warrant on Eddie's home tomorrow," he told Florio.

"You want to find a place to spend the night?"

"No, you're taking me home after we meet with the girlfriend. You can drive back down tomorrow by yourself." Stellar saw the concern on his face. "You can handle it."

Stellar stared out the window as Florio drove. The next-of-kin announcement wasn't something he was going to leave to Florio, no matter how much he hated it. Stellar would be ruining two people's lives tonight. Although he knew he wasn't to blame, he was taking a man from a woman and a father from his son. He would always be remembered as the cop who had destroyed their night and their lives.

Stellar took a deep breath and tried to prepare himself. People handled loss differently. Some cried or fell apart. Others sat stoically and said nothing. It didn't matter to Stellar. It felt the same to him. Breaking the news to the family made the death more real. It made catching the killer much more important.

Chapter 12

O'Sullivan's was less than a mile south of the Death Valley Motel, but Alex had never been there. In fact, she hadn't had a drink in over ten years. The walk to the bar did more to clear her head than the swim, but what she really needed was sleep.

First a name. Then, hopefully, sleep.

She had expected a young, hip crowd to surround the bar at O'Sullivan's, but it was an older somber crowd that filled the booths along the walls. The air conditioning was working full blast to keep the heat outside. A lonely pool table sat unused in the corner. The bar was in the back, manned by a tall man who appeared pleasant and efficient as he handed out drinks and collected tabs. There was a door to the kitchen on the left, a hallway on the right, a sign indicated an emergency exit and restrooms. Only a few lone people sat at the bar, so she was able to find a stool with a perfect view of the people and a fast track to the exit. She worried she would run into a problem with the bartender, but he smiled as he walked toward her.

"What can I get you?" he asked. He didn't look Irish, but he looked comfortable behind the bar. He wore a tee shirt that read "House of Pain." He looked to be in his early thirties, with shaggy hair, a thin nose, and green eyes. He put his palms on the bar. Alex wondered if he was O'Sullivan.

"How about your best Irish whiskey?"

"Jameson?"

She shook her head. Too predictable. "You have anything from Bushmills?"

He smiled brighter. "You got it."

He put a clean tumbler down, poured two thumbs. Glanced at her. She drained it and put the glass back on the bar.

"What is it?" she asked, eyeing the black label.

"Bushmills twenty-one-year single malt."

"Impressive." She pushed the empty glass toward him.

He poured more this time, but before pushing it back to her, he added, "Might want to take it easy on this one."

She smiled at him and drained the glass again. "Might be a good idea to leave the bottle."

He laughed, poured a full glass, and handed her the bottle. "I hope you're not driving. This bottle's my best, reserved for a very few, but it will kick you in the ass."

"I think I can handle it." She glanced around. "Full bar, but why's it so quiet?"

He nodded. "There was a funeral today. A young boy. Too young."

She eyed the mourners in the bar as they nursed their beers. "Aren't they always?"

He didn't need to answer. She didn't want to talk about death.

"You're Ric's sister, right?"

Alex grinned. Leave it to her brother Ric to make friends at the local bar. He wasn't a drinker, but he always made friends with the right people. It was the cop in him.

"Alex," she said. She didn't offer her hand. He didn't expect it. "Are you the owner?"

He smiled again, brightly. "Call me Liam."

"Liam, you don't look Irish."

He put his finger to his lips. "Don't say that too loudly. I'm actually more French than Irish."

She laughed. "How'd you come to own an Irish pub?"

He leaned against the bar. "My mother won it in a poker game when I was a kid. My older brother was still living at home at the time, and he came down to check it out and fell in love with it. My mother thought the name was cute and nicknamed my brother Mick and me Liam. They stuck, I guess. I was sweeping floors here when I was just fifteen. Graduated to bartender and never once thought of leaving it behind."

"And your brother—Mick?"

"Fell for the love of his life a couple of years ago. Still owns half the bar, but spends most his time with his growing family."

"Good for him. I'll drink to him tonight."

He pushed the bottle back toward her. "Then it's on me."

She thanked him. He nodded and then turned to help another customer down the bar. Alex pulled the picture out of her bag and waited for him to walk back to her. She watched him talking to a blonde, blue-eyed woman. She was tall, probably in her mid-thirties, with a beautiful smile. She could have been a model or an actress. She stole several glances at the door but kept in full conversation with Liam.

Alex was bumped on her left. Startled, she jumped up.

A man had fallen into the stool next to hers. He grinned from beneath the bill of his baseball cap, showing off a smile in desperate need of a dentist's care. He was a beefy man who reeked of stale beer.

He reached out and grabbed her arm. "Thanks, sweetheart. You got a nice body to be falling into."

She pulled her arm away. "*Cabron.*"

Liam yelled down the bar at him. "Bobby, don't make me throw you outta here."

"This fine lady caught me," he muttered. He reached for her arm again to steady himself.

"Don't touch me again, Bobby," she warned, stepping back.

He drew his hand away, muttering to himself. She ignored him and sat back down. Liam walked over and scolded Bobby, then turned to her.

"Sorry about that, Alex."

"Not your problem," she said.

Liam smiled at her as if they were old friends. She used the opportunity to push the photo toward him.

"You probably know this town pretty well. I'm fairly new, and I'm trying to find an old friend. I think she lives here. You recognize her?"

He looked at the picture. "Maybe, but this isn't a great picture. What's her name?"

Alex found herself in a tight spot. She had to know her own friend's name, but no matter what name she used, it would only ensure he didn't know her.

"My friend's name is Jane, but I'm not sure if this is her in the picture. It may be just someone who looks like her. Someone said she was in here last night."

He shook his head. "Doesn't sound familiar. I don't remember seeing anyone like that yesterday." He looked down the bar. "Hey, Erika, come here."

Alex cringed but remained frozen in her seat. Erika could either help or hurt her. She took another drink and watched as the blonde he had been speaking with walked over. Erika dropped onto the stool to her right.

"Bobby bothering you?" she asked Alex. The woman was much prettier up close.

"I can handle myself."

"You're Alex, right? You work at the motel down the street."

Alex nodded. She now wanted to hide the picture.

"Erika Mack." She offered her hand but was distracted by the picture on the bar.

"Recognize her?" Liam asked.

"Yeah, I do. Where'd you get this picture?" Erika studied it, ignoring Alex. "This is a security camera picture. I can't tell the background."

Alex concocted a quick lie. "A friend sent it to me a while back. She looked like a friend I went to college with. I thought I would ask around."

"This isn't your friend." She looked at Alex, then back at the photo. "This is Leanna Nunez. She's not the college type."

Alex sighed. "Oh, well. I was hoping it was Jane." She took the picture from Erika's hands. Erika kept her eyes on the picture, frowning. Alex stuffed it back in her bag.

"I've never been to O'Sullivan's before. Is this a good place to meet people?" Alex asked, trying to distract the woman.

Erika grabbed a glass from behind the bar and winked at Liam. She spotted someone across the bar and waved. Alex wondered if she was drunk.

Erika poured her own drink. "I know a few better places. If I wasn't meeting my boyfriend here tonight, I'd take you out on the town. Maybe we can meet up later, discuss the action you've seen at the motel lately. Give me a call tomorrow," Erika said. She dug through her purse. "Here's my number. I'm sure we'd have lots to talk about. Starting with that picture."

Alex watched her walk away.

"I can show you a good time," Bobby said, grabbing Alex's shoulder.

Those were the last words he would say to her. Her mind now blank and her instincts taking over, Alex swung her right arm around so fast she snapped his head backward. He tumbled off the stool, his back flat on the bar floor. Blood poured from his nose, and his eyes rolled back into his head.

The entire bar shrank into silence. Bobby didn't move.

Fear rippled through her. She clenched her fists and slowed her breathing. Closing her eyes, she cursed silently. Every nerve in her body was tingling. Adrenaline was spiking and pushing her to escape, to run. Instead, she softened her face and looked at Liam. She took a deep, calming breath.

"Sorry."

"No need to be," said Liam. "Not the first time I've seen Bobby misbehave—although I have to say I've never seen him flattened by a woman so ... small."

A broad man with chubby cheeks and sharp eyes walked over and looked down at the drunk lying unconscious on the floor. He was the only man in O'Sullivan's wearing a suit. It looked cheap and worn, which told her he wasn't a wealthy man, but she couldn't explain why every eye in the room was on him, as if he owned the place.

The man turned to the bartender. "Liam, what happened?"

Alex started to explain, but the bartender interrupted her. "Sorry, Chief. I was just about to handle it, but the woman's a sprite faster than me."

Alex cursed. She was supposed to be inconspicuous. She wasn't supposed to get into any trouble. *In and out*, she had told Ric. Now an entire bar was staring at her, and the chief of police himself was asking the questions.

"Get him into a cab," the chief told Liam. He turned to Alex. "You're Alex Delgado, right?" He offered her a meaty hand. She considered ignoring it, then thought better of it. She shook his hand quickly then glanced toward her bag to make sure the picture was still hidden away. She leaned against the barstool and emptied her face of emotion.

"I've met your brother," he said. "A very respectable man." He stuck a cigar in his mouth and studied her. She had a sinking sensation that this man knew too much about her, so she kept her mouth shut.

"I'm sorry about the situation at the motel this morning. I have all the faith in Detective Stellar to close this case quickly so we can all go back to our quiet lives. I trust you're assisting him in every way you can?"

"Of course," Alex said. She was saved from saying any more when Erika rushed over.

"Chief!" Erika shouted. She saw the chief cringe.

He turned to her. "Erika, my dear."

"I gave you something. You give me something."

"Let's make this quick," the chief said. "I got a job to get back to."

Erika smiled at Alex and then wrapped her arm around the chief's arm. "You're not the man I hoped to meet, but you'll do for now."

Apologizing, Alex dropped a twenty on the bar despite Liam's protests. She rushed back to the motel, wondering where she could find Leanna Nunez, Eddie's mystery woman, and desperately trying to ignore the fear gripping her throat.

Chapter 13

It was midnight when Detective Stellar knocked on Joy Ochoa's door. Eddie's son Ollie answered. He was a good-looking kid, except for the mop of hair that covered most of his face.

"Is your mother home?" Stellar asked.

The boy looked past Stellar to the patrol car on the street. "He's dead, isn't he?"

Stellar squatted to level his eyes at the boy and saw the sadness in them. "You should be in bed. It's late. Why don't you get your mother?"

Stellar and Florio sat on Joy Ochoa's flea-infested couch as she lit a cigarette. With her hands shaking and her eyes closed, she inhaled deeply. The police intrusion hadn't surprised her, but she had been surprised with Eddie's murder. He had seen tears, but she quickly wiped them away. She invited them in and rushed off to grab a small photo album and her cigarettes. She passed the photos to Florio. She had been through the process before, maybe a brother or cousin.

She stared at the cigarette in her hands as if it would keep the tears away.

Stellar stared at the child across the room playing a handheld video game. He needed a haircut and a bath, but Stellar could tell the child was probably more mature than the woman they were talking to.

Joy had told the boy three times to go to bed, but he had ignored her each time. Stellar hoped he was out of earshot, but it didn't matter what the boy heard. His father was dead. He was a smart kid.

Stellar knew what it was like to lose a parent. His father was still alive, but Alzheimer's had taken everything but his life. He no longer recognized his children. He no longer recognized his wife. And, similar to this boy, Stellar had dealt with death early. His brother Sam's death had shocked everyone. He wanted to do something for the kid, help him get past the pain and guilt.

"Eddie was a good father," Joy said. "He was a good man." He could hear the tears in her voice.

"Did you know he was out of town?"

She sucked on the cigarette and ignored the smeared makeup on her face. Her eyes were bloodshot, her pupils large.

"I don't know where he went. He just said he had something to do and dropped off Ollie. Summer is too hard for me. I can't keep him here when I'm at work. Eddie knows he's supposed to take care of Ollie in the summer."

The redness in her eyes wasn't the result of crying or sadness. She was high. From the huge suitcases under her eyes, the sores on her face, and the numerous missing teeth, he suspected methamphetamines—and not just recreational use. If he searched the house, he'd find drugs.

"When did you move out?" Florio asked.

She rubbed her arms to hide her shaking. "He bought this apartment for me last year."

"Why?"

Stellar turned to watch the child at the dining room table, continuing to punch the buttons on the game console. His face was concentrated and determined. A black Labrador retriever lay at his feet, watching Stellar. The dog scratched its neck. Stellar resisted the urge to do the same.

"The drugs," she said.

Surprised by the honesty, Stellar turned to look at Joy. Both men waited for her to explain. She looked lost for a minute. Stellar listened to the sounds of the video game from across the room.

"We both grew up around it," she said finally. "In L.A., the only way to survive was to be a part of it. We left, and he had no problem leaving it behind. He wanted a fresh start in his momma's house. I didn't think he was serious, but his momma wanted him clean. So he went clean. He wanted to make her proud, even though she was dead. When Ollie came 'round, it just made him stronger. He didn't want Ollie to grow up like he did."

"But you didn't stop?" Stellar asked.

She shook her head and scratched her arm. "It's hard. I've been in and out of every facility he sent me to. I can't kick it."

"If he didn't want you around Ollie, why is the boy living with you?"

"He dropped him off a few days ago before he left. He said he'd be back by the weekend. I thought maybe he was meeting some old friends."

"In L.A.?"

She shrugged. "He don't know anyone here."

"Could he have been seeing someone else? Another woman?"

She shook her head and rubbed her eyes. "No, he's not cheating on me."

"Does he know anyone in Lake City?"

She scratched. "Where's that?"

Stellar shook his head and decided to move the conversation back to Eddie's past. "What was he selling in L.A.?"

"Cocaine mostly, but whatever he got his hands on was okay with him."

"Do you know his contacts?"

She shook her head, avoided looking at him. "No, I don't." He could have pushed, having spotted her lie, but he already had a list of his known associates, so he moved on.

"Did Eddie have any enemies?"

"Cops," she said. "They don't like him."

"Did he ever hit you? Or Ollie?"

She stared at Stellar. "No. He's not like that. His momma taught him to respect women. He never raised a hand to me or Ollie. You can ask him. That boy loved his father."

Stellar looked at Ollie. He was still focused on the game, but his eyes were red and moist.

"Was Eddie upset when he dropped Ollie off?"

She shrugged. "He wouldn't tell me if he was."

Stellar looked down at Ollie and found the boy watching him.

"Where were you on Tuesday night?" Florio asked.

Her eyes narrowed on him. "Sitting in the drunk tank. You can check with your friends."

"Did Eddie own a gun?"

"Yeah, one like yours."

Stellar glanced at the Glock at his waist. "Like this? Are you sure it wasn't a revolver?"

She shook her head. "No, he didn't like the older guns. He had an AK back in L.A., but he got rid of it."

"Did he have a cell phone?"

"Who doesn't?" she answered.

"I'm going to need the number."

"You don't have his phone?" she asked. Stellar didn't answer. "He was always forgetting it. He usually left it in the car."

Stellar took down the number. As he and Florio left the apartment, Stellar realized he was no closer to figuring out why Eddie Chavez had visited Lake City, let alone who would have wanted him dead. He looked back at the house and saw the little boy staring out the window at him. Stellar waved, but Ollie didn't move. The kid was lost between death and pain.

"Call Social Services tomorrow," Stellar whispered to Florio as they walked back to the patrol car. "Make sure they take the kid."

Florio nodded. "Do you want me to subpoena the phone records?"

"I'll have Morgan run it. Check on her alibi too. She had to be pissed to learn he was going to take her kid away from her."

"And my bet is she's going to get whatever's left of the settlement money too."

Eddie Chavez had apparently gone clean and now he was dead. But just because drugs were no longer in play didn't mean his past hadn't come back to kill him. It was important to find out why Eddie Chavez was in Lake City. The condom wrapper in the room suggested he had a visitor. If Eddie Chavez had a girlfriend in Lake City, Stellar needed to find her. The cell phone records could help. So would finding Eddie's car. But his priority was still the surveillance video. He needed to find a way around the Delgados' roadblock.

Chapter 14

Ric stood in the office doorway listening carefully to the desert sounds outside. There would be no movies tonight. He needed the deathly silence.

Alex was his sister—his only sister, his only family. She had been only ten when their mother had died, seventeen when their father had been killed. Ric, almost ten years older, had become her only living family member, and she his.

They had survived together. He had given up his life in L.A. for her. She felt bad about it, but no matter what she said or did, he wouldn't have it any other way. They needed to stick together, to be there for each other. No one else could ever take their places in each other's life.

He had heard nothing, seen nothing. That bothered him. Some killer had been mere feet away and he had done nothing. He couldn't help wondering what would have happened if the killer had chosen room 200 instead.

This was no random killing, but that didn't provide much comfort. A killer had deceived him, tricked him as he sat in his uncomfortable chair watching movies and wishing he was back in Los Angeles.

Alex needed her sleep. She looked tired, sickly, too thin. She needed something to reinvigorate her. He was the one who had pushed the idea of working out. Swimming laps at night helped ease her mind as well as strengthen her body. But she needed more than just the workouts to get her healthy again. She needed rest. She needed her peace of mind back. She needed safety and security. She needed the quiet, no matter how much she hated it. She needed time to forget. To heal.

It's why he had picked Lake City. The small town on the border of Nevada and California was only known for the man-made lake and was just outside the Death Valley National Park. He thought they could just disappear and live a quiet existence. Away from her past and their bad memories.

Ric took another glance around the empty parking lot and pool. He left the office door open and unlocked his filing cabinet. Sitting on the ground, he leafed through the folders. Every case he'd ever worked on started with good research. Information on all the players was vital. If you knew all the players it was easy to spot the guilty.

The first folders contained his personal information, his years spent as a detective with the Los Angeles Police Department. He had old case information. Some were famous cases he had closed. A few were unsolved cases he hadn't been able to let go. He had lists of contacts from LAPD to FBI and ATF. He had been a successful cop. He had been respected, even after he had cut loose.

As far as he was concerned, those years of carrying a badge were in the past, but he was still a cop at the core. His training had put him in a position to protect and serve the people he came into contact with. With or without the badge, he always thought like a cop.

Ric had spent his first month in Lake City, Nevada, scouting the terrain and learning the names. The background searches on the players in the city were essential to ensuring his sister's safety. He knew what made Mayor Lyons upset. He knew about the police chief's incompetence and how smart the chief's daughter, Erika, was. He knew how dedicated Detective Will Stellar was to his job.

He debated pulling Detective Stellar's file to review his notes. He had first seen Will Stellar as he was scouting the expensive ranch compound that surrounded the lake. The detective had been riding a horse with a couple of dogs running after him. He looked completely comfortable on a horse, with a cowboy hat covering his eyes.

Ric had almost dismissed the rider completely, except the man's posture told him this man was significant. He hadn't been surprised later to learn he was a cop. Despite the cowboy attire, the man looked like a cop. Probably lived and breathed the badge, just as Ric had.

But Ric had been more interested in the other half of the Stellar family. Will's brother Lincoln had followed in their father's footsteps, being the town savior. Lincoln funded everything in town and had a finger in every project. Money was coming in as never before. He had his father's business sense, pouring money into one project after another. Ric had been told Lincoln was as ruthless with his businesses as he was generous with the town. Ric found the paradox interesting—two sides of the same coin.

He pushed past the folders, looking for Leanna Nunez. The name sounded familiar, but he couldn't place it. There was no folder for Leanna Nunez, which meant she wasn't important, just as he expected, but there was a folder on Daniel Nunez. He pulled the folder.

Danny Nunez, nineteen, was already a repeat offender: breaking and entering as a juvenile, possession and distribution more recently. He had no violent arrests. Ric didn't expect there to be. Danny had been a small kid when Ric had first arrived at Lake City. His hair was shaggy in the pictures Ric had snapped of him during a few weeks of surveillance. Ric had included another picture of Danny's friend. He hadn't been able to identify him. He was a bit taller, but he followed Danny around like a harmless puppy.

They were a small operation, Ric remembered. They grew pot in the garage of a house he believed belonged to the puppy. He had seen

Danny with a small nine millimeter, but it was mostly for show. Ric didn't think he was capable of pulling the trigger. They were punks. Ric had calculated their threat as low.

He wouldn't have put them on the same scale as Eddie Chavez. Then again, Eddie Chavez appeared to have gone clean. He hadn't expected that.

Ric replaced the folder, pushing all the files forward. He stared down at the .44 hidden at the bottom of the drawer and then stood, walked back to the doorway, and gazed out at the dark night.

His father had taught him honor. His mother had taught him honesty. His training had taught him composure. Yet in the past twenty-four hours, he had broken into a stranger's house, stolen a picture from the residence, paid a prostitute for information, and deceived a detective. He had changed too much too fast. He wasn't sure if he was ready to make the next step.

But he had no choice. The gun was a necessity now. He was a good shot. He had never once shot a man, but he had pointed his weapon at a number of criminals, and he had no doubt that he could. He wasn't the type to hesitate when a life was on the line, but he had never been put in that position. He was much better at planning. His well-developed judgment and his ability to process all possible outcomes were powerful forces in keeping him out of danger.

The next four hours Ric spent reviewing the pages of information Detective Becker had e-mailed on Eddie Chavez. He researched the known associates and was pleased to see most were back behind bars. Some were dead, some missing, but none appeared to be living in Nevada. It was a dead end, but it would help narrow Ric's search.

Ric also did a search of Eddie's known girlfriend, Joy Ochoa. He found her living in Las Vegas, with numerous recent drug arrests. She was a key lead, but he would have to leave her to Detective Stellar.

Financial records were harder to come by, but Detective Becker had pulled some information for him. Eddie Chavez was doing fine financially due to the money the city of Los Angeles had paid him.

Beneficiary information showed the money would go to his son. The only information he wanted but didn't have was phone records. Ric knew Eddie had a cell phone and he was positive he was making or receiving calls during the four days he was in town. Those calls might explain what he was doing in Lake City or who he knew here. Since no phone had been found, he would keep digging in other areas.

He got up to stretch his legs and grabbed a protein bar from his stash in Alex's desk. He watched the horizon as night faded into dawn. There was a chill in the air that only came right before dawn. He closed his eyes and enjoyed the quiet, cool air.

Before the sun rose, he walked slowly back to the cabinet and pulled out the Colt Anaconda revolver. It was heavy. He tucked it in a pant holster at his back. Carrying the gun seemed to balance him again, but it didn't feel comfortable. Carrying a gun had never felt comfortable. The day it did, someone would end up dead.

The tee shirt he wore wouldn't cover the weapon. Locking the cabinet, he walked to his room and changed into a roomier Hawaiian shirt.

Although he wanted to leave her out of this, he went upstairs to wake Alex. He wasn't surprised to find her studying the map of Lake City. He could tell she hadn't slept again. She pulled out the earbuds and dropped the iPod on the bed.

"Let's go," Ric said, throwing her a protein bar.

Alex ignored the food and eyed the shirt. He knew what she was thinking but said nothing. She moved past him down the stairs to his truck and then she climbed into the passenger seat and watched him.

"What makes you think she's going to be home?" he asked as he climbed in and started the truck.

"She was raped, Ric. Going to work is the furthest thing from her mind."

He pulled the truck out onto the road. "But what if she wants to forget about it? She'd go to work to get her mind off of it. Maybe we should try finding out where she works."

She looked at him. "Will you trust me on this?"

He stared straight ahead. Alex looked out the window.

"I don't think she killed him," Ric finally said.

"Why, 'cause she's a woman and he was big and scary?"

He grunted. "Don't start that. I think he was killed later." He didn't explain how he knew this. He didn't want to have to explain his reason for staying a step ahead of her. "Are you sure you didn't hear anything?"

"I told you, I didn't. Now you don't believe me?"

"I believe you." He was quiet the rest of the trip. He needed to stop thinking like a brother and start thinking like a cop.

Chapter 15

Alex and Ric caught Leanna as she was on her way out. She opened the door before Alex could knock. Ric decided to let Alex to do the talking, figuring a male voice would only scare her into silence.

Leanna wasn't an attractive woman. Spats of makeup had been pasted to her face that would only melt when she walked into the desert heat. Thick mascara caked her eyelashes like spider's legs. Her lips were speared with bright red lipstick. Long black hair fell down her back. The tight skirt did little to improve her look. A stud nose ring protruded from her right nostril, and large hoop earrings hung in her ears.

Ric held back and let Alex do the introductions. She showed Leanna the picture of Eddie Chavez, her hand covering the little boy's face.

"Do you know him?"

Ric saw the flash in Leanna's eyes. Confusion, fear, but definitely recognition. Then she composed herself.

"I never saw him before. Sorry." She walked out the door and turned to close it behind her. "I have to get to work."

"We know you were at the motel with him," Alex said. "I need to know what happened. I need to hear your side before the cops find out you were the last person to see Eddie Chavez alive."

She started to protest again, but Ric held up his hand.

"We don't have time to stand in your doorway listening to you stall." He kicked the door back open and pushed Leanna backward through it.

"Ric!" Alex said.

"No need to shout," he said in barely a whisper. "We don't want to be seen here." He walked through and waited for Alex to follow. Closing the door with his foot, he locked it behind him. The room reeked of cheap rose perfume. It reminded him of seeing his great aunt in her coffin.

Alex moved closer to Leanna but didn't reach to touch her. Ric stood with his back to the door, listening for movement elsewhere in the house. He looked around the small living area. A leather couch the color of dog shit faced a 52-inch television. Hi-def, surround sound. He needed to get a better system for the office.

"*Bien*," Alex said. "We're not here to hurt you. I want to help you."

Leanna shook her head but still said nothing. Her eyes were wide, bags underneath pulling them down her thin face. He knew an addict when he saw one.

Alex cleared off the couch and sat down. He waited for Leanna to sit.

"Leanna, let me help you—"

"Danny will be here any minute," Leanna warned.

Alex looked up and caught Ric's stare. He looked at his watch but said nothing. She was probably right.

"Who's Danny?" Alex asked. "Is that your boyfriend?"

"My brother. He's on his way."

"Sit down, Leanna. Tell me what happened in Eddie's room."

Leanna seemed to wake up. She was shaking now. "I don't know what you're talking about. I've never seen that man. I have to get to work."

"I know something horrible happened to you," Alex said lowering her voice. "I need to know the details. I can help you. You have to trust me. I'm on your side."

Ric watched as Leanna started to relax. She was studying Alex. The more Alex talked and soothed, the more Ric found himself relaxing, too.

Leanna shook her head. "I swear I didn't do anything wrong."

Ric studied her hands. They twitched. Marks on her wrists could have been ligature marks. Or burn marks.

"Tell me what happened," Alex continued. "Where did you meet him?"

Leanna sat silently. Finally she sighed. "I saw him at O'Sullivan's. He bought me a drink."

"What did he say?"

Leanna didn't answer. Ric guessed she was thinking of the right answer instead of the truth.

"What was he drinking?"

"Alex," Ric interrupted, "we don't have a lot of time."

Alex persisted. "I know this is difficult, Leanna, but I need to know what happened."

"I don't know. We were talking one minute, and then the next..."

"Tell me what you remember. Do you remember going to his motel room?"

At the silence, Ric watched Leanna's face closely. It wasn't fear he saw in Leanna's eyes. Her pupils were wide, her eyes darting around. He could see she was telling the truth. She didn't remember. It confirmed his suspicion that she'd been drugged.

"Leanna, a man is dead," Alex continued. "The cops are going to come knocking any minute. I can help you with them. I can keep them away. I can protect you. I know what you're going through. You have to trust me."

"I don't know you. I didn't do anything."

With this denial, Ric saw the lie. She didn't look stupid or frightened. She looked guilty, a criminal caught in a lie.

Alex sighed. "I know."

Ric had seen enough. He left the women in the living room and walked toward the hallway. He found the kitchen first. The floor was sticky, the sink full of dirty dishes. The room smelled of spoiled milk.

He found a coffeepot and opened the top to find the grounds still wet inside. He closed the lid and then opened the low cupboard. Everything looked normal. He closed the cupboard and opened the refrigerator. A half gallon of milk and a six-pack of Budweiser sat on the top shelf. He checked the expiration on the milk. Finding nothing else of interest, he closed the door.

Walking down the hall, he peeked in the bathroom. It looked clean, so he moved on. He found Leanna's room first. *Untidy* was a nice word for it. He kicked at some clothes on the floor and uncovered only a lighter. He scanned the closet and opened the dresser. He found several knock-off Coach purses and some poorly made fake identification. He found a bag of pot tucked in with her bras. She was a hustler and probably a recreational user. Again, he was caught with the notion that she was unimportant.

He could hear Alex speaking. Despite their low voices, he could hear the sadness and desperation.

He saw movement in the corner and saw a fur ball emerge from under the bed. He thought it was a rat, then realized it was too big. A black cat. Worse than a rat, this animal was encouraged to come back. He never understood people who let filthy animals freely walk around their homes. He backed up before the cat could get any closer to him and moved on to the next room. A bedroom.

It clearly belonged to Leanna's brother. He wasn't as neat as his sister. Danny was worse than a slob. Ric wondered how a human could even live in the room. The room reeked of cigarettes and mildew. Something repulsive was growing beside the dresser. He had searched worse rooms before, so he ignored the smell and tried not to touch anything with his bare hands. He opened the drawers in the dresser, found a checkbook in the name of Daniel Nunez. He was broke. No surprise. Ric had never met a dealer with a savings plan.

A shelf in the corner held several sports trophies. At closer look, there were eight, all for soccer. Danny had been an athlete most of his childhood. Given the consecutive years of MVP trophies, he was also a hell of a player.

Ric found a beat-up cardboard box in the corner containing schoolbooks and yearbooks. He considered looking up what position Danny had played but knew it was merely curiosity and not something that would help with Eddie's murder, so he skipped it. However, he did spot a faded newspaper in the stack that interested him enough to read through.

It featured an article on a car accident that had killed Danny's parents, dated three years earlier. During a flash flood, their car had been swept from the road, killing both instantly. Danny had only been sixteen.

Too young to lose one's parents. He knew.

Ric replaced the article and found several report cards, also tucked in the box. Based on the grades, Danny had been a good student. Somewhere along the way, he'd taken the wrong road. That road may have forced him to cross paths with Eddie Chavez.

Ric searched the bed next. Underneath, he found a black duffel bag with the letters *L.I.* embroidered in white cursive writing. Curious about why it was under the bed, Ric pulled it out. He opened the bag and found hundreds of bags of white powder. Methamphetamines. He estimated close to a quarter of an ounce in each little bag. Probably over one hundred bags in the duffel.

He had known Danny sold pot, but the meth was new. He pushed the bag back and lifted the mattress. Two guns lay in the center of the box spring. A Glock and a Smith & Wesson revolver. Eddie Chavez was missing a Glock.

Ric didn't touch either weapon. He dropped the mattress and walked back down the hall. This time, he stopped at the bathroom to inspect more thoroughly.

He opened the medicine cabinet. Toothbrush, toothpaste, deodorant. He opened a package of allergy medicine and found no pills missing. He replaced the box, then looked under the sink and found several bottles in the corner. Shower cleaner. Tile cleaner. He stopped at the bottle of drain cleaner. Lifting it, he found it half empty. A single bottle of hydrogen peroxide was hidden behind it. He grabbed the dirty bottle and found the expiration date. Two years old. He put the bottle back and scrubbed his hands until they were a brilliant red.

Making his way back to the living room, he expected Leanna to be crying by now. Her face revealed something akin to fear. Ric wondered what Alex had said to her. Meanwhile, Alex's face showed no emotion. They were speaking Spanish now as if they were old friends.

He walked outside, leaving the two alone. On the porch, he watched the street and waited for his sister to finish. He wanted to find Danny.

Ric looked back at Leanna's car and then back to the house. The neighborhood wasn't great, but the house was kept up. Paint fairly new, windows unbroken. There was little trash outside. He hadn't seen scales or pots set up in the kitchen. He saw no evidence of a meth lab, no sign anything was being manufactured here. Despite the disorder, it was clean.

Twenty minutes later Alex walked out. She said nothing as she headed toward him. Ric leaned against the truck, still eyeing the house.

"She was high."

"Doesn't mean she wasn't raped," she said, grabbing the door.

"Doesn't mean she was telling the truth, either." He stopped her hand. "You know you led her."

"This isn't a trial. She needed someone to talk to."

"Did she confess?"

"To killing him? No. I don't think she killed him."

He said nothing.

"She says she doesn't remember anything after talking to Eddie at the bar. She just happened to be in the wrong place at the wrong time."

"Did you push?"

"I didn't have to. I believed her."

He rolled his eyes. "Maybe someone wanted him to pay for what he did to her."

"Her brother?"

He shrugged then opened the door for her. "Get in. I have a stop to make before I drop you off."

Chapter 16

"You're going to find Danny?" Alex asked.

Ric pulled into the parking lot of Schneider's Computer Store. He eyed a red Jeep in the lot. He ignored Alex, hoping she would leave him alone with his thoughts for a few minutes. He parked next to the Jeep and peeked inside. School books were stacked in the passenger seat.

"I want to go with you."

"No." Ric jumped from the truck and slammed the door behind him. Alex did the same.

"I want to talk to him," she persisted. "I know Leanna didn't kill Chavez. The police will be coming after her. We need to think of her."

"It's not up for debate. You're not my partner. When it comes to drug dealers, I go alone."

With Alex trailing behind him, he walked into the store and grabbed a blue basket. Schneider's was a small shop filled with electronics. It was the only place in town that was up to date with the latest technology. He wasn't surprised to find the store mostly empty—another reason it was his favorite store.

He walked down the third aisle and picked up some batteries for his digital camera. He found a box of DVD recordable discs and dropped them in the basket.

"She was high, but that wasn't a mom-and-pop lab," Alex said as she trailed behind him.

Ric glanced at the front counter. The teenager working it was listening to his iPod. He was there every time Ric came by.

Ric turned back to Alex and lowered his voice. "Danny has over thirty thousand dollars worth of meth ready for the street. It's just sitting under his bed. Why don't you go next door to the mini-mart and get something to eat?"

"I'm not hungry."

"I didn't ask if you were hungry." He pointed at the door.

Turning, he headed for the camera section. He needed to think without Alex hovering over him. He didn't know why Eddie had picked Leanna, yet a chance meeting was too much of a coincidence. Her brother just happened to be the only serious drug dealer in the city. Eddie had chosen his sister to assault. It didn't add up. He hadn't pegged Eddie as stupid or reckless.

Searching the shelves, Ric found a teddy bear nanny cam and checked the specifications. It offered color video and remote viewing, but no audio. Knowing it would be hard to hide in a drug dealer's den, he put it back on the shelf. He felt uncomfortable with the bear's eyes staring back at him. It looked sad and lonely and Ric wondered if a child would want it nearby.

He found a small clock radio with a pinhole lens. The clock radio had similar specifications and if placed properly, it could be missed. But audio was still a problem. He picked up a wireless microphone. He put both in the basket and added up his total. It was more than he wanted to spend on a drug dealer.

Alex reappeared, holding a newspaper instead of food.

"Do you even attempt to listen to me?" he asked. He put the camera back. He needed audio more. He glanced back at the lonely bear on the shelf.

Alex stepped in front of him. "You're thinking it's not a coincidence that two drug dealers crossed paths?"

"You need food."

When she didn't respond, he shrugged.

"Eddie's an Eighteenth Street banger," he said, keeping his voice low. "You know they have connections to the Mexican Mafia. They deal in high-end product. Danny grows low-rate pot in his garage. They're not in the same league. We're missing someone in between."

She tossed the newspaper at him. "The paper claims no one in town knew him."

He looked at the paper. The front page featured a picture of a young Eddie Chavez. Erika Mack worked fast. He read the article under the caption. It was thorough. She had listed Eddie's arrest record, as well as a quote from the chief promising to find the murderer. Sergeant Morgan offered some very basic information. The stranger had been killed by a gunshot wound to the head early Wednesday morning. The investigation was ongoing. There was no quote from Detective Stellar.

Ric skimmed the rest of the newspaper. They hadn't talked to everyone. Erika hadn't bothered to interview himself or Alex. There was no mention of Danny or Leanna Nunez.

"We need to find out why Eddie was in town," he said.

"Maybe Eddie came to take over Danny's customer base."

Ric shrugged. "Too small, and it doesn't explain how Danny has that much meth sitting under his bed."

"You already said he's a dealer—"

He shook his head. "It hasn't been touched, which means two things. Leanna doesn't know it's there—"

"Or she would have dipped into it," Alex muttered.

"And he's too scared to touch it."

"So it's stolen. Maybe from Eddie. Maybe Eddie's moved into methamphetamines. It's not too much of a stretch. The market is growing fast."

Ric agreed, but something still bothered him. If Danny stole the dope from Eddie, Eddie could retaliate by assaulting the sister. And Danny, like most brothers, would come after anyone who attacked his sister.

"You don't think Danny pulled the trigger?" Alex said.

He shrugged. "Danny was there. He had Eddie's gun." He handed the paper back to her and walked to the counter.

The kid smiled too brightly when he spotted Ric, revealing a mouthful of metal. He took the earphones out of his ears. "Hey, Mr. Delgado, how's it going?"

He wasn't sure of the teenager's name, so he always called him Buddy. "Hey, Buddy. Have you seen Danny around here lately?"

"No way, man. Haven't seen him around in a couple of weeks. I owe you."

Alex stepped up. "What did you do?"

"Oh, dude, you gotta show it off," he said as he began ringing up the items from the basket. "He installed some cameras outside. It's kept all kinds of trouble away. The system's sweet."

Ric shrugged. "It was nothing."

"Nah. My friend Carly works next door at the mini-mart, and she says she feels so much safer now. I totally owe you, dude."

"Is that your Jeep outside?" Ric asked.

"Yeah, just got it last week. My dad bought it for me. He said it's 'cause you keep buying stuff here. You like it?"

"I was just wondering where you got it. My sister here needs a car so I don't have to drag her everywhere."

The kid looked over at Alex, blushing. "Hey! Sweet. I didn't know you had a sister. That's cool, dude. We don't have a dealership or anything here, but my dad's friend Harvey fixes up old cars and resells them. I'll tell him you might be interested in something."

As Ric handed the kid a wad of cash, Alex dropped the newspaper on the counter. "I'm Alex. Nice to meet you. Do you know this guy?"

The kid looked down at the picture, and his smile faded. When he looked up, he spoke to Ric.

"No, man. I heard about that guy at the motel. Sucks for you, huh? I didn't know him. I don't think anyone did, but I heard a customer say they saw him at the church the other night, for the thing with Ann Wesley. Maybe she knew him."

"Go get something to eat," Ric told Alex.

"Where does Ann live?" she asked, ignoring him.

"Just down the street. Lake View Apartments." He glanced at Ric and smiled. "I don't know why they call it that. They don't have a lake view. I guess the guy thinks with a name like Lake View, the people won't realize it's a dump."

Ric pointed Alex toward the door. "Get something to eat." He turned back to the kid. "You got a sister who talks too much?"

The kid chuckled and blushed again. He handed Ric his change.

When Alex didn't move, Ric grabbed her arm and his bag of electronics and walked her to the door. "You need to eat something," he growled.

"Why stage Eddie's death as a suicide?" she whispered.

Ric pushed open the door and they stepped out into the heat. "Danny wants to move up in the business world. Meth is easier and cheaper to produce and is increasing in popularity, but if he gets caught the result is the same. He needed to make Eddie's death look like a suicide so he doesn't end up in prison."

"You think he's that smart?"

"Street smart maybe."

They climbed in the car.

"Then tell me, how'd he get in the room?" she asked. "There wasn't a struggle. You said they weren't in the same league. You think he's smarter than Eddie? I saw Eddie. I don't think he's stupid enough to open the door for Danny. He wouldn't have asked him in. He wouldn't have sat quietly as Danny put a gun to his head and pulled the trigger."

He saw where she was going with this. Danny had to have help. Ric couldn't see Eddie opening the door for Leanna after what he had done to her. He ruled out Danny's puppy-dog friend as well. Opening your door to one drug dealer was stupid. Opening it to two was suicidal.

He realized he had overlooked the crucial piece of information. Maybe listening to his sister would prove useful. He closed his eyes and recalled the scene.

"I'm wrong," he said. "Danny couldn't use Eddie's gun, because it wasn't in the room. I think he left it in the car when he carried Leanna to the room. When she takes off with the car, she takes off with his gun. It makes him vulnerable to anyone knocking on his door."

"Which puts us at square one again. Anyone could have killed him."

He shook his head. "Danny's involved."

"Just because he had meth under his bed?"

"That much meth is worth killing for."

"I'm going to see Ann Wesley."

He considered this. She wasn't asking for his permission. It had been a long time since he had worked with a partner. He wasn't sure if he liked the idea of his partner being his sister.

"Eat first. You go see Ann and find out if she knew Eddie. I'll watch Danny. We'll compare notes later." He studied her. "We're in this together now."

She hugged him, but he pulled her off of him.

"Don't ever do that again," he said.

Chapter 17

It was a bit of a walk, but Alex knew the fresh air would be good for her. Still, it was hot and dry as a bone. She found the Lake View Apartments easily despite the dilapidated sign. Few cars were out. The street was empty except for a black Dodge Magnum parked across the street. It reminded Alex of a hearse. The building looked less cared for than the sign. She had seen similar rundown apartments in South Los Angeles. She found Ann's apartment at the top of a set of muddy, dingy steps. The door was open. She heard movement inside but opted to stay outside.

"Ms. Wesley?" she called while peering inside.

Boxes were stacked near the door. Furniture had been moved to the center of the room. A middle-aged woman came to the door, holding a roll of tape. Her blonde hair was flat and pulled back in a loose ponytail. She wore no makeup on her plain face. Her gray dress hung loose on her thin form. She stared at Alex through round glasses.

"Where's Lincoln?" she asked in a husky voice.

Confused, Alex looked around. "I don't know. Who's Lincoln?"

Suddenly, Ann looked frustrated. "I thought you were with Lincoln. I'm waiting for him to bring the truck." She pointed back to the boxes. "I have to get back. I don't have much time to get this stuff all boxed up."

Alex shrugged. "I can help."

Ann considered this, then waved her inside. "I can use the help, but there's no air. It's been out for a week now. You're new in town, huh?"

"Yeah, how'd you know?" She looked at the woman's small round face.

"You don't know Lincoln. Everyone knows Lincoln. What's your name?"

"Alex Delgado. My brother and I work at the Death Valley Motel. Are you moving?"

Ann sighed. "I have no choice. I can't afford the rent here anymore. I have nothing to stay for, anyway."

Alex said nothing as she followed Ann's lead and opened the cabinet and started wrapping the glasses in paper. She noticed Ann didn't have a set, just a couple of tall glasses and a few short ones. She had a lot of plastic cups, some of which advertised local clubs or parks.

The air was stale and warm. The woman didn't even have a fan running. Ann grabbed another box and started packing. She seemed friendly, allowing a complete stranger in her home, but Alex wondered why the woman hadn't asked why she was there.

"How long have you lived here?" Alex asked.

"All my life." Ann stopped filling the box and looked out the door. "It's sad to leave. Growing up, I thought things were going to be so different. I graduated with Lincoln. He was in my class. I had a huge crush on him." She smiled, remembering. "I used to picture us getting married, having kids."

"What happened?" Alex asked. She saw no rings on the woman's hands, no jewelry of any kind.

"Oh, it was just a girl daydreaming. Every young girl dreamed of being with one of the Stellar boys."

"Stellar? Is Lincoln related to the detective?"

"Oh, yes, dear. They're brothers. Will was just a bit younger than me, but he was always completely devoted to his girlfriend. Although they have their issues, too. If only he could see her for what she truly is. He might have never come back to Lake City. Lincoln, he's still single. Probably always will be. Since taking over the family business, he's been totally focused on growing the city."

Alex saw a bug scurry past her hand and decided she was done packing the cabinet.

The woman paused in thought. "I think it's the dimples. Will shows them off more than Lincoln, but when you see them, you just fall in love."

Alex hadn't noticed any dimples. Ann was offering some interesting information, but it wasn't useful. Not sure how long she would continue gabbing, Alex grabbed another box and decided to move the conversation along. "Did you hear about the murder at the motel?"

Ann stopped, but didn't look at her. "Yeah, I saw it in the paper this morning."

Alex sensed irritation in her voice. "Did you know him?"

She shook her head. "From what the paper said, it doesn't appear anyone did. A total stranger is killed, and the town can't stop talking about it. How quickly everyone moves on. I went to the post office this morning, and Charlie and Debbie were talking about it." She waived her hands as if they didn't matter. "They're neighbors from down the street. They said he was shot in his own room." She mulled this over, then added, "It's sad. No one's safe anymore."

Alex closed up her box and grabbed another one. She took the long way around the boxes so she could get a good look at Ann's face.

"His name was Eddie Chavez," Alex said.

Ann didn't react to the name. Alex heard a truck outside.

"It's about time. Lincoln can help with the rest of this. Thank you."

Alex knew when she was being excused, but she wasn't satisfied yet. Alex pulled out the picture and showed it to Ann. "This is him. Have you seen him before?"

Ann shook her head. "He doesn't look familiar. Probably not a local, but you can check with Erika Mack. She knows everyone in town." She glanced at the door.

"Someone mentioned they saw him at the church the other night. With you."

She shook her head. "There would be no reason for him to be there. No, whoever said that is mistaken."

Alex looked up as a man walked in the door. He rushed to Ann's side and helped her up.

"Who are you?" he asked, glaring at Alex.

The man was big and intimidating. Alex stood and faced him but kept out of his reach. He wore a white starched shirt with the sleeves rolled up, as if used to hard work, but his black slacks were definitely Armani. His hands were calloused, but his wrist was adorned with an expensive watch, similar to Detective Stellar's. He also wore a big, expensive ring, probably commemorating some championship. In the eyes she saw the resemblance to his brother.

She scanned the room, the exits and the angles. Then she turned to face Lincoln Stellar head on. He stood tall, his back straight and his chin up. He controlled the room much like his brother had controlled his crime scene the day earlier. But Detective Stellar's power had come from the badge. Lincoln's self confidence came from the wealth he flaunted.

"I'm Alex Delgado. You must be Lincoln. I was just asking Ann if she knew this man."

He stepped toward her, but Alex didn't flinch. As she focused on his dark eyes, he snatched the picture from her hands. She saw the recognition, then saw it change to anger.

"Ann, I'll show Alex out, and then we can start packing the truck."

He released Ann only to take hold of Alex's arm. Even though his anger had settled, Alex shook him off. She disliked being touched, even if she didn't feel threatened. His stature and demeanor pushed her toward the door.

He handed the picture back to her once she was out the door. He had the same great hair as his brother, but his was speckled with bits of gray.

"You tell that bastard to stay away from Ann," he warned. "Let him know if I see him in Lake City again, I'll take him down personally."

"He's dead."

Surprise replaced the temper, and then it was gone, leaving his face unreadable. In that split second, Alex was positive he really didn't know.

"The man they found at the motel?" he said, his voice softening. "I didn't realize they'd identified him yet."

"How did you know him?"

Lincoln sighed, glanced back toward Ann. "I don't know him. Neither does Ann. He showed up at the church the other night. It was a private gathering, and he decided to crash. He was belligerent and was bothering my guests. I had him removed from the property."

"Did he say anything to you or to Ann?"

Lincoln shook his head. "I kept him away from her. I only saw him for a minute before he was escorted outside."

"Did you see him after this?"

Lincoln shook his head again. "No, but I'm not sorry he's dead. He didn't belong in Lake City. We don't like his type here."

"What type is that?" Alex asked.

He didn't answer. Ann was calling him. "I need to get back to her."

Why was a rich powerful man interested in this poor, lonely woman?

Alex started her long walk back but stopped at the street. Lincoln's truck was open. The words *Lincoln's Ice* were painted on the truck's side. She peered into the empty truck and wondered why he would carry ice in a truck with no refrigeration. She looked up at the house and saw Lincoln watching her.

Alex was distracted as a cat bolted through the neighbor's yard. She thought she saw movement in the black Magnum still parked at the curb and wondered how far along Detective Stellar had gotten in his investigation.

Chapter 18

Six months earlier, Ric Delgado had spent considerable time staking out the house on Ember Glen Road. It was a normal-looking home sitting only a few feet from the freeway overpass, where junkies often converged.

The house was painted light beige with teal trim. The paint was starting to fade and flake, but not so much that the average passerby would notice. There was nothing interesting or unique about it. The windows were clean, and the drapes always closed to the hot sun. There were no plants in the planter boxes, but there were no weeds either.

The house was unremarkable, even to Ric. What drew his attention was the garage, a stucco building set back away from the front of the house. The glass windows in the garage door had been covered, a sure sign something was worth hiding.

Six months earlier, he had watched Danny Nunez open the garage. The rows of marijuana plants hadn't impressed him. It wasn't a large operation—a local kid growing weed and selling to his friends bored Ric. He had left the drug hole without much thought.

Now, Ric questioned that decision. He sat low in his truck and watched a young man walk from the house, wearing a white tee shirt with the word *Cutter* printed in large black letters. Ric had seen him on the last visit, wearing the same shirt.

Cutter grabbed an old Huffy bike from the lawn and cruised around the street. No sign of Danny. He rode the bicycle up and down the street. Whenever a car slowed, Cutter cruised to the driver's side door. Money moved out the window, and a baggy was passed inside. The exchange wasn't covert. Cutter kept the dope in his pockets, a sure sign of a rookie.

Ric easily identified each bag, size, and amount that was changing hands. Cutter wasn't as smooth as Danny had been. He had yet to see any meth changing hands.

Cutter was less observant, so Ric considered moving closer to the house. The garage was closed, and he hadn't seen any other activity other than Cutter going in and out. He wanted to see Danny, but if he didn't, Cutter would do.

Ric slid down lower in the truck as Cutter rode the bike back into the yard. A white sedan turned onto Ember Glen, coming straight at Ric. He focused on the driver for a split second before turning his head away.

Cop.

The car cruised past Ric's truck. Ric glanced at Cutter, who hadn't moved from the lawn. Cutter was watching the car, too.

Ric's first impression was that the cop was dirty. Why else would he cruise right past a known drug hole and not stop to hassle Cutter? Why else would Cutter not have reacted?

Ric trailed the Taurus in his rearview mirror and watched the unmarked car slow at the intersection. The driver turned to look down both streets, then slowly crept forward. Ric turned to watch Cutter. He had watched the cop, too. He dropped the bike and rushed inside the house. He had given too much credit to the kid. He hadn't spotted the cop until it was too late. The cop didn't stop because he had more pressing matters at hand. Detective Stellar probably had every officer searching for Eddie Chavez's missing Mercedes.

With Cutter hiding, Ric considered giving up the surveillance. A moment later, Cutter returned with Danny. Ric sat up to get a better angle. Cutter grabbed the bike and took off down the street. Ric didn't bother to watch him. Danny was his focus now.

His hair was longer and his clothes were dirtier. He was starting to look like the street punk he was. He glanced down the street where the cop car had disappeared. He was looking for movement, so Ric was safe from being spotted. Danny stood on the lawn for another minute, making Ric think he was waiting for someone. Instead, he turned toward the garage and unlocked the padlock. He waited a second, then put on gloves.

Ric watched as the garage door lifted. He expected to see the same setup as before, with lines of plants and florescent lights, but the plants were now gone. Ric opened his glove compartment and rummaged through the junk until he found his camera. He slipped in the new batteries and took two quick shots of the Mercedes sitting inside the garage. Danny had now upgraded from street dealer to professional criminal.

Danny used a screwdriver to remove the license plate. Tossing the screwdriver and the plate aside, he jumped into the car and pulled out slowly. As soon as he hit the street, he changed gears and drove west, past Ric's parked truck. Ric watched in his side mirror until Danny turned left. He started the truck, cranked a quick U-turn, and rushed off after him. With the streets empty, it was going to be hard to follow him. He turned left where he had seen the Mercedes turn. Spotting the car three blocks down, he started his slow pursuit.

Ric kept his car at least three blocks away at all times. He expected Danny to scan the roads, but his worries would revolve around a cop car or an unmarked. Ric's dirty pickup shouldn't draw attention, unless the pursuit lasted longer than a few minutes.

Luckily, the pursuit didn't last long. Ric watched as Danny slowed at a dirt road. Ric didn't slow and came up behind him as Danny turned right into a mobile home park. Danny wasn't paying attention to anything behind him. He was focused completely on the road ahead. Even if he spotted Ric, Danny would have no reason to fear him. They'd never met.

Ric drove straight past for another minute, his eyes on his rearview mirror, waiting to see if Danny would come back out. When he didn't, Ric pulled over and parked alongside the road. He grabbed the camera, stuffed the Colt revolver in the glove compartment, and ran back toward the mobile home park. He opted to jump the short brick wall surrounding the park instead of walking directly on the dirt road, in case Danny was watching it. The wall was covered in thick ivy. Trying not to think of the rodents living in the ivy, Ric jumped up and over. Once over, Ric had no idea which way to go. He listened, hoping to hear the Mercedes, but all he heard was the hum of air conditioners. He would have to do a row-by-row search. At the same time, he kept an eye out for any video cameras.

He avoided the main road in case Danny had parked alongside. The park seemed small, only three mobile homes wide. He stayed east of the entrance and made his way between the first two homes. The alleyway was narrow and filled with garbage, which would hide him well if necessary.

Ric began his methodical search, scanning the alleys, dirt roads, and driveways for the Mercedes. After the first three rows, he heard voices and stopped to listen. He couldn't make out the words but identified a man and a woman to his right.

Making his way down the alley, Ric spotted the Mercedes parked alongside the dirt road, behind a white Toyota Corolla that had seen better days. The two cars looked odd sitting next to each other.

Ric inched his way closer. Danny and a blonde woman were too preoccupied with the car to notice his approach. When the woman turned from Danny, Ric got a clear look at her.

Rick shook his head and smiled. Erika Mack.

He pushed his back into the alley and watched as she walked to the Mercedes. She opened the door, got in, and leaned down, looking for something. Ric aimed the camera, ready to get a clear shot of her stepping from the car. He snapped two shots of her searching the front seat. He could tell she was frustrated as she did the same to the back seat. Danny waited outside the car, staring out to the street.

Erika emerged a minute later. She pulled an envelope from her pocket and handed it to him. Ric snapped another picture, but he missed the exchange. Ric didn't move from his spot as she walked back to her Toyota and drove out. Danny watched her go.

Danny walked around the Mercedes with a dirty red rag and wiped it down. He made his way methodically along the edges of the car, taking the same kind of care Ric had taken to find him. Ric was impressed by his patience. Wiping a car of every print was a tedious process.

Chapter 19

Alex Delgado stood in her open doorway and stared at the destruction. Her bed had been tossed aside, and the drawers thrown from the dresser. The mirror above her dresser had been shattered into thousands of little pieces. Each sliver grabbed the sunlight from the open door, shining across the carpet.

If the mess had ended there, she would have considered it a simple break-in, but the writing on the wall told her differently. Someone had spray-painted above her bed in blood-red paint: *Go home.* As she looked at every letter in detail, the threat against her was almost palpable. A murderer had been in her motel. Now he had been in her room. She should feel scared. Instead, she was furious.

She stared at the last word on the wall and wondered where home was. She had once thought it was Los Angeles, but the home she had shared with her parents and brother had been shattered too early. She was too detached from her past to remember a home. The only home she had was her hotel room, and someone had destroyed it.

She leaned down and flipped through her CDs. Each one was cracked. Not a single one had been spared. Not that it would have mattered. Her stereo was smashed. Given the destruction, she guessed a baseball bat or metal pipe. Something strong, wielded by someone with a lot of hate.

How had she made someone so angry with her?

She stepped over the scattered clothes and shattered glass to the bathroom. It had been spared. Under the counter, she found the leftover paint she had kept in case any of the rooms needed a touch-up.

After erasing the words from the wall, she spent the next twenty minutes searching the remaining rooms and the front office for any evidence of an intruder. Only her room had been violated.

She considered calling the cops, but she didn't want to see Detective Stellar. He was too dedicated; he would need to question her. That would lead to more problems than solutions. It was time for Alex to take care of herself. She had stood motionless for too long. If someone wanted to fight, she sure as hell was ready to fight back.

Although she had wiped them off the walls, she couldn't erase the words from her mind as she unlocked the office door. She was thankful the office had been spared. She scanned her files and made sure nothing was missing. Ric's laptop was still sitting on the table. The safe under the desk was untouched. She checked Ric's cabinet, but it was locked tight.

She pulled out the security discs she had hidden in her drawer. If the break-in was connected to the murder, the thief would have been looking for the discs, but he hadn't found them. Either he had given up, or he was after something else.

Alex opened the small fridge and pulled the security disc from the recorder. She sat down to see who it was that hated her so much.

Chapter 20

Detective Stellar paced with the phone to his ear. He had spent all morning scouring the internet for information on Carson Realty, Inc.

The office began closing in on him. He was tired of looking at the taupe walls. He had worn a path in the carpet as he paced, but he couldn't sit down. He hadn't slept in twenty-eight hours, hadn't eaten in nine. He was long out of coffee. It wasn't even noon yet, but he wasn't going to give in. The Delgados would not win this round.

His cell phone rang. He glanced at the readout and hit the ignore button. It was his mother, likely calling to confirm the spreading gossip about his breakup with Erika.

As he waited for Nicolas Carson's assistant to come to the phone, Sergeant Morgan walked in and sat down in the chair.

"Tell me you got the warrant signed," Stellar said.

"Not yet. Judge Brown isn't in yet. Any luck with the owner?"

Stellar shook his head. "Getting closer, though." He saw the folder in Morgan's hands. "What did you find?"

"One of the prints from the room came back. Ric Delgado."

Stellar looked at the folder. "He's got a jacket?"

"Not as a criminal. He used to be a cop in Los Angeles."

Stellar straightened. "You're kidding." But it made sense. The attitude, the stance, the composure. "A beat cop?"

Morgan shook his head. "He's a retired detective. He spent eight years in patrol and nine as a detective in vice and narcotics. Retired at the young age of thirty-six."

Cradling the phone against his shoulder, Stellar grabbed the folder from him. Things were moving now. He couldn't hold back a smile. "Why'd he leave early?"

"Just up and quit. His record is spotless. No complaints against him, through seventeen years on the force. This, I was reminded several times, is pretty damn impressive in L.A. After quitting, he worked as a bouncer at a couple of different bars, then moved out here."

Stellar skimmed the notes. "To run a motel in a town where he has no connections. Why Lake City? What brings an L.A. narcotics detective out here?"

Morgan shook his head.

Stellar had a dead dealer and a retired narcotics detective. The drug connection could still be in play. He should focus on the victim, but the Delgados looked much more interesting. They were hiding secrets, and he wanted to know what they were.

He heard the scratching at the window and glanced at the bird as it watched him. Morgan stood. He stopped and turned around.

"I was at Lincoln's last night."

Morgan had something on his mind. "Yeah?"

"Danny Nunez showed up."

Placing the phone on speaker, Stellar put down the headset. Hold music filled the office.

"Why?"

Morgan shook his head. "I don't know. Lincoln talked to him for a few minutes, and then the kid left. Lincoln said he's trying to help him out."

Stellar rubbed his head, feeling his good mood evaporate. "Lincoln needs to stop trying to save everyone."

He remembered the man he had seen with Lincoln at the cemetery. "Do you know the new guy that's hanging around him? A. J."

Morgan nodded. "Yeah, cool kid. He's from Reno, I think. He's staying in the guesthouse."

"Do me a favor. See what you can find out about him. Lincoln didn't give me a last name, but if you can find out, run him."

"You want to run background searches on your brother's friends now?"

"I don't trust strangers. Not around Lincoln. I'll talk to Lincoln about staying clear of Danny."

Stellar turned back to the information on Ric Delgado. He needed to know why Delgado had left the force. He wanted to know if the ex-cop had ever crossed paths with Eddie Chavez.

His thoughts were interrupted by a crackle in the phone. He snatched it up as the music faded.

"Detective Stellar?" A woman's voice.

"Yes, I'm waiting to speak to Nicolas Carson."

"I'm connecting you now."

Another minute passed before a man's voice picked up.

"Detective, this is Nick Carson. I have a team of attorneys that can help you with whatever you need. Is it really necessary for you to speak to me directly?"

Will caught the underlying message. Nicolas Carson was a busy man, an important man. But Will was more important. He jumped up so he could pace again.

"Mr. Carson, I appreciate the few minutes you can spare for me. I'm interested in one of your properties here in Nevada. The Death Valley Motel."

"Doesn't sound like one of mine. If something happened on the property, you can reach my attorneys."

"I'm not looking for a guilty party here, Mr. Carson. You're listed as the owner."

Stellar heard the man sigh, then clicking on a keyboard. "Here it is. Death Valley Motel." The tone in the man's voice changed. He seemed relieved and relaxed. "I don't own that one."

Will breathed in deeply, exhaled slowly. "Mr. Carson, I have a business license with your name on it."

"Well, yeah. It's a technicality. My ex-wife is in the process of moving it over to her name. It was just put in my name to reduce the red tape. I was trying to avoid the legal and financial issues that would have come up. You know."

"No, I don't know." Stellar rubbed his temples. "I'm investigating a homicide on the property, Mr. Carson. I need to speak to your ex-wife."

"A homicide? How exciting. Is Allie not there?"

"Allie?" Will stopped pacing. Something struck him hard in the chest. "Alex. Alex Delgado?"

"Oh, I didn't realize she'd dropped my name. Can't blame her, though. Too many memories as Alex Carson. She's a great woman, Allie. Have you met her?"

"Yes. I have, indeed." Will thanked Mr. Carson and dropped the phone on his desk.

Staring at his computer, his temper began to rise again. The woman was not to be trusted. She had deceived him again, causing him to spend half the morning chasing his tail. Will was done playing games with the Delgados. He opened his office door. Erika Mack smiled back at him.

"Got a minute?" she asked.

"Not really. I've got a million things to do right now."

She stepped in his way and put her hand on his chest, stopping him in mid-stride.

"You'll make the time for me." She continued to smile.

He couldn't tell if it was the dejected girlfriend smile or the journalist smile. Either way, he didn't want this conversation. Not now. He glanced around the room and saw several cops staring at him. Officer Morgan stood in the corner, smirking.

"Damn it, Erika, I don't have time to play games right now."

"Oh, I think you made that clear when you broke up with me. I'm not here to rehash." She pushed him back into his office. He reluctantly allowed it and watched her close the door.

"Erika—"

"I'm not here to take, Will. I have information to trade. That's how it works, I know. I give you information, you give me information."

He laughed and sat on the edge of his desk. He couldn't resist staring into her beautiful eyes. "And here I was thinking you were here on a personal call."

"You stood me up last night."

"I have a dead guy in our morgue. He's got a bullet in his skull."

"I'm sure Wags can get it out for him. I can't believe you would give up a drink with me for a guy who's not going anywhere."

"A drink with you would have led to more, and you know it. I don't think we want to go there again."

"Why not? The sex was always good."

He smirked and stuffed his hands in his pockets. "I won't deny that, but the morning after was always too painful."

"We're still friends."

He nodded slowly. He knew where this was going. They had known each other too many years to count. Grade school. High school dances. The endless fights. The big break-up. The rumors. Too much history for a clean break.

"We can still have a drink together once in a while," she pressed.

He continued to nod but didn't interrupt her. He focused on the ground between their feet. It was safer that way.

"And friends help each other."

Now, he raised his gaze to hers. "And how are you going to help me?"

"I ran into a woman at O'Sullivan's last night asking all kinds of questions. I was wasting time waiting for you."

"I never told you I'd meet you."

"You're not going to ask who the woman was?"

He shrugged. "I don't know how it's important, other than to remind me I stood you up on a date we never set."

"She had a photo. Black and white. From what looked like a security camera."

He straightened. "Alex Delgado was at O'Sullivan's last night?"

She pouted. "How'd you guess?"

"Who was in the photo?"

"I can't recall. Tell me how you knew."

He knew the routine. "I'm a detective. It's kinda my job. She has surveillance footage from the motel on the night of Eddie Chavez's murder. I need that footage. Tell me who was in the photo."

Erika pulled out her notebook and wrote quickly. "What makes you think I knew who was in the photo?"

He wanted to strangle her. "Because you know everyone in town and you wouldn't have come here with just Alex asking questions. Tell me who's in the photo and I'll give you a quote for tomorrow's paper."

Erika's face lit up. "And drinks tonight?"

Sergeant Morgan walked in. He smiled then winked at Erika. Stellar rolled his eyes.

"Patrol found Eddie's car in a mobile home park near the old mines."

Stellar cursed. "I'm on my way now."

Erika jumped to follow. "I'll beat you there."

Chapter 21

"We have a problem," Ric said as he walked into the office.
Alex stretched her legs and rubbed her tired eyes. "You have no idea." She pointed to the screen. "Take a look."

Intrigued, Ric walked over. She pressed play, and they both watched as a man walked onto the screen. He wore a brown baseball cap and kept his head down. With the sun behind him, his face was nothing but a shadow. He held a bat in his right hand and a spray can in his left.

"Who the hell is that?" Ric asked.

"Apparently a fan of mine," she said as the man walked up the stairs toward her room and then disappeared from the screen.

"What did he do?"

She could hear the fury in his voice. It was so overpowering, she almost didn't hear the worry.

"Just trashed the place. Nothing appears to be stolen. I guess someone didn't know we had cameras."

"*Mierda.*"

Alex looked back at her brother. He rarely cursed, and he never reverted to Spanish.

"He was in your room?" he asked.

His eyes were still focused on the screen. The man reappeared and walked calmly down the steps. Just at the camera's edge, he took off the hat and wiped sweat from his forehead. He replaced the cap backward.

Ric reached over and paused the video and zoomed in on the frame. The cap read *Lake City Lakers.*

"He didn't come in the office?" He looked around the office. "This wasn't for money. It's personal."

"Doors were locked, but he didn't even look interested."

Ric grunted. "The security discs you pulled were in here, right?"

"And perfectly safe. All of my CDs are destroyed, though."

She saw the rage boiling in him. She pressed play, and he watched the man throw the spray can toward the pool.

"We could get prints from the spray can, if we involve the police," she said. "If we keep them out of it, our only evidence is the video. There's no clear shot of his face at any time. Just shadows."

"We've pissed someone off. We need to get you out of here."

"I can take care of myself. I'll spend the night cleaning, but it'll take more than a trashed room to make me jumpy."

"This is the just the beginning. I can't see the whole picture yet, but too much is going on that I can't explain yet. One wrong step and you'll be back behind bars."

"What?" she asked. He was upset about more than just the break-in. She watched him attach his camera to the printer.

"Danny's operation is changing. The stash of meth at the house means he's planning on moving up in the big bad world, but I didn't peg him for auto theft. I followed him as he dumped Eddie's car, but the cops happened upon it, and I had to bug out."

As the photos began to print, he said nothing. He turned back to the still-video image of the man in the baseball cap.

Alex picked up the photos. A man on a cell phone. She guessed he was Leanna's brother, Danny. The missing Mercedes. She stopped at a picture of the blonde.

"That's Erika," she said. "She's the one who identified Leanna in the bar."

"Erika Mack. She's the chief's daughter—and Detective Stellar's girlfriend. She has an interest in Eddie's car. She took a few minutes to search it before leaving it for patrol to find. If she's in this, so is Detective Stellar. This is bigger than the two of us can handle. It's time for you to leave."

Alex stared at the picture. "I'm not leaving."

"I'm not asking. It's only a matter of time before Stellar finds out about you. You'll be the perfect scapegoat."

"What if he doesn't know Erika's involved in this? I think he's really trying to find Eddie's killer."

"Alex, if he doesn't know, he will soon enough. He's going to do whatever he can to protect her from getting caught in the middle. This is a small city. He can turn this investigation in any direction he wants. Hell, he'll have the police chief pushing him to cover it up. This is bigger than a dead drug dealer from L.A. It's no longer important who killed Eddie Chavez."

She fingered the necklace in her pocket. "That's exactly why I'm not leaving."

He cursed again. "Okay, but you have to promise me we do things my way. Your way gets people killed." He grabbed the photos and pushed the door open. She watched him drive away, still thinking of Erika Mack.

Chapter 22

Detective Stellar stared at the Mercedes. The license plates were missing, but he was positive it was Eddie Chavez's car. Several officers surrounded the car, working like ants in the hot sun. Stellar chose to stand in the shade and watch.

An officer updated him. "We have an eyewitness. She says a white pickup truck sped out of here just a few minutes before I pulled up." The officer closed the notebook. "We couldn't get a better description."

Stellar nodded, but he had a strong instinct he knew who this white truck belonged to. The wind kicked up. The crime scene tape snapped in the wind.

"We're knocking on doors, but it's the only lead we have. We haven't found anything in the car except the registration belonging to Eddie Chavez."

Stellar scanned the mobile home park. "Find out if there are any video cameras in the area. And get the car towed back to the garage."

He heard the crunching gravel of a car approaching and turned to see Officer Florio pulling up.

"What'd you learn at Eddie's?" Stellar asked Florio through the open window.

Florio shook his head. "Nothing there. Metro confirmed Joy Ochoa's alibi. While I was there, I thought I'd run a few names through the LVMPD system." He climbed out of the car and handed Stellar a folder. "You'll find this very interesting."

"I'll go over it later," Stellar said. "I need to finish up with the car." He tried to hand the folder back, but Florio refused to take it.

"You're gonna want to read it now, sir."

Stellar watched as the officers scurried around the car. The wind punched at the dust circling around them, sending a dust devil sweeping past him. One of the officers turned to him and shook his head. They weren't finding any prints.

It was time to start beating down the doors. Someone had to know something. He glanced past the crime scene tape and saw Erika standing patiently next to her photographer as he snapped pictures.

Opening the folder, Stellar scanned the pages. Then he stopped and reread the page more carefully. He looked at Florio, who remained silent. His eyes revealed nothing.

"Why didn't we see this earlier?"

Florio shook his head. "Someone didn't want us to."

He read it again. He suddenly felt unsteady on his own legs. "Help them finish processing the car."

"Are you sure you don't need backup?" Florio called to Stellar's back. He didn't bother to answer.

~~~

Alex was alone in the office when Stellar walked in. She wore a thin tank top and jeans. She offered him a smile, but she seemed uneasy.

"*Hola*, Detective."

"I don't have time for your fake hospitality, Mrs. Carson. I want the tapes and I want the truth." He slapped the folder on the counter.

The smile fell away as her eyes dropped to the folder. Her face whitened, and she bit her lip, but it was a bit too scripted. She was a hell of an actress. Stellar waited, staring her down. She took a deep breath, but she didn't crack.

The fan clicked as it stirred the stale air.

"It's Delgado." She said it slowly, stressing every sound with a hint of an accent. "I'm a legal citizen of Lake City, Nevada. I believe I deserve a little respect from the city *employees*."

"Respect?" Stellar's voice went up a notch. "You're a murderer. You executed a man in cold blood." He opened the folder and read, "Two shots at close range in the chest, and once in the head as the man died on the ground."

"I pled out and took my punishment. I will not have you treat me like I'm still in prison. I'm not a criminal." She spoke slowly, pronouncing each word.

"You killed another human being. You're a disgrace to humanity."

She stepped up to the counter as her face flashed red, her eyes cold and dark. Her voice turned to a low growl. "I won't apologize to you or anyone for my past."

"You should still be in prison. Instead, some bureaucratic asshole releases you early to kill again. Not in my city. I'll do whatever I need to put you back behind bars or drive you out of my town."

He saw her eyes pierce him like knives, and her jaw clenched tightly. He wanted the anger. Anger brought confession.

"How dare you stand there and pretend you're better than me?" she said. "You don't know me or what I've been through. You don't know what that man did to me, so you don't get to judge me. You're not God."

"Neither are you. You don't get to determine who deserves to live and die, but that's what you did, didn't you? You decided this man *upset* you, so you decided to play God and kill him."

"Shut up, Stellar. That *man* shot a Taser in my back. Do you know what it feels like to have fifty thousand volts of electricity coursing through your body? Did they show you that at the academy? It paralyzes every muscle."

He fell silent now, offering her time to vent her rage. He wanted her to speak without watching her words.

"He hit me three times in a row. Do you know why the academy teaches you to pause between shots? Because it's too painful for anyone to handle. It hits every nerve and keeps going. Over and over, bouncing and jabbing like hot spears, but the pain is nothing compared to the fear of knowing what's coming next. It makes you completely vulnerable. Do you know how that feels?"

He didn't answer. He heard a siren in the distance. Alex was no longer looking at him. She was staring down at her hands.

"Do you know how it feels to hurt all over, but feel nothing?" She shook her head, as if shaking the thought away. She looked back up at him, her eyes hollow. "That *cabron*, who you think deserved to live, almost killed me to teach me a lesson. He didn't like women, especially me. He threw me in the back of his pickup truck. I couldn't move, couldn't fight back. Did you even read the report?"

He'd heard enough. The anger was gone. "I'm sorry—"

"Don't!" Her eyes narrowed on him as if he was her prey. He thought he saw pure evil there. Stellar said nothing and remained still.

"If you think I was wrong in taking his life, then you need to know what he did to me." Her anger back, she continued with her chin up. "He drove me to a construction site and dumped me on the ground. He tied my hands and legs to poles stuck in the ground. Then he pulled the knife out. I don't know why he took his time cutting away my clothes. He wasn't careful."

Alex folded her arms over her chest as if she were cold. As she rubbed her shoulders, Stellar noticed a long scar on her right shoulder. He felt uncomfortable looking at her. As he stared at the scar, he knew what was coming next.

"He raped me. When I didn't scream or cry or beg for him to stop, he raped me again."

"Alex—"

She shook her head. Her face had grown pale. Her eyes held only one color, blood red.

"He left me there, walked away clean. I was left there alone. Naked and cold …"

Her voice trailed off, but he knew the ordeal was still playing out in her head. He said nothing. Not because he didn't know what to say, but because anything he said wouldn't be enough.

The creaking of the fan was the only sound. Stellar waited for the tears to come, but they never did. He stepped up to the counter. He wanted to reach over to comfort her, but she was a liar—worse, she was a murderer. She was his suspect, and he refused to cross the line. He still didn't trust her.

"You should have told me," he said.

She shook her head. Her eyes still held rage and hate, and they were directed at him. "My past has nothing to do with your investigation."

"You're wrong. You killed a man, and I have another dead body just feet from your room."

"I didn't kill Eddie Chavez."

"You're a killer. You shot a man twice in the chest and then stood over his body and put a bullet in his brain. You executed him. Cold and calculated. You're a killer."

"And I'd do it again in a heartbeat," she screamed at him.

He slapped his hands on the counter, matching her anger. "Damn it, Alex, don't you see? That's why you're a suspect."

The door behind him opened before Alex could respond. Stellar reached back for his gun but didn't pull it.

"What the hell is going on?" Ric walked in and moved quickly to his sister's side.

Stellar took a step back and watched Alex. She didn't look at Ric, didn't lean on him for support.

"Allie," Ric reached for her, but she pushed him away.

Alex tried to walk past Stellar, but he clamped his hand on her wrist. She stopped and stared at his hand.

"Let her go, cowboy," Ric said.

Ignoring Ric, Stellar looked down at her bare arm. He expected her to shiver at his touch. At the least, he had expected her to tense up. But when he looked into her eyes, she was steady. Calm.

"I'm not done," he said. "I need to ask you some questions."

She spun her arm around and he lost his grip. She was lightning fast. He didn't see her other hand come up. Ric jerked forward and grabbed her wrist just inches from Stellar's face.

"Alex!"

Stellar smiled. He had been seconds from having his nose broken. He could see it in her eyes.

"You want to ask me questions, get a warrant." She pulled her arm away from Ric. "And bring backup." She shoved the door open and ran up the stairs.

"You're pretty bold, even for a cop," Ric said.

"I could arrest her. Her parole officer won't look too kindly on an assault charge."

"And I can produce surveillance video of you grabbing her first. She's trained in self-defense. I would suggest not laying another hand on her. She'll just shove your badge—"

"You were a cop once, too, Delgado. You should have been straight with me."

Ric folded his arms across his chest. Stellar had expected anger from him, but he looked smug. "Your police chief was notified about Alex's parole. He decided that you didn't need the information. I suggest you back off."

"Don't threaten me."

"I won't let you pin this on Alex just because she's got a record. You want to cover up this murder, you find someone else."

"Cover this up? I'm the only one trying to find the truth. If you two stop getting in my way, I might actually find out who killed Eddie Chavez."

Ric laughed. "If you want the truth, you should watch who you sleep with."

"What the hell does that mean?"

Ric studied him. "You're so far behind, aren't you? I can't blame you too much. She's pretty. Could make a dumb man blind, but I'm not helping you until you take your beady little eyes off my sister."

Confused, Stellar said nothing. Did Ric think he was sleeping with Alex?

"I don't know what you're talking about," said Stellar, "but the more you talk, the faster you move to the top of my suspect list. I want the tapes."

Ric handed him a brown package. "Three weeks of tapes. I haven't had a chance to label them, so you can just make a stab at where to start. Don't waste too much time with them. You're already too far behind, cowboy."

Chapter 23

Alex let the anger wade through her as she slipped into the pool. The water was still warm, despite the setting sun. Darkness would be arriving soon, and she wasn't sure she was ready for it.

She dipped her head underwater. Her eyes closed as the bubbles rushed around her head, relaxing her tight muscles. The weightlessness settled into her body as the cool water pulled at the hatred and anger stored deep inside. She let it take her away, both body and mind.

She didn't want to think of that night, the night everything had changed. She wanted to focus on the anger—the anger Detective Stellar had brought out. It would make the swim easier.

She wanted to hit someone, to strike someone down. She wanted to feel the rush of winning a fight. If given the choice to swim or fight, she would always choose to fight. She could take down anyone who challenged her. It had a lot to do with technique, she knew, but it had more to do with necessity.

Pushing up out of the water, she took a deep breath of air. Then she dove back under, kicking her legs, looking for the release of tension. Up for a breath and into a freestyle stroke.

Detective Stellar had a lot of nerve coming there and confronting her about her past. He had no right yelling at her. Threatening her. Calling her a killer. He had come close to knowing how dangerous she really was.

He had ignored the fact that she had been a victim. She had taken her life back in the only way she could. She had fought back. Her life, her choice.

She tore through the water, her arms straight as the daggers in her blood. She dove down, twisted, and pushed her feet against the pool wall to spring forward once again.

She remembered seeing Davy Knight in her academy class. She hadn't met him before that night in the bar, but she had recognized him when she saw him. He had been kicked out a few days earlier. She didn't know why, nor did she care. She was too focused on her own progress to care about the other members. She needed to succeed. She needed to graduate. Needed to be someone.

She was disappointed Ric hadn't been able to meet her that night. She had already ordered her second beer when he called to cancel. She should have just walked out. It probably wouldn't have changed what had happened that night, but it might have changed the outcome.

Instead, she finished her beer and said good-bye to the bartender. She saw Davy Knight in the corner, drinking alone. She paid him no attention as she walked out to her car.

It was dark, and the cool Los Angeles night air was creeping in. The breeze chopped at her long hair. She didn't have to look for her car—she had a great memory and remembered where she parked—but she was stopped before she got there.

The sting in her back shot her forward. She dropped to the ground. Her purse and keys slid out of reach. She didn't scream.

I should have screamed.

She felt the pain zip through her. Unable to move, she closed her eyes and waited for the current to stop. She became nauseous and feared she would throw up.

She never wondered what was happening to her. Her entire brain was focused on stopping the pain and regaining control of her body. After that, she would think about fighting back.

As her muscles relaxed from the spasms, she realized she was lying in the parking lot. Gravel dug into her face. She opened her eyes and saw Davy Knight standing beside her.

He was smiling.

Fear and rage spiked through her at once. She pushed past the pain and willed her body to move. She reached out and grabbed his ankle. She was too weak to pull him down, but he was surprised by the move.

He stepped back and stared down at her. He had yet to say a word.

Unable to control her movements, she relaxed and waited for her strength to return. When it did, she could attack. She heard talking and listened hard. Someone was walking from the bar. Davy looked away. She was so close to taking back the control. She should have screamed.

Her eyes watered. She squeezed them shut and tried to talk. Before a sound could escape, he shocked her again. Her body went rigid and silence descended. The voices were gone. Reality was gone.

She never felt him pick her up and drop her in the bed of his truck, but when the third shock jolted her head against the truck, she hoped he would kill her. It wasn't the last time that night she had begged for death.

In the pool, Alex came up for a breath of air, but she didn't stop. The anger was still there. She dove back under, enjoying the fact that she had control of her legs as they kicked fiercely through the water. She sprang off the edge, then dove deeper, cutting the water with strong strokes.

She needed air, but she forced herself to continue, pushing herself further until the burn in her lungs hammered in her head. Still she refused to come up for air. She strained her tired legs to pump faster and faster. Her eyes clenched tightly, and she felt the life being sucked from her body.

I should have screamed. Why didn't I scream?

Dr. Cruz had told her she needed to express her feelings. During her prison sessions, Dr. Cruz had insisted Alex tell the story to someone. Ten years later, she had no idea why she had chosen Detective Stellar. Cruz had told her it would make her feel better. It would bring her closer to the people around her if she broke down that last wall. But Alex didn't feel better.

Her head burst upward, her lungs gulping for the dry desert air to replace the pain in her chest and the ache of pressure in her head. As the oxygen shot through her body, she let go of her emotions and allowed herself to breathe. To live.

I should have screamed.

She wiped the cool water and the warm tears from her face. She laid her arms out of the pool. She let her feet dangle and watched a horned lizard scurry past her fingertips. She felt nothing now. Just like that night.

She looked up at the sky. Billions of stars shined above her. Alex had never felt so small. So unimportant. So meaningless. Stellar had every right to be combative with her, but she hadn't killed out of rage or revenge. She had killed for her own survival.

Maybe Ric was right. She should have left Lake City before Stellar had learned of her past, but she had nowhere to go. Los Angeles held too many bad memories for her. Although this was only a hotel in the middle of the desert, she had nowhere else to go.

Someone needed to find Eddie Chavez's killer. She didn't care about the drugs Danny was dealing. She didn't care that Stellar wanted to protect his girlfriend. Eddie Chavez had a son. A boy, now fatherless, needed answers, needed justice. She didn't want to admit it, but she knew finding Eddie's killer would erase all doubt that she was somehow responsible for his death. She had yet to find any concrete evidence she was involved, but her memory of that night hadn't returned. The memory lapses were a side effect of the Taser attack, but she didn't want her brother to know about them. She didn't want to explain to him that Davy had also taken the trust she had in herself.

She looked at room 110 and wondered what had happened that night after Leanna had left. Why hadn't the cameras caught the killer coming or going?

She stared at the cameras. Ric was right. They were nearly impossible to see, unless you knew exactly where to look, because she had placed them herself. Ric knew. But how had the killer known? She glanced at the camera above her room, then at the camera on the far end of the roof.

She stood up straight. Something was off.

"What's wrong?"

Alex jumped at Ric's voice. She didn't answer. She trudged through the water toward the steps.

"What's wrong, Alex? You've been swimming nonstop for two hours."

"Stop watching me." She stepped from the pool and grabbed her towel. The warm air would dry her skin in mere minutes, but she needed the towel to control the chill that was about to run through her.

Alex glanced at her watch and realized he was right. Two hours had passed. She only remembered twenty minutes at most. She shook her head, refocused on what had drawn her attention from out of the murkiness of her memory.

"Don't worry about Stellar," Ric said. "I'll have him removed from the case."

"Forget about the detective." She pointed to the cameras. "Someone moved the camera."

Ric didn't look. "I told you, the camera's not important."

"It is. Someone moved camera three. I had them placed perfectly so there was no overlapping. Someone moved camera three so it overlaps camera two. We didn't need two cameras watching the staircase outside my room. It leaves a blind spot."

Now Ric looked. "What are you talking about?"

Alex closed her eyes and remembered the camera angles on the screen. Opening her eyes, she reached for the gate and walked to the parking lot. Ric followed behind.

She stopped. "Here. A blind spot. Neither of the cameras can see this exact spot."

Ric sighed and looked up at the cameras. She could tell he saw it. He glanced back at the rooms, rubbed his eyes, and muttered a curse.

"Someone moved the camera. Only you and I knew about the cameras."

Ric shrugged. "And whoever told Detective Stellar."

She could tell he wasn't excited with this discovery. "You still don't think the cameras are important?"

"Eddie Chavez is dead. The cameras didn't capture the killer. You figured out why, but it doesn't get us anywhere. "

She eyed him. "Do you even care *who* the killer is or are you only interested in the drugs?"

"Drugs often lead to murder, but no, it's not high on my list of priorities right now. I'm more interested in the fool who took a bat to your room."

"Don't you think it's connected?"

"I'm going to find out. Are you okay by yourself for a while?"

She narrowed her eyes. "I'll try not to hurt myself while you're gone."

"I'm more worried about you hurting someone else."

Chapter 24

O'Sullivan's bar was packed when Ric walked in. People were spread out in the booths. Some played cards; others talked. He noticed they were all older than him. When Liam noticed him, he carried over a ginger ale. The bartender was close to Ric's age, and they had become friends almost as soon as Ric had moved to Lake City, despite the fact that Ric didn't drink.

Ric sat at the bar, pushed aside a newspaper someone had left behind. "How's it going, Liam?"

"It's been a busy night so far. What brings you in?"

"You guys have a local adult league for baseball or softball called the Lake City Lakers?"

Liam nodded. "Yep. Thirty and over. A few of us old farts from high school put it together a couple of years ago. I'm catcher."

Ric nodded, immediately calculating his age range. He remembered the way the man in the video had taken the stairs. The man was definitely over thirty, but he didn't seem as old as Liam and himself.

"Got any standouts on the team? Guys who love to swing a bat?"

Liam studied him, but Ric kept his face straight. He wouldn't show his hand this early.

"Will Stellar plays centerfield. He usually can knock 'em out of the ballpark, especially after a bad day. He usually bats cleanup."

Ric nodded and said nothing. He took a drink to ensure he wasn't giving away any reaction. Detective Stellar didn't look like the type to destroy property, especially since a warrant would get him everything he needed. He didn't seem like the violent type. He was analytical and untrusting, but not stupid.

"His friend and fellow badge holder, Morgan, plays second base. You may have seen him around. He's a short guy, talks big, though. And then you got Lincoln, Stellar's brother, town mascot and hero. He plays first base. They're both decent at bat."

He knew both men and the stature was wrong on both. The guy was wide, not short or stocky like Morgan. Lincoln was broad, but he was lean and cut.

"Anyone on the team causing more problems than they're worth?"

Liam laughed and looked down the bar. "Guy at the end," he pointed. "That's Bobby Jacks. He got kicked off the high school team when we were kids. He drinks a little too much, but he can hit the ball when he wants to. When he shows up, we put him out in right field and hope he's sober enough to see the ball."

Ric watched the man sitting at the end of the bar. He was talking a bit too loudly and looked cockeyed. He wore a faded Marines tee shirt, but the man's bad posture told Ric he'd never served a day.

"Doesn't look that threatening," Ric muttered.

Liam smiled. "Your sister didn't think so, either. She flattened him good the other night when she came in."

Ric put his glass down. "Did Bobby touch her?"

Liam's smile faded as he caught Ric's tone. "I don't know the specifics, but he was drunk and didn't know what he was doing. She handled herself just fine. We escorted him out to sober up."

Ric finished the ginger ale and ordered another. His stare returned to Bobby as Liam stepped away. The build was right. Wide, but not too bulky. Bobby turned his way, giving Ric a good look at the man. Ric grinned as he recognized the cap on his head. Lake City Lakers.

Bobby was bigger than Ric, by twenty or thirty pounds. Ric hadn't seen the inside of a gym in a few years, but if he had to, he could take him. Bobby was probably drunk, after all. Ric was a decent brawler, but he didn't want to get his hands dirty tonight. He didn't want Bobby to get any ideas of his own, either.

Ric picked up the newspaper and saw Erika Mack's story on Eddie Chavez's murder. He read it again, then flipped through the rest of the newspaper, looking for her name.

Bobby stood and walked past Ric toward the bathrooms. Ric kept his eyes on the paper as he passed, then folded the paper neatly and placed it back on the bar. Following the same route Bobby had taken, Ric found the bathroom doors. He nudged the door open with his foot and pulled out his Colt Anaconda.

The bathroom reeked of piss and vomit. Bobby was in the single stall, adding to the latter. Ric scanned the room to make sure they were alone. He held the gun in his right hand, down at his thigh. He flicked the safety off in case Bobby was sober enough to look.

Ric grabbed some towels with his other hand and locked the door. He waited for Bobby to finish emptying his stomach. After a couple of flushes, Bobby Jacks swung the stall door open as if he were smacking a fly out of his way. He was bigger up close. Ric hoped Bobby wouldn't try to swat him away.

He ignored Ric as he stumbled toward the sink and splashed water on his face. Ric moved to keep the door in view while maintaining his focus on Bobby.

"My name is Ric Delgado."

Bobby looked up at Ric but continued to wash his hands. There was no recognition in Bobby's eyes. Ric saw Bobby's eyes drift to the weapon. Ric lifted the revolver and trained it on Bobby's chest. Center of mass.

The Colt revolver is a big gun. Not as big as a Desert Eagle, but it's accurate, and no one could mistake it for a toy. Ric had chosen it because it made a statement. People listened when you pointed a .44 at their chest.

"My sister is Alex Delgado. I believe you two have met."

First Ric saw recognition, then guilt and fear. Bobby straightened and squared himself. His eyes were still trained on the barrel, his mouth closed tightly.

"You like baseball, Slugger?" Ric said.

Bobby took a step back. A sound similar to a grunt came from deep inside, but Ric didn't recognize any words. His face twisted like a disfigured mime.

"I didn't appreciate the mess you made. And I'm not someone you want to annoy."

Finally Bobby released a spew of words. Ric caught only a few. "I didn't … she started … please, no …"

"I'm not going to hurt you. If I was going to hurt you, I'd have brought a bat and made a statement." He lowered the gun. "This is so I'm sure you're listening."

Bobby seemed to relax a bit, so Ric took a step forward and held the gun up to his head.

"Get on your knees. I have some questions for you. And you're going to answer real fast and real honest. You got it?"

Bobby looked at the floor. Ric wondered if he was going to vomit again. "The floor?" Bobby asked.

Ric didn't want to waste any more time. He swung his right foot out and took out both of Bobby's legs. He landed on his hands and knees. Ric cringed as Bobby's palms splashed what he hoped was only water.

"I ask, you answer," Ric said. "Not too hard. How do you know Eddie Chavez?"

"Who?"

"Are you kidding me, here? How drunk are you? I ask a question, you answer. You don't get to ask me anything."

"I don't know who you're talking about."

"Eddie Chavez," Ric repeated. "Hispanic male, big build, slight limp on his right leg. He was killed at the motel early Wednesday morning. You had to have heard. The whole town is talking about it."

"I heard about the murder, but I swear I didn't know him." Bobby wiped his hands on his pants.

"Okay, Slugger. How about someone easier? What do you know about Daniel Nunez?"

"Danny? He's a dealer out near the freeway. Pothead."

"Do you buy from him?"

He looked surprised. "I don't do that stuff, man. He's scum. Him and his lying sister."

Ric nodded, convinced Bobby was too drunk to lie coherently. He lowered his gun. Bobby had nothing to do with Eddie's murder. He was just a waste of Ric's time.

"You met my sister, right?" Ric asked.

Bobby nodded, but his eyes were still focused on the gun.

"I understand that meeting didn't go well. She embarrassed you, right? You retaliated by trashing her room. I haven't missed anything, have I?"

Bobby's face took on an even more desperate look. "I'm sorry."

"Don't apologize to me, Slugger. It wasn't my stuff you destroyed. I'm calling it even, understand? Don't come near her again." Ric paused to make sure he was listening. "Pay attention. If you come near her again, I can't guarantee you'll live. Do you hear me?"

Bobby shook his head up and down as fast as he could.

"I'm not convinced. Tell me you understand me."

"I … I understand."

"I'm still not convinced. I know your type. You can't stand to have someone hold something over you." Ric holstered his gun. "Your conflict with her is over. When you're sober, if you still feel like a fight, you come for me."

Ric turned toward the exit and stared at the door handle. "Open that for me," he ordered.

Bobby looked confused as he stared at the door. Ric slapped him on the back of the head.

"I don't know what's on that thing. Open it."

Bobby rushed forward, fumbled with the lock, and opened the door. Ric walked out, hoping Bobby Jacks understood his warning.

Chapter 25

Will Stellar reviewed the final disc for the third time. The screen showed Eddie Chavez's car pull into the parking lot. The car parked and Leanna Nunez emerged from Chavez's passenger seat. They both disappeared from the camera. He let the tape play, but turned back to his notes. There was something wrong. Per Ric Delgado, Eddie Chavez had checked in on Saturday. He was killed early Wednesday morning. That gave him four nights at the Death Valley Motel, but only three discs showed Eddie Chavez at all. Without date stamps, he was having a hard time putting them in order. He had one tape with Eddie checking in. He pushed that aside. He had discounted another tape that showed Eddie buying the Sunday paper. So he was missing Monday and Tuesday, and had only one tape left that showed Eddie at all.

He stood and paced. He needed to see Ric again.

The Delgados were still at the top of his suspect list. Like every cop he had ever known, Stellar had built a brotherhood with the badge. No one understood the lifestyle, the dangers, and the stress of a cop's life except other cops. The brotherhood was so strong that it included cops he'd never met. He'd defend them and protect them when necessary.

But he'd also seen his share of bad cops. Cops tested by the pressure and tempted by the opportunities. Ric had been a narcotics cop in L.A. He had dealt with gangs and guns and money. He had probably seen large amounts of drugs and money on any given day. Ric had tried to control the devil's playground. It wasn't a hard stretch to believe he had pulled an apple from the tree.

Stellar heard the pecking on the window and ignored it. He turned back to the tape and watched as the final tape wound down. Alex Delgado appeared on the tape as she walked down the stairs to the office. Will shook his head. On tape, she looked even thinner, tired even after a long night's sleep.

Her routine had been the same every day for the past three weeks. Each tape showed her leaving her room around dawn. She relieved Ric at the desk and sat there staring into oblivion. She rarely ate, except when Ric brought her food. Around seven in the evening, she would disappear in her room for a few minutes and reemerge to do laps in the pool. She swam for an hour straight, pushing herself harder each day. She never left the property, and she didn't speak to anyone other than her brother.

Stellar watched as she entered the office where Ric was watching his television. She opened the refrigerator and the disc went black. He grabbed the remote, rewound, and froze on the image of Alex Delgado opening the fridge. She was wearing a black sweatshirt and jeans.

He searched the room for the ugly pink sweater he had seen her wearing that morning. Why would she have changed clothes?

Florio knocked on the open door. "Leanna Nunez is on her way in. Chief Mack wants to see you first."

Stellar grunted and turned off the tape, rubbed his temples.

"Also, I got an interesting call a few minutes ago. Ms. Alex Delgado."

Stellar looked up.

"She said to tell you to ask Leanna about the shoe laces."

"What?"

Florio shrugged. "She said it's been bothering her. Don't forget to see Mack."

Chief Mack was at his desk, his jacket off, his sleeves rolled up. "Close the door. Sit," he said, motioning Stellar to a leather chair.

"Leanna Nunez is here." Stellar saw the concern on Mack's face. "But Florio can handle the introductions. What's wrong?"

"You sent trace evidence to the Las Vegas crime lab for DNA testing?"

Stellar remained standing. "A hair we found at the crime scene. It could be a crucial piece of evidence."

"A hair in a dirty motel room? Do you have any way of knowing this hair belongs to the killer, or are you just trying to deplete my budget as fast as you can?"

Stellar straightened at the chief's tone. "My job is to find Eddie Chavez's killer. I'll do whatever it takes to close the case."

"And my job is to keep this department under budget and out of scrutiny by the city council and our tightwad mayor."

"Fine, I'll pay for it. Is that it?"

"Don't get smart, and don't throw your Stellar money around me. This is my department."

Stellar saw the fight coming. "You want to say something, so say it."

"I've been hearing complaints about the way you're handling this investigation, Detective."

"From who?"

The Chief leaned back in his chair. "That's not important. Your ethics are being questioned."

"My ethics? I think I have the right to know who's questioning my ethics."

"You've been harassing the Delgados."

He couldn't help but laugh. "Ric's upset because I questioned his sister? She's a convicted murderer. I think I have a right to question her."

The chief folded his arms over his chest. "You should have run it by me first."

"Why?" Stellar asked. "So you can stop me from finding Eddie Chavez's killer? Is that why you didn't tell me about her past?"

"The parole board informed me she was planning on moving to Lake City. Her brother set up residency here, and since he's her only living relative, they felt it would help her transition. I met with several people, including her brother. We all felt it was in her best interest to keep her past in the past. She's trying to move on."

Stellar stared at the chief. He let the silence drag while he composed his thoughts. "She killed a man ten years ago. I have another man dead in the motel she now owns. She's a suspect. You can't stop me from interrogating her."

"You're right, but you should have brought her down here and done it properly. You should be using your officers, not running by yourself on this. It makes people concerned that this department is run by one man."

"And I'm sure you convinced Mr. Delgado that there's more than one cowboy in town. Everyone knows you're the police chief."

"But you're dating my daughter, Will."

"Not anymore. And with all due respect, sir, my relationships are not a police matter."

"It's over?"

Stellar didn't answer. He wasn't all too sure of the answer, but he didn't want to let Mack rub his face in his failure.

"You know how it looks, Will. I need you to lay off the Delgados. You have other leads to follow. Follow them."

Stellar shook his head. "I'm not altering the way I run my investigation. Alex and Ric are both suspects. I can't ignore that, even if I *used to* date your daughter."

"I'm giving you a direct order, Will. Stay away from Alex Delgado."

Stellar felt a nervous tick in his stomach. "Does Ric have something on you?"

Mack laughed, but he didn't meet Will's glare. "Do what you need to, Detective." The formality was back. "But be careful. We don't need anyone thinking this department can't be trusted. If I hear another complaint, I'll have no choice but to remove you from the case. Detective Jonas can take it from here."

"Detective Jonas can't handle death scenes, and you know it. He can't stand the sight of blood."

"If Jonas can't handle it, I'll bring in the State Police. Either way, you'll learn your boundaries."

Stellar left without another word.

Chapter 26

S tellar found Leanna Nunez slouching in a metal chair in the interrogation room.

"Leanna, it hasn't been that long, has it? You clean?" he asked.

Leanna shrugged. She had bags under her eyes. Will handed her a glass of water, but she ignored it. He noticed she was sitting on her hands, probably to keep herself from shaking.

"Have you ever seen this man?" Will slid the picture of Eddie Chavez across the table to her.

She only glanced at it, then looked away. "Like I told the other officer, I've never seen him before."

"Funny thing, Leanna, I've got surveillance video of you getting out of his car. Then he carries you to his motel room."

Leanna remained silent.

"That's right. There were cameras at the motel. You know what the cameras caught?"

Leanna looked at him. "That girl from the motel talk to you?" She didn't wait for an answer. "I saw him at O'Sullivan's," she said. "He was drunk, so I thought he was harmless. We had a couple of drinks. He must have put something in mine."

Will jotted a note down to check with Liam at O'Sullivan's. "What were you drinking?"

She shrugged, looked at the ground. "I don't remember."

"When was this?"

"Monday night, after the memorial."

Will smiled. The final disc showed Monday night. He was missing Tuesday night's tape, the tape that could reveal Eddie's killer. He made another note to contact Ric for the missing disc. "You were at the memorial service?"

"For a few minutes."

Will hadn't seen Leanna at the memorial. She must have left before he got there. "Why were you there?"

"I knew the boy. I saw him at camp."

"You were at Camp Courage?" he asked.

"Your brother got me a job there. I register the kids. Cole was a cool kid."

Will said nothing. He didn't want to talk about the boy. It was irrelevant to his current investigation.

"Then I left for O'Sullivan's," she said. "Eddie was at the bar."

"Back up, Leanna. You're forgetting something. How did you know Eddie Chavez was at O'Sullivan's?"

She shook her head.

He leaned forward and got in her face. "I know you, Leanna. You're a con, and a stranger in town is a perfect mark. I'm not looking to bust you. Just tell me how you met Eddie."

She leaned back, her hands wrapped around the glass of water. He noticed red marks on her wrist and scratches on her hand. He leaned back and waited for her to talk.

"He was at the memorial service."

"Eddie was at Cole's memorial service? Did he know someone there?"

Leanna shrugged. "Don't know. He went up to Lincoln and said something, and Lincoln got pissy. Your brother's friends threw him out."

He felt his stomach knot. He didn't want his brother anywhere near this investigation, even if it was just as a witness.

"So you followed him to O'Sullivan's? Why? What did he say, Leanna?"

She slumped further in the seat, knowing she was digging herself further. "He said he was looking for a hit."

"And you followed him so you could offer some of Danny's dope."

"I offered, but he didn't bite. He said he wanted something stronger. Or maybe he just wanted to make sure I wasn't a cop or something. I figured he just didn't want to buy in such a public place."

"A bit too public for you to rob him, huh?"

She shook her head. "No. It wasn't my idea to go back to his room. He slipped something in my drink."

"You're not that stupid, Leanna. You pretended to be drunk so he would take you to the room. It gives you the chance to rob him."

"I didn't pretend, and I didn't rob him."

"You stole his car. His cell phone and wallet are missing, too."

She rolled her eyes and shifted in the seat. "Whatever. I didn't steal from him. I woke up and got the hell out of there. The car was just an easy way to get out."

He remembered the tape of Leanna leaving. She was disoriented. She didn't know which car she had arrived in. Maybe Will was wrong about the act. He looked at her wrists again.

"What happened in the room, Leanna?"

She looked away, wiped her nose. "I don't know what happened. I don't remember any of it."

"What happened to your hands? Did he hurt you?"

"I don't know." Her hands returned to her lap.

Will couldn't be sure if she was telling the truth. Leanna was a known liar—a good one, in fact—but the ligature marks on her wrists told a different story than the one he had expected. She wiped her face again. Will didn't see tears. There was something she wasn't telling him.

He switched tactics. "We don't seem to be getting anywhere. Why don't I tell you what I know and see if it helps you remember?"

Will stood up to walk the small room and tried to picture the crime scene. He remembered Alex's message.

"I'm trying to figure out why he drove you to the motel. He didn't rape you." He looked at Leanna, but there was no reaction on her face. So far he was right. "That wasn't his intention. There's nothing in his file that shows he's a sexual predator. His ex-girlfriend had nothing but nice things to say about him, stuff about respecting women and honoring his mother. So he didn't bring you back to his room for sex. He wanted something else from you. Does this sound about right so far?"

She didn't answer.

"Okay. So he slips something into your drink, and he brings you back to the room. He sits you in the chair."

She looked up. Will was on the right track.

"He sits you in the chair and ties your wrists. With his shoelaces, right?"

She looked down at her wrists. Rubbed them.

"You woke up from whatever he slipped in your drink, and he wanted something from you. What did he want from you?"

"I don't know."

"He asked you questions. What did he want, Leanna? Drugs? Money? Did he want Danny?"

She didn't answer.

"Okay, I'm done." He looked at Florio. "Process her." He reached for the door, but she stopped him.

"He wanted to know where I got the drugs."

Stellar smiled and turned around. "What happened then? How did the chair end up broken?"

"He got in my face. He was screaming about drugs and how I was killing people. He didn't tie my feet, so I kicked him. Hard. I was just protecting myself."

"Go on."

"One of the arms of the chair broke. Somehow I got untied, but he was fighting to keep me down. I punched him, kept punching him until he let go of me. Then I ran."

"Did he follow you?"

She shook her head, rubbed her wrists again. "I don't think so. I didn't look back. I grabbed the keys, but I didn't mean to steal his car. Seriously. I just wanted to get outta there."

"Did he hurt you or cut you? Were you bleeding?"

She shook her head. "I saw blood, but it was from hitting him. I don't think any of it was mine. He was alive when I left. I swear I didn't kill him."

He nodded. "Okay. Where's Danny?"

"I don't know. I haven't seen him since yesterday."

"Does he know what happened to you?"

She nodded. "I told him. He said he needed to get rid of the car. I haven't seen him since."

Stellar left Leanna in the interrogation room.

"Are we charging her?" Florio asked.

"No. I don't think she was there when Eddie died, but get some photos of her arms for the file. We'll need to set up interviews with everyone at the memorial service." He paused, thinking of his brother. "Lincoln's not going to like it, but we're going to have to talk to Ann and his new assistant. Put the APB out on Daniel Nunez. We'll speak to him before bothering Lincoln."

Chapter 27

It was past midnight when Stellar pulled into the parking lot of O'Sullivan's. He didn't talk to anyone when he walked in. He didn't go to O'Sullivan's for the ambiance or the crowd. He wanted one thing. The following day's newspaper was already being printed, which guaranteed Erika wouldn't be there to bother him. He walked behind the bar and grabbed his bottle. He looked at Liam.

"My bottle feels a bit light."

Liam smiled. "You're not the only one in town anymore who likes a good Irish whiskey. You're gonna have to learn to share."

Stellar said nothing. He was brooding, and he was procrastinating. He should have gone straight to see Lincoln. He needed to hear what he knew about Eddie Chavez crashing the boy's memorial, but questioning Lincoln wasn't easy. Lincoln didn't enjoy being put on the defensive, and he sure didn't feel he should answer to anyone, especially his little brother. He tended to protect his friends just the same.

Again, Stellar's mind drifted to Lincoln's assistant, A. J. He would love to put the murder on a stranger in town—it would be easier for the town to handle—but what was the motive?

"How's the case going?" Liam asked.

Stellar shrugged. "I can't get ahead of it." He settled into the bar stool and poured himself a glass. He stared into the glass without drinking and then pulled out the picture of Eddie Chavez. The guy had caused so much damage in such a short amount of time. He felt for Leanna and what she had endured, but his gut told him her brother was involved somehow.

Stellar's phone rang. He thought about ignoring it, but the display read *Dr. Wagstaff.*

"I just received the blood screen back on Eddie Chavez," Wags said. "He had alcohol and methamphetamines in his system."

"Enough to kill him if the bullet hadn't done it first?"

"I can't make that call until the full toxicology report is complete."

Stellar didn't believe Danny had moved up to selling meth. If he believed Eddie's girlfriend, Eddie wouldn't have brought the drug with him.

"I reviewed the X-rays as well," Wags continued. "It looks as if your vic's nose was broken. It doesn't appear to be a result of the bullet."

"Can you tell if it was a recent break?"

"Probably within twenty-four hours of his death."

"Thanks, Wags." He snapped the phone shut.

Leanna's story was matching up, but he was leaving room for doubt. Danny was clearly moving to the top of his list. The longer he remained missing, the stronger Stellar's suspicion became.

Liam was watching him. He pointed at the glass. "You're not drinking."

"I'm missing so much of this puzzle that the pieces look foreign."

"You're distracted. We barely put the boy in the ground, and you're off on a new case."

He could blame only part of his distraction on Cole. Someone far more interesting was distracting him.

Alex Delgado was also still high on the suspect list. He couldn't picture her as a cold-blooded killer, but he had learned otherwise. Opening the folder, he found the arresting officer's name and dialed the Los Angeles Police Department. He stared at the full glass of whiskey as he waited for Detective Ryan Dade to pick up. After a few minutes, he was patched through to Dade's cell phone.

"Detective Dade, this is Detective William Stellar out in Lake City, Nevada. I'm calling for some background information on a woman you arrested ten years ago."

He heard the man laugh. "I can remember some of the girls, but it would have to be a regular for me to remember the details."

"A regular?"

"I was vice ten years ago."

"No, this was a murder. Maybe I have the wrong paperwork."

Silence fell on the other end. The silence interested him, so he pursued.

"You were listed as the arresting officer on the crime scene report."

"Ten years ago?" Dade's voice changed. It was lower, the amusement gone. Something was there. Stellar waited.

"Alex Carson."

Bingo. "Yeah, that's her. You arrested her for homicide. Was she a prostitute?"

"No. God, no. Is she there? Where did you say you were calling from?"

"Lake City, Nevada. I have a homicide here at the Death Valley Motel she owns. I'm just looking for some background information on her."

"I'll get your background information. I'll be there first thing in the morning."

The line went dead. He stared at his cell phone. Now that was great service. Stellar waved Liam down the bar.

"You remember this guy?" He pushed the photo of Eddie Chavez across the bar. "He was in here a couple nights ago."

Liam nodded. "Yeah, I remember him. Came in a couple nights last week." He pointed down the bar. "Sat down at the end, kept his eye on everyone. Is that the guy that died?"

"You remember him with anyone?"

"I didn't watch him all night. You might want to talk to Erika. She's been asking around about him, too."

"Erika?"

"Yeah, she came in earlier. You two should really talk."

He threw a twenty across the bar, even though he hadn't even tasted the whiskey.

Stellar knew what Ric had been referring to now. Stellar had been too focused on Alex. He thought about apologizing to her. Or he could pick a fight with another strong woman.

~~~

Ten minutes later, Stellar knocked on Erika's door and waited. He had a key but refused to use it. He caught sight of a piece of glass in the bushes. He kicked at it and found it was an ashtray.

When did Erika start sneaking cigarettes?

She answered her door with a smile and a sparkle in her eye. "It's too late for a quote now, Detective."

"I know," he said, putting the cigarette from his mind. He heard jazz playing behind her. She always played it when she was working.

"You're here on a personal level?" she said, opening the door to let him in. She had already changed into a long shirt. Her bright red robe covered her legs and was loosely tied at her waist.

"Not here for that either." Keeping his eyes on her face, he walked past her into the house, straight to the kitchen. He'd been unable to have a drink at O'Sullivan's and now he needed one desperately.

The dishwasher was open. He had caught her in the middle of cleaning. She only cleaned when she was anxious or on the verge of a big story.

Jazz. Cleaning. She's working on the Chavez story.

He grabbed a clean glass and the bottle of whiskey from above the fridge.

"You're in a mood," she remarked, grabbing the bottle from his hands.

He watched her pour the drink. Steady. She was always steady.

"You've been asking around about my vic," he said. "And you stood with your photographer as we searched Eddie's car."

She hesitated slightly, and then returned the bottle to the top of the fridge. "I have a job, too." She handed him the drink.

"You don't have time to chase stories anymore. You hand them off to your staff. Yet your byline was on my murder investigation this morning." He sipped the whiskey and waited.

"I didn't realize you still read the paper."

He downed the remaining liquid, then reached for the bottle again. The alcohol didn't settle well in his empty stomach.

She pulled the bottle from his hands. "Why are you here?"

"Why do you care about Eddie Chavez?"

"It's my job." She poured the alcohol in the glass. She wouldn't look at him. "Same as you."

"Your job is to get a newspaper out every day. You're taking a special interest in this story. Why?"

"Why don't you spit out what you're trying to ask me?"

He looked back at her. She looked beautiful even when she was annoyed. She was the only woman he had ever loved, and yet he couldn't trust her.

"How well did you know him?" he asked.

"I didn't—"

Stellar shook his head, stopping the oncoming fight. Her denials were worse than the lies. He drank and felt the burn all the way down to his soul.

Their relationship had never been easy. His mother thought she was a gold digger. Her father thought the Stellar money would corrupt her. Even the little disagreements had always erupted into yelling matches.

Their largest fight had led to a breakup of two years, right after her father had been elected police chief and she made managing editor at the paper. She worked all day, and Chief Mack transferred Stellar to the graveyard shift. They barely saw each other, but when the chief started handing out promotions only to those who needed the money, Stellar made a choice. He transferred to the Las Vegas Metro Police and asked Erika to move with him. To start a new life, just the two of them.

She had said no.

He hadn't seen her those two years he was in Vegas, but he'd heard rumors that she was seeing someone. After making detective, he'd decided to return to Lake City and to the woman he loved. They had resumed where they left off. Neither had talked about the two years he had been gone, but there had been another man in her life. Stellar couldn't stop thinking about it.

"I don't care what you do in your spare time," Stellar said. "We're not together anymore. I'm interested in my dead vic. Tell me how well you knew him."

She laughed. "You think I was sleeping with your victim?"

He said nothing. Instead, he watched her face for any sign.

"You're too insecure, Will. Why didn't you meet me at O'Sullivan's last night?"

"We broke up."

He rinsed the glass and dropped it in the dishwasher. Piling in the remaining dishes, he poured in some soap and set the timer on the dishwasher to come on in three hours. She would be asleep by then.

Erika leaned back against the counter with her arms folded over her chest. Watching him. "Why are we fighting now?"

"I asked you to marry me," he said. He didn't look at her. He didn't want to see her face, but he heard the sigh that caught in her throat. The answer was the same.

"You know you're asking a whole lot more than that."

"I'm not asking you to quit your job."

"But you are. You want an open relationship, and I can't promise that. My job requires confidentiality. So does yours. We both know you're not planning on leaving the force."

"I don't want secrets between us."

He looked at her now. She said nothing. After a moment, she looked away.

He walked from the kitchen, flipping the switch off as he left. Maybe he should come to grips with the fact that their relationship was never going to work, but he just couldn't turn it off that easily.

"Where were you Tuesday night?" he asked as he walked to the sliding glass door, making sure it was locked.

She didn't answer.

"Nothing to say?" he prodded.

"Am I a suspect?"

He shrugged. "You always go to the paper. You have to be there to supervise your staff, approve the stories. You work until one, when the first paper comes off the line. You head home after and sleep for six straight hours. I know your routine. You didn't go Tuesday night."

"Are you following me now?"

"Answer the question, Erika, and I'll leave."

"I never met your victim. I swear. Never spoke one word to him. It's been a hard week with Cole's death. Excuse me if I needed a night off. As you always remind me, my staff can handle a little time without me. And you, you were unavailable. You were still mad at me."

He was still mad. He checked the windows to make sure they were locked. She always forgot to check them, too busy looking for the story to watch her own back. As always, he would be there to clean up after her.

He wished for another drink as he stared at her through the darkness.

"You didn't know Cole, did you?" she finally asked.

He shook his head. He had seen Cole around town. He knew a few of the boy's friends. At the memorial service, his teachers said Cole was the smartest kid in the class. A dreamer and a schemer. Always one step ahead. Some had compared him to Lincoln.

Will had attended the viewing, as most in the town had. He had no intention of actually seeing the boy. But despite his better judgment, Will had waited in line behind the other families and took his turn to say good-bye at the casket. The boy looked different from the kid he had seen walking around town. He was dressed in a baseball uniform. Stellar didn't even know he had been on the team. He wondered what position Cole played.

The boy's face and hands looked too big for his body in the tiny casket. As Will stared at the boy in the casket, he realized he had never spoken to the kid. Several people had mentioned going to O'Sullivan's afterward to honor the lost childhood. He had headed home to drink alone, thinking of the brother he had lost.

"It's like I'm twelve years old again." It was all he could say. The anger was gone. Only despair remained.

She reached out for his hand. "Do you want to talk about it?"

He shook his head and took her in his arms. The smell of her hair was comforting. Despite it all, he would be staying.

Chapter 28

Alex couldn't sleep. At six o'clock, she rolled out of bed and showered, rapping along with Dr. Dre and Snoop Dogg. With her hair still wet, she pulled on a light blue tank top. It wouldn't cover the scar, but the blue would bring some color to her dark skin. Gray sweatpants and her old flip flops completed her relaxed look. She grabbed her room keycard and walked outside, letting the heavy door slam behind her.

She looked back at the motel door. A jail cell, nothing more.

She shielded her eyes from the sun and gazed at the Death Valley Motel. The parking lot was empty, except for Ric's lone white truck. The swimming pool was still, the street deserted. There was no breeze in the deserted sky. She listened hard and thought she might have heard a car in the distance. Or a plane. But she saw no movement. The place was dead.

She walked down the cobbled steps and into the undersized office. Ric had left a note about needing sleep. She figured he deserved it and decided to leave him alone. It was time she picked up some of the cleaning chores.

Room 110 had been stripped by the officers. The sheets from the bed were gone. Only the mattress and box spring remained. They had taken the few items Eddie had brought with him. The cleaning crew had done a decent job of removing the blood and smell of death, but Alex could still sense it. She could see a discoloration on the carpet that looked like a large teardrop where Eddie's body had crumpled on the floor.

There was no other trace Eddie Chavez had lived in this room.

A new day was a new start; that was what they had taught her in prison. For Eddie Chavez, it wasn't. For Alex, the new start was cleaning up a room where death had been.

She stared into Eddie's room, thankful that at least she could be alone with her thoughts. She should try to enjoy the silence. As she cleaned, she would try to make sense of Eddie's death, including how Leanna fit in.

She believed Leanna was telling the truth about not killing Eddie, but she wasn't as quick as Ric to put the blame on her brother Danny. There was only one exit to the room, only one door. Had Eddie let the killer in? Did he even bother looking through the peephole or out the window? There had been no sign of a struggle and no sign of forced entry.

Maybe Eddie knew the killer and didn't think he was a threat. Maybe he trusted him. Or maybe he felt he had no choice but to open the door. Alex thought about Erika Mack. Would Eddie open the door to an unthreatening female? Alex doubted she could overpower Eddie. What if she were accompanied by her boyfriend? Would Eddie open the door if Detective Will Stellar flashed his badge? A badge was always a good way to open doors.

Then what? Trapped in a room with a killer. What were his final thoughts? Had he thought of his son or his family? Had he begged for his life on his knees? Had he prayed? Or had he given up?

The room couldn't answer the questions. Ric would try to get the answers from Danny, but Alex knew the answers wouldn't come from him. Maybe Ric was right, and Detective Stellar and his blonde girlfriend were involved. She couldn't exactly confront the detective, but she could talk to Erika. She had seemed interested in talking to Alex at the bar.

Before she could confront Erika, Alex had to clean room 110. The carpet would have to be replaced, and the room would need a fresh coat of paint before it would be ready for new guests. She looked at the dresser. It would have to go, too. It looked clean, but it was hard to remove blood, especially from so many crevices.

She pushed the chair toward the desk and noticed the arm of the chair was broken. She would have to buy another chair, too. She opened the bathroom window. Fresh air would help, even if it was hot air. When she returned to the room, the sunlight from the open doorway was blocked.

Bobby, the man who had bumped into her at the bar, stood with his arms folded over his chest. He glared at her with a scowl on his face. He was bigger than she remembered, his shoulders almost spanning the entire doorway, but she had last seen him on the floor of O'Sullivan's bar. They always looked small when they were drunk and sprawled out on the ground.

She realized he was blocking her only exit.

I should scream, she thought.

"Where's your brother?" he asked. His voice was harsh, but she could tell he was sober now.

Ric was four doors down. If she was loud enough he would hear, but she didn't scream. Instead, she analyzed his posture, studied his face. He was there to prove a point. He was standing square, threatening. She was cornered. She should scream. End it before it started. But she didn't.

"About the other night at the bar," she started.

He shook his head, stepped closer. She felt the room getting smaller. She felt her heart beating faster. She counted the beats, hoping to slow them down.

"I did warn you not to touch me," she said raising her hands, her palms level with her head.

If she didn't scream, she should at least run. If he continued closer, the door would open up, but she would have to jump over the bed to run for it.

She didn't want to run, but she didn't want to go back to prison.

She dragged her right foot back, exhaled. She shifted so her left shoulder now faced her attacker. She scanned the room, the dresser, the bed, the nightstand. They could be obstacles or they could be weapons.

"Where's your brother?" he asked again.

He took another step. He was within reach, and her breath caught.

"You should go," she warned, but it wasn't heartfelt. She wanted him to stay. She wanted him to fight. She continued to count her heartbeats. They were steady.

"You and your brother don't scare me. I was drunk—"

"When I knocked you on your ass?"

His eyes narrowed on her. "You should apologize."

"You have me cornered, big guy. You want me to apologize? Why don't you make me?"

He reached up with his right hand to backhand her. In one move, using only her right hand, she grabbed his hand, twisted his wrist, and bent his fingers back toward his chest. He screamed in pain as she bent them back further than God intended. He doubled over and fell to one knee. She listened for the snapping sound, but just before, she eased her grip.

"You should leave now. I don't want to hurt you."

He cradled his right hand and stared at her. "You don't want to—"

She could no longer hear him. She couldn't hear anything but her heart pounding. She couldn't feel anything. She didn't see him. She saw Davy Knight staring down at her in that dirty construction site. She pictured forcing her knee into his chin or slamming the palm of her hand into his nose.

She forced herself to count again. Bobby's pained face returned and Davy Knight was just a memory.

"I don't want to hurt you," she said again. "I've warned you twice now. If you push me again, I may not be able to stop. And if I kill you, I'll have a hell of a time explaining it to Detective Stellar."

A familiar deep voice cut through the fog that surrounded her. "Police. Back off."

Alex jerked back and looked in the doorway. She saw the outline of a tall, lean man and knew immediately it wasn't Detective Stellar. She recognized the smooth bald head and the dark goatee. He had his jacket pulled back, posture turned slightly to the side, his hand on his service pistol.

Her stomach flipped as she watched Detective Ryan Dade.

Bobby didn't miss the message or the tone. He put his hands up, his hurt hand slightly lower than his good hand. "Officer, we were just talking."

Dade nodded. "I bet. Take a step back before she hurts you."

Alex was thankful he kept his eyes on Bobby. She didn't want his blue eyes examining her before she had time to compose herself.

"What's your name?" Dade asked.

"Bobby. Bobby Jacks. I'm friends with Will Stellar."

Dade nodded again. "Go home and ice the hand." He kept his hand on his gun until Bobby walked past him out the door. He turned to watch him leave.

Alex took a deep breath, but she still felt as if she were drowning. When he turned back to her, she realized her heart was beating too fast. The fight was over. At least, she hoped it was.

"Looks like you're getting along well with the locals," Dade said, his blue eyes softening with his smile. He wore a black suit and a power red tie. Professional as always. It didn't appear the hundred-degree sun beating at his back bothered him a bit.

"You didn't call," he said when she didn't answer.

He took a step toward her. Instinctively, Alex took a step backward. Her back smacked the wall behind her. She cringed from the pain and the embarrassment.

Dade stopped where he was. "Are you okay?"

"I'm fine," she managed to say. She took a deep breath, remembering her breathing exercises. "How'd you find me?"

"It seems you're causing problems." He flashed an easy smile, then sat on the bed and looked at her. "You're scared of me?"

She shook her head. She could never be scared of him. She leaned against the wall for support. She wasn't scared of anyone—except herself. "I needed space. I needed time."

He nodded, but she could tell he still didn't understand her. She wondered if he ever would. He leaned on his knees and rubbed his palms together. She was thankful for every minute his eyes weren't studying her.

"I thought you'd come back after you got out of the CC," he said.

Alex had spent the past two years in the Southern Nevada Correctional Center in North Las Vegas. She had spent some of her time there in education programs and therapy sessions. Most of the time she had spent alone in her cell. Ryan Dade had visited her every month.

She rested her back against the wall and tried to relax her muscles. "I needed to get my life back. There's nothing I can do about my past. I just want to forget it. You remind me of everything that went wrong. I'm sorry."

He looked at her. "But Ric doesn't?"

"Ric's family."

"I thought we were family. I was planning on helping you get back on your feet. I know you have Ric, but I was hoping I could be a part of that, too."

He was feeling the guilt. He had arrested her. He had done his job, had done what she had asked him to do, but he was still feeling guilty about that. She could see in his eyes that he still cared about her.

For a second, she forgot the past and thought of the future. With him. A home. Not a motel room in the middle of the desert. Maybe children. She could teach them to swim. He could teach them to be honest. Ric could be an uncle. She wondered if Ric was good with children.

Reality soon replaced the excitement. She wasn't the type to get caught up in fairytale dreams. Ryan Dade wasn't her prince charming. He wasn't hers at all. She stared at his hands on his lap, the gold glistening on his ring finger. He wasn't here to change her future.

"We're friends," she said. "We always will be. I just need some time to center myself again." She felt the tears coming. She closed her eyes as she held them back.

He stood and reached out to grab her arms. She didn't fight him. She couldn't. He pulled her into his arms. His sweet cologne enveloped her and flooded her with memories.

"It's been four months," he whispered as he held on tight. "Was that enough time?"

Obviously not, she thought as the sobs came.

"You should go," she said.

"Did you kill someone?"

She smiled through the tears. "Not recently."

"I have to meet with Detective Stellar. I'll help clear this up."

"I don't need your help."

"I think you do. You don't have to fight on your own."

Even though she was tucked tightly in Ryan Dade's arms and her brother was only a few doors away, she felt so alone.

Chapter 29

Ric wasn't in his room. After putting his sister to bed the night before, Ric had decided he needed to keep a close eye on his prime suspect. Instead of taking his truck, he set out on foot and walked the two miles from the motel to Schneider's Computer Store. Buddy was behind the counter as usual. He was more than happy to lend Ric his Jeep.

There were two reasons Ric took the Jeep instead of his truck. The first was to ensure his sister had no idea he was gone. The second was to ensure Danny Nunez didn't get suspicious when he saw a white truck following him around.

It was just after midnight when Ric made it to the home Danny and Leanna shared. He waited in the darkness. He couldn't remember the last time he had slept. As he fought the fatigue hitting him at all angles, he tried to remember why he was doing this. Why was he helping his sister with the fruitless search for the killer? He didn't care that Eddie Chavez was dead, but Alex did. So he forced his eyes open.

There was no sign of Danny. Leanna came home around two o'clock, alone and obviously a little drunk. She parked crooked and went straight to her bedroom. Ric was starting to doubt every part of the story she had told to Alex. If Leanna hadn't been raped, then it placed serious doubts on Danny's role in Eddie's murder.

Ric wondered if Danny was avoiding his house. He had to know the cops were sniffing close to him, or maybe they had already picked him up. The tapes given to Detective Stellar showed a definite connection from Eddie to Leanna. Stellar would have already interviewed her, but Ric would have heard if the investigation was close to an arrest.

So Ric decided to forgo the house surveillance and head for the drug hole. Everything was quiet there, too. Ric settled in for a long night of waiting.

After three hours, he was hungry and about to fall asleep. A barking dog kept him awake. There had been no movement inside or around the drug hole. He watched as the stars disappeared and the sky grew lighter. The air turned from crisp to dry. The sun peeked over the mountains and pink clouds formed on the horizon.

Pink sky in the morning, everyone take warning.

Time was running out. As he sat in the warm truck, his mind wandered back to Alex's initial reaction. She was right—he did doubt her innocence. She had killed before. It would be stupid to not consider her a suspect, but she had seemed confused with the news of the dead guest. If she was confused, then he had a problem. If the evidence pointed at her, then he had to make a choice, one he was not comfortable making.

He needed to get his blood moving. It was time to see what Danny was hiding. Since Ric had left his gun locked in the motel office, he really didn't want to come face to face with Danny unless they were on his terms. So Ric was especially careful as he approached the house. He listened but heard nothing from inside.

He made his way to the back yard. The neighbor's mutt barked, making Ric cringe. It was an ugly dog that looked malnourished and foul. No lights came on in the neighbor's house. He wasn't too worried about a neighborhood watch. Drug holes only existed where the neighbors didn't care about each other. He growled at the dog, and it stopped barking.

Ric tried the back door and was surprised to find it unlocked. Not sure what to expect, Ric proceeded slowly into the house. The door opened into a small kitchen. Without touching anything, he looked for signs of a meth lab but found none. In fact, it seemed pretty clean. The cabinets were bare, the refrigerator had been unplugged and stood empty.

He continued into the living room. It was empty—stark empty. He walked down the hall and found the bedroom almost as empty. Just a bare mattress on the floor. He leaned his back against the wall.

He'd seen drug holes this empty before. It meant only one thing: Danny had known the cops were onto him. He had probably been tipped off to an impending search warrant. Detective Stellar and his team could be on their way right now. Ric would need a hell of an explanation if he was caught here when they served the warrant. He glanced at his watch. Instead of leaving, he sat down on the mattress and laid his head in his hands. He tried to think what this meant, other than Danny was in the wind. Maybe he had underestimated the boy. He was a small-time pot dealer, but he was also a good student, just as Ric had been. A star athlete, just like Ric. He had just taken the wrong road when his parents died.

Had the same happened to Ric? His father had told him the two most important things in life were taking care of your family and respecting the badge. Ric had failed his family and quit the force. He had been left with nothing but an empty house. He had nothing in his life. His sister wouldn't let him help her because he hadn't been there for her the one night she needed him. When he had tried to help her with the investigation, he'd lost the trail of their only suspect. He wanted more than watching movies in the hot, cramped office of a motel in the middle of nowhere. His only highlight was the local prostitute who smiled at him as if knowing his loneliness. This was his miserable life.

Was it any better than Danny's? If he had killed Eddie Chavez for raping his sister, at least he had the balls to take care of his family. Ric had done nothing. He had respected the badge until it was too late.

He wasn't sure where to go from here. His old partner would have known. Maybe Danny had the right idea. Maybe it was time for Alex and Ric to hit the road. He just had to convince Alex that Eddie's death was no longer their problem. They could start over somewhere new and hope death wouldn't keep following them.

He knew Alex would be up soon and wondered what her next step would be. He knew she was still searching for a motive, searching for the why. Maybe she was right. He should stop looking for a killer and start looking for the reason. Maybe the reason Eddie Chavez died was more important than who killed him.

Chapter 30

Will carried the two mugs into Erika's bedroom. He was feeling relaxed and revived, ready to tackle a new day. Erika was already up and showered.

"Coffee?" he asked.

She looked at him as she slipped into a black skirt. "I don't have time. I need to get to the office."

He put the mugs down and reached over to zip up the skirt. Erika slapped his hand away.

"I've got it. I can manage to dress myself."

He smirked at her. "I know. I can help, though."

She zipped up the skirt and walked into the bathroom. He followed her. She wore a deep purple blouse. He liked purple on her.

"What's wrong?" he asked, fingering her blonde hair.

"Nothing." She leaned over and kissed him quickly. "I need to get ready. I'm late."

"You can't live on only six hours of sleep. You can afford to take a minute for yourself every now and then."

He watched her jam the earrings in her ears. *Why is she always rushing?*

She watched him in the mirror. "My career is just as important as yours."

He held up his hands in surrender. "Whoa! I never said it wasn't."

She pushed past him and out of the bathroom.

He grabbed her arm, stopping her. "Why are you picking a fight with me? You asked me to stay last night."

"Yes, I wanted you to stay last night, but I don't need your help now. I've been doing fine without you hovering over me."

He released her arm. "I can't believe you pulled me right back into this."

"It was your choice to stay," she said, walking from the room.

"It's never my choice."

~~~

Stellar scanned the evidence report. With a few hours of sleep, a hot shower and a shave, and a fight already behind him, Stellar was determined to find his killer by midnight.

"All the blood on the sheet is the victim's?" he asked.

Sergeant Morgan nodded. He didn't sit.

Stellar refused to let the evidence get him down. He had pulled strings to get the DNA on the sheet analyzed quickly. He had been positive it would lead to a suspect. Instead, it had led him in a circle. He threw the paper down and waited for better news.

"The prints on the chair in the motel room match Leanna Nunez," Morgan said, shifting his weight from one leg to the other. Stellar noticed he wasn't looking at him.

"What else?"

"Despite the car being wiped, we were able to recover two prints from the car. We recovered Leanna's from inside the passenger door."

Stellar noticed Morgan's hesitation and wondered why he looked nervous. Confused, Stellar watched him as he stared at the papers in his hand. He leaned back in the chair. It wasn't Morgan's personality to be quiet or shy around him.

He heard a scratching at the window and ignored it. "You said two sets of prints, didn't you?"

Stellar waited. Morgan nodded but didn't look up. Stellar watched as Morgan took a deep breath, letting it out slowly. He refused to demand the information. Morgan needed to have the strength.

Morgan held out a piece of paper. Stellar stared at him for a minute and then grabbed it.

"Those were found on the outside of the driver's door."

Stellar glanced at the page. Confused, he read it again, then set it down. "Are you sure?"

Morgan didn't respond.

Stellar looked up. "How did Erika's prints end up in AFIS?"

Morgan coughed, then shifted his feet. Stellar rubbed his head that was just starting to ache and waited.

"She was arrested in college for drug possession," Morgan explained. "The charge was dropped, but she'd been officially booked."

Stellar didn't know about the arrest, or the drugs. They had dated all through college. How had he not known? *More secrets.* Now her prints were on his victim's vehicle. Why the driver's door? He reread the report.

"Who else knows about this?" Stellar asked.

"Just you."

Stellar folded the paper. "Keep it that way."

"Sir?"

Stellar stood and stared at Morgan. "Is there anything else, Sergeant?"

"No, sir."

"Then find Daniel Nunez." Stellar stared at Morgan's back until he disappeared. He buried the report in his desk and grabbed his keys.

He needed a vacation, one that included umbrella drinks and tall, dark women in skimpy bikinis. He deserved it. He'd never taken a real vacation since making detective. After this case was closed, he could drive off to some Mexican resort and ignore his girlfriend's lies, his mother's meddling, his brother's antics, and the rest of the town's rumors. He could forget about the entire Mack family. Mexico was sounding like a dream.

He could practice his Spanish by ordering room service. Or maybe he'd invite Alex as his personal translator. *Ooh, bad idea*, he thought. *Can't go there.* Maybe Canada was a better option. Or Europe. Much farther away from everything. Once he solved this case, he would definitely look into a vacation.

~~~

When he pulled into the lot at the Death Valley Motel, Stellar noticed the door to room 110 was wide open. Ric's truck was parked near the office door. A blue Toyota Prius was parked across two slots. The driver's door was wide open.

Stellar parked next to Ric's truck. He needed to talk to Ric, possibly without Alex in the room. The missing disc was Ric's doing. He tried the office door but found it locked. He made his way slowly to room 110.

He heard Alex's voice, and then a man's. Not Ric's. Then he heard her crying. Stellar pulled his gun and held it to his side. He looked in and saw a man holding Alex.

Stellar hadn't made a sound, but the man spun around, shoving Alex behind him. He pointed a gun at Stellar's face.

The man was quick, but Stellar had seen the badge before the gun, so he didn't bother to raise his own weapon.

"Detective Ryan Dade?" he asked.

The detective was wearing an expensive suit. Stellar wondered who he was trying to impress.

Dade nodded and lowered the gun.

"I thought you'd stop by the station first," Stellar said.

Dade holstered his weapon. "Detective Will Stellar? I apologize. I haven't seen Alex in several months. I wanted to make sure she was okay first."

Stellar noticed he hadn't moved away from Alex. He looked at her now. She had tears in her eyes, but she didn't look sad. He felt he had just stepped into an argument.

"Alex, are you okay?" he asked.

"Peachy." She smirked. She wiped at her tears, and any sign of weakness was gone. "Even I didn't expect you to call Detective Dade and drag him from L.A. to appease your sick curiosity."

"Just doing my job. No matter how many speed bumps you put in my way, I'm going to find Eddie's killer. Even if it's you."

Dade raised his hand now. "That's not necessary, Detective."

He was defending her. Another person to put a barrier up. Stellar holstered his own gun and clenched his fists. "Detective Dade, did you come here to see her or to assist me with my investigation?"

Alex threw up her arms. "Ah, *Dios.* He's here to help you, Stellar. He'll tell you everything you want to know."

Dade turned to Alex. "Allie, please. Let's not get dramatic. Let me talk to the detective, and then I'll come back to see you."

She looked at him. "I'd rather you didn't come back. Please, just leave me alone." She looked at Stellar. "Both of you."

Chapter 31

Detective Stellar wiped the sweat from his brow. It was another hot one. He opened the café door for Detective Dade. Stellar couldn't help but notice that the heat didn't seem to bother him.

"You two seem to be old friends," Stellar said after they found an empty booth. He noticed the wedding ring on his finger.

Dade didn't answer the implied question. He leaned back in the booth, rubbed his bald head as if he was used to having hair. "You seem to have a problem with crime in this city," he said finally.

Stellar studied the man. He was older than Stellar, maybe mid-forties, which probably meant he'd been a detective longer than Stellar had owned a badge. It was obvious Dade knew this, too, but it was experience, not arrogance, that he saw on Dade's face. He reminded himself they were on the same side.

"It's a small city," Stellar said. "We all seem to get along just fine. Every now and then, someone steps out of bounds. When they do, we take care of it."

Dade didn't say anything as the waitress dropped off a glass of water for Dade. She put a mug of coffee and a glass of ice in front of Stellar. He ordered an omelet, extra onions. Dade just shook his head.

"Do you know a man named Bobby Jacks?" Dade asked when the waitress had gone.

Stellar leaned forward. "I do."

"He trespassed onto motel property and cornered Alex. He threatened her. When she didn't back down, he attempted to strike her."

"Attempted?" Stellar asked.

"You should pick him up. Warn him of the consequences of such an attack."

Stellar made a call to Sergeant Morgan to pick up Bobby Jacks. He closed the phone and looked at Dade. "He won't hurt her."

Dade laughed, his whole body shaking. "I wasn't worried he would. You don't know Alex. First bit of advice, don't underestimate her."

Stellar leaned back and studied Detective Dade. He wasn't sure about him yet. All he knew for certain was that he was too old for Alex, yet their embrace said there was a relationship there.

"Tell me about her. How do you know her?"

"Her brother and I were partners."

"Partners?" Stellar couldn't hide his surprise.

"LAPD narcotics and vice for five years. He was a great detective, great undercover too. Probably the best partner I ever had. I always knew he had my back, no matter what. I realized I didn't have to worry with him. He was always a step ahead of everyone, especially the addicts. It made me feel slow sometimes, but I respected him."

Stellar understood. It was a cop thing.

"Ric's pretty observant. He doesn't talk much, but when he does, he can be a bit—"

"Blunt?" Stellar added.

Dade laughed again. "That's just a nice way to say he's an asshole. It worked well for him undercover. He fit with the gang life well. They feared him and respected him at the same time. He was straightforward and in your face. Half the guys he busted still respect him."

"And the other half?"

"Probably want him dead, but he was clean, and he was smart. If they were busted, they knew it was because they were outsmarted."

"Same in vice?"

Dade nodded. "The girls always liked him. He was a gentleman undercover and a hardass on the arrests. He wanted to make a difference to the girls." He shrugged. "Sometimes it worked. Most of the time we were busting them a week later."

"What about the brass? Seems like a guy with a sharp tongue is bound to cut the wrong person."

"Like I said, he's smart. He learned to keep his mouth shut. When it came to the politics, he observed and I talked. We were good partners, kept each other out of trouble."

"You're no longer keeping him out of trouble. Why is that?"

"He hasn't spoken to me in over ten years. Since I arrested Alex."

Stellar waited for Dade to continue. He used a spoon and dropped several ice cubes in his coffee. He needed the caffeine.

"The two of them weren't that close growing up," Dade said. "The age difference was too large for them to be friends. By the time she needed a big brother, he had moved out of the house and was in the academy. When their mother died, they grew further apart. Their father didn't take the death well. He was devastated and withdrew from both of them. Ric stayed away from the house, and Alex started spending time with the wrong type of people.

"By the time their father died, they were barely speaking. Within a few years she was engaged. Ric never got into details, but from what I understand he thought the guy was a thug. He was five years older than her and there was some question about his family background. There was an argument about it, and she told him he wasn't invited to the wedding. Two years later, everything changed. She told him she was getting divorced and was ready to let him in her life. They were just starting to get to know each other again."

He glanced around the café as if looking for someone. He seemed distracted by the only other patron, a young man reading the newspaper and sipping his coffee. Then he leaned back in his chair. "Ric and I were working a case late one night. We were supposed to meet up with Alex after her training."

"Training?" Stellar asked.

"She had just joined the LASD. Her way of starting a new life."

"She was in the Sheriff's Academy?" The surprises kept coming.

He nodded. "When she had an evening free, she'd call us and try to hook up for a drink. That night, she was waiting at the bar for us, but we got called in on a case and didn't get to meet her. The guy, Davy Knight, was a fellow trainee. He'd been separated out a week earlier—an integrity issue, they said. She had been assigned class sergeant the day he was kicked out. I don't know if there was a connection. You can smoke here, right?"

Dade pulled out a cigarette. Stellar didn't bother to answer. He watched as Dade's hands shook slightly as he lit the cigarette.

"Why the Taser?" Stellar asked.

"Despite how she looks, Alex can be very dangerous. She's a good shot, and she's a black belt in kenpo."

"Her brother mentioned she was trained in self-defense."

Dade smiled as if knowing a secret. "Their father used to say she was a handful. She was always getting in trouble at school. He was too busy to deal with a rebellious child. He shoved her off to boxing class. He figured she'd learn some discipline. She did. Over the years, she graduated from boxing to karate. She found some master in Kenpo and in time she became extremely good. She still ran with a bad crowd, Latin Kings, MS-13, but now she could hold her own against any of them.

"She was trained to fight, to attack when threatened. And if given a fighting chance, she would have killed Davy Knight in the parking lot that night." Dade looked back at the man in the booth. "It's quiet here."

Stellar nodded. The waitress dropped off his omelet. She asked Dade again if he wanted anything. He only shook his head. Stellar waited for Dade to continue the story. When he didn't, Stellar started in on his omelet. He didn't realize how hungry he was.

"What happened?" he finally asked. "How'd he get off?"

Dade blew out smoke. "The detectives did everything by the books. They had to, with Ric and me all over their back. But they had no knife, no Taser, no DNA, and Davy had a hell of a lawyer. All we really had was her ID. They dug away at her. Eventually they got their reasonable doubt."

"Are you sure it was the right guy?"

"Positive. No doubt about it. I sat in that courtroom and watched the bastard stare at her. It was hell for her, every day. He enjoyed watching her pain, and I don't think he doubted for a second he would get off."

Stellar lost his appetite. He pushed his plate to the center of the table and folded his arms over his chest. "So when the court let him go, she took his sentence in her own hands?"

"She had a faith in the system. I think it's still there. At least I hope it is. But this definitely was a blow—to all of us. She knew when she pulled the trigger she would have to pay for it. She called me as soon as she did it. She stayed at the scene and handed me the gun when I pulled up. She gave a full confession. Prosecutor cut her a break due to the circumstances." He shrugged. "She knew what she did was wrong, but she was willing to live with her actions. She doesn't regret it, though. Probably never will."

"She's stubborn and determined to fight me."

"When her back's against the wall … when she feels she has to fight, she'll fight. Treat her like a suspect and she'll fight you."

"Do you think she's capable of killing again?"

Dade leaned back, sucked on his cigarette. "Killing, absolutely. She's been trained to protect herself. But murder?" He shook his head.

"I swear, I didn't think she was capable of murder the first time. Now I know differently. Everyone's capable of murder."

Not everyone, Stellar thought. "What about Ric?"

"If put in the position, Ric could kill, but he's not capable of murder. His official training and his good judgment prevent him from doing anything stupid. He may push on the line, but he'll never be a bad seed."

Stellar was still stuck on the fact that Alex had called Dade, and not her brother after shooting her attacker. He wiped his hands and decided the truth was important enough to risk pissing off an LAPD detective.

"Were you two sleeping together at the time?" Stellar asked.

Dade seemed genuinely surprised. "God, no!" He pointed to his ring. "I'm happily married, thank you very much."

Stellar said nothing, merely studied Dade.

"Fifteen years, and I've always been faithful," Dade said. "Alex and I are only friends. She's Ric's little sister."

"I'm not Ric."

Dade looked confused. Or hurt. Stellar could tell the thought of sleeping with Alex hadn't crossed his mind. It didn't make any sense.

"I apologize if the question bothered you," Stellar said. "You two looked closer than friends back at the motel."

Dade relaxed. "Yeah, well, I haven't seen her in almost five months. I went to see her every month when she was locked up." He smiled. "I used to bring her cases I was working on. She's great at reading a crime scene. She would always find the one piece of evidence everyone else had missed or discounted."

Stellar took his time drinking his coffee.

Finally, Dade continued, "I heard she was going to be released early, but she never called. They both just disappeared. I've been worried about her ever since."

"So why the silent treatment from Ric? Does he hold you responsible for his sister?"

Dade shrugged. "He's refused to talk to me since her arrest. I transferred to homicide shortly after. I felt it was best for everyone. A few years later, Ric quit the force, no explanation to anyone. My only information about him came from her."

Stellar decided to lay it on the table. "So are you here to see her or to help me?"

Dade looked at him. "How about both? She told me she didn't do this, and I believe her. I'll do whatever I can to help. I gave you the background information. What else can I do?"

"Tell me how I can get them to talk to me. I need to know what they know. I have a guy murdered in one of her rooms, and they refuse to let me find the killer."

Dade looked confused. "She won't help you?"

"She lies every chance she gets."

"She does that so you won't get too close or ask too many personal questions. She keeps too much to herself. Ric and I still don't even know what happened the two years she was married. You'll need more time than you've got to break her. You'll have to use him."

"He refuses to talk to me."

"Like I said, he's not the social type, but I can get him to talk."

"You have an idea?"

Dade smiled. "Of course. I know Ric better than anyone."

Chapter 32

Ric sat in the bare room and stared at the surveillance camera on the wall. It stared back at him. It was a cheap brand, probably bought in bulk by a department struggling with finances. He figured it was a black-and-white model. Detective Stellar was probably watching him on a monitor smaller than his unit at the motel. He hadn't lied when he told them the air was on the fritz. It really was a sweat room.

Ric was pretty sure it was after noon, even though they had taken his watch. He was hungry and he needed sleep. The fatigue would make it hard to keep his mouth closed. With his cuffed hands, he pushed the table away from him, giving him a bit more room to breathe.

There were no windows in the room. He was always impressed that every police agency in America had the same interrogation room. Bare and uncomfortable. The walls needed paint and some new furniture. It could use an air freshener, but it was part of the ambiance. In a way, it was nostalgic for him. It brought back some great memories, so he wasn't too upset that he had been left alone to reminisce.

He was surprised when Detective Dade walked in, but he made sure not to reveal it. His former partner sat down across from him. He said nothing, merely stared at Ric, waiting for him to say the first word, to beg for his freedom. He was so predictable. Whatever his plan was, Ric would stay a step ahead.

Ric played out a few scenarios in his head, then went with his first option. "I'd like to see the arrest warrant."

Dade shook his head and smiled. "We didn't need one. You made it easy for us, driving around in someone else's car. Probably stolen. That's probable cause."

"If you speak to the Jeep's owner, he'll tell you I borrowed it. And you'll have to release me."

"I believe someone's trying to reach Bud Schneider right now."

Ric was sure no one was trying. "Take these off, Dade. They're making my wrists itch."

Dade leaned over and uncuffed him. "You need to talk to me."

"No, I really don't." Ric grinned, rubbing his wrist. "Last time I checked LAPD doesn't have jurisdiction in Nevada."

"I'm assisting Detective Stellar on his case since the victim used to reside in L.A. Talk to me."

"I know my rights, Dade. Or did you forget I was once a better detective than you?"

Dade's booming laugh echoed in the small room. "Detective Stellar's a good detective, but he needs your help. He had no choice."

"Bullshit. This stinks of you. Stellar wouldn't risk hooking me up. My guess is the police chief himself doesn't know yet. So tell me why you're doing this."

Dade leaned back. "You won't talk to Stellar. Alex lies to him. You're both suspects. For murder, Ric. This isn't a spitting contest to see who has the biggest marbles or who's the best detective in this little town. A man's dead."

"And he'll have a hard time proving I did anything wrong."

"Probably, but he has enough to arrest you. He has enough to arrest Alex. He could've dragged either one of you in for obstructing justice. You and I both know what that would do to Alex. I don't want to see handcuffs around her wrists again. Do you?"

Ric said nothing. He stared at his own wrists.

"So talk to me. We were partners once."

Ric shook his head. "Not anymore, Judas."

"I know you're pissed at me. I let the silent treatment go for the past decade. I understand it, even though it's not warranted. You're hurting, Delgado. I understand."

Ric kept his mouth closed. He knew the importance of listening instead of talking.

Dade leaned back in his chair. "I visited her in prison. Did you know that?"

He did. He would have kept him away from his sister if he thought the visits were harmful, but she needed to see him, needed contact from the outside world.

"I won't apologize for what I did," Dade continued when Ric didn't respond. "You know I wasn't at fault. Someday you'll admit that to yourself, but you had no right to take her away from me. We're friends, Alex and I. You could have called me when she was released. I wanted to see her."

"That night, she called you as a friend, Dade. She needed our help and you hauled her off to jail. Believe what you want, but you're not her friend."

Dade shook his head. "You never asked yourself why she called me and not you?"

"I'm done talking to you. Tell Stellar to book me or let me go."

"She didn't want you to fix what she did. She didn't want you to have to choose between the badge and family. She wanted to be arrested. That's why she refused to leave the scene. She called me and sat there with the gun in her lap and waited for me. I asked her to stay quiet and talk to a lawyer. But it's Alex. She does what she wants. She wanted to be arrested, convicted. She wanted to pay for what she did, without dealing with a trial. Don't blame me for doing my job, Delgado. I did what she asked me to."

"But she needed someone to take care of her." *And I wasn't there.*

Dade shook his head. "That's the last thing she needed, then or now. Why didn't you call me when she was released?"

"Because she didn't want to see you. Her choice, not mine. Like you said, she does what she wants."

Dade thought about this.

Ric looked up at the camera. "Hey, cowboy, get in here. You want to talk, let's talk."

~~~

"Tell me about the security discs," Stellar said.

Ric glanced at the table. Stellar had spread out several still pictures from the surveillance videos. Detective Dade was sifting through them.

Ric leaned back and fought the urge to put his feet up on the table. It would piss Stellar off. Dade would push them off just like Alex often did. They thought it was a sign of disrespect. He just found himself more at ease with his feet up.

"The discs are unimportant," Ric said. "We need to move on to motive."

Stellar shook his head. "I'm the homicide detective, not you. I'll worry about motive when I have my killer. Tell me about the discs."

Ric shrugged. "You saw them. You tell me."

Stellar leaned back. "I saw what you wanted me to see. Now tell me what you didn't want me to see."

Ric remained silent.

"Where's the other disc?"

Ric sighed. Detective Stellar was asking the questions, which meant Detective Dade was watching Ric for body language. It was hard keeping track of the answers he wanted to give to Stellar and not give away anything to Dade.

"There's a disc missing," Stellar pressed. "The night of the crime is missing. I asked for all the discs. Where is it?"

"Destroyed."

"How?"

"I hid it in Alex's CD collection. Her room was broken into. Everything was destroyed."

Stellar stared hard at him. "A robbery? That's convenient."

"For who?" Ric asked.

Stellar folded his arms. "When was this?"

"Yesterday."

"What did the disc show?" Dade asked. "I know you watched it."

"Eddie was in his room all day," Ric said directing his answer to Stellar. "His car wasn't in the lot, since Leanna Nunez took it the day before. Like I told you, he never came out of his room."

"What else?" asked Stellar.

Ric shook his head and looked at Dade. "Hey, Judas, how many cases have you solved by surveillance cameras?"

Dade didn't answer.

"That's right," Ric said. "None. The missing disc isn't important."

Stellar raised his eyebrows. "Why not?"

Ric shook his head. "The camera doesn't catch the killer. The third camera, the camera showing the middle of the parking lot, was moved slightly and overlapped with camera two. Unfortunately, it left a blind spot in the parking lot. Anyone could have approached Eddie's door and not been caught on camera."

Dade glanced at the still shots and nodded. "I see it."

"Shut up, Judas," Ric snapped.

Dade looked back at Ric, confused. "Who moved the camera, Ric?"

"Good question," Ric said. He looked back at Stellar and waited.

Stellar was thinking. "Tell me about the cameras," he finally said.

"The cameras aren't visible. You didn't even see them when you were there."

"Whoever killed Eddie Chavez knew the cameras were there."

"Only two people knew about the cameras. Myself and Alex."

Stellar thought about this. "And the killer, right? So the killer jumped up on your roof and moved it?"

"I didn't say that. Forget the cameras. Chalk it up to bad luck. Forget the discs. You need to move on and look for motive. Why the hell did someone want Eddie Chavez dead?"

Stellar shook his head. "The cameras are important."

Ric sighed, then shrugged. He was done here. He needed to get out of this room. The best way was to get Dade on his side. "Fine. Tell me who told you about the cameras."

Stellar didn't answer. Ric smiled. He now knew exactly who had told him about the cameras. The question was how she knew. Ric wanted to know.

"Whose prints did you find on Eddie's car?"

Stellar's head snapped up. He could tell from Stellar's eyes that he knew about Erika. He had guessed right. It was hard to wipe a car completely clean.

"So the cowboy is finally catching up."

Dade looked at Stellar. "Who told you about the cameras?"

Stellar shook his head, apparently confused with the question. "What?"

"Only Alex and Ric knew about the cameras. Who told you there were cameras?" Dade repeated.

"The chief told me."

Ric looked at Dade. *Always a step behind*, Ric thought. "How did the chief know?"

Stellar didn't answer.

Dade turned to Ric and waited for the answer. He saw the curiosity in Dade's eyes. He knew he had him now.

Ric raised his hands in surrender.

"Chief Mack's too smart to be involved in something this stupid, but his daughter Erika sure knows more than she's telling you."

Chapter 33

Stellar felt he was going in circles. He released Ric Delgado to Detective Dade, who promised to push for more. In reality, Stellar had no choice. Besides, he was starting to believe Ric. The video wasn't useful, and he should have been looking at Erika all along.

He stepped into his office to find Gail Lyons lounging in his guest chair and staring out the window at the bird on his windowsill. He had known Gail a long time. She was friends with his parents, but they hadn't kept in touch over the last few years. She had been elected mayor two years ago, and she was a busy woman. Because of this, he suspected the visit wasn't a personal one.

"Mayor," he said politely. "What brings you here?"

She shook his hand, stern and solid, like every politician he'd ever met. She was a beautiful woman, with ebony skin and brilliant brown eyes that twinkled when she wanted something and drilled through you when you screwed up. He had seen both sides of Mayor Lyons and both amazed him. She looked as if she was in her forties, but he knew she was in her mid-sixties.

"I understand you arrested Ric Delgado," she said, sitting down in the chair.

He cocked his head at her. He had no idea Ric was so well connected. "He was brought in for questioning. He's since been released."

Stellar remained standing. "How did you hear this?"

"I was under the impression the cuffs around his wrist were a sign of incarceration."

Stellar grinned, but he felt no happiness. "That would be incorrect. And why would his arrest concern you, ma'am?"

She shook her finger at him. "Don't *ma'am* me, Will. I've changed your diapers."

"I've since learned to clean my own shit, Gail. Tell me why you're really here."

She folded her hands in her lap. "You know I like you, Will, but I have to keep an eye on this city."

"As you should. You are our mayor."

"Mr. Delgado alerted me yesterday that this case of yours, the murdered stranger, was getting complicated. He was worried about the way you were handling it."

Stellar folded his arms over his chest and kept his mouth shut.

"I support you and this department completely. However, he asked that I keep an eye on it in case there were any slips in procedure."

"And I'm sure you've seen I've been above board on everything. As I told the chief, I had every right to question Alex Delgado. She has a history of violence. I can't ignore a murder rap. As for Ric, he was brought in for a completely separate incident. He agreed to speak to me. He cooperated, and I released him."

"Has the chief pressured you into suppressing evidence?"

"Of course not. I don't mess with evidence, Gail. I'm insulted you would even ask that."

She shifted in her seat and kept her eyes on him. "Your relationship with Erika Mack is common knowledge. So I have to ask this. Are you covering for her?"

Stellar sat down and stared at Mayor Lyons. *What does she know?*

"I promised Ric I would keep on top of this," she explained. "I asked Wags for his notes, and the lab has copied me on their notes. I get notified when prints are run and when there's a match in the database."

She knew everything.

"I'm working a complicated homicide case," he said. "It takes time to compile all the evidence in order to translate it correctly."

"Why hasn't Erika been arrested? Her prints are on the victim's car, Will."

"She didn't murder Eddie Chavez. Besides, I don't have enough for an arrest warrant."

"But you had enough to bring Ric Delgado in? You should bring her in and question her. You can't keep ignoring the fact that she's involved. She's not like us."

He knew what she meant, and it disgusted him. The city was split between the haves and the have-nots. Although Stellar was clearly in the haves category, he spent most of his time protecting and serving the have-nots. Despite her recent success at the newspaper, Erika Mack wasn't in the elite club. She wasn't wealthy, and she was looked down on because of it.

"Erika Mack has the entire media behind her," he said. "If I pull her in, even for questioning, I have to face the ready-made pulpit she has, not to mention the chief of police on my back. It's a sticky situation that requires delicate maneuvering—one I am fully capable of handling. Let me do my job, Mrs. Lyons. If I don't find Eddie Chavez's killer by the end of the week, you can bring in the state police, but I need to know you have my back on this."

She stood. "You have until tomorrow."

~~~

Will Stellar was on his way out to his car when he saw Lincoln's old pickup pull into the station parking lot. He waved and waited for him to get out.

"Where's the Hummer?" he asked when his brother opened the door.

Lincoln grinned. "Got pulled over in Vegas with the expired tags. Maybe you can help me with the ticket?"

Will shook his head. "You're on your own. Is that why you stopped by?"

"Jeff keeps leaving his stuff at my place. I figured I should drop it off for him, but I also needed to talk to you. Do you have a minute?"

Will looked at his watch. "Need a brother or a cop?"

"Both."

Lincoln leaned against his car and lit a cigarette. Will didn't understand the point of smoking in the desert heat.

"You've met Alex Delgado, right? The new woman at the motel?"

Will nodded. "I have indeed."

"What's your take on her?"

"She's irritating, manipulative, and extremely dangerous. Why?"

"Well, now that I know you like her, I was wondering if you thought I had a chance with her."

Will looked at Lincoln and was relieved to see the humor in his face. "She's just your type. Just a bit of warning, though, the last guy who pissed her off ended up with a bullet in his skull."

The grin faded from Lincoln's face. "Serious?"

"As a heart attack."

Lincoln sucked on the cigarette. "What happened?"

Will looked at his watch again. He had some time. "Short story. Guy raped her. When the jury didn't buy her story, she figured she'd take matters into her own hands."

"Good for her. She should have cut his balls off first."

Will wiped the sweat from his forehead. "You forget who you're talking to?"

"No, but I understand where she's coming from. I'm all for law and order, but when things don't fall into place as neatly as you'd like, every now and then a person needs to step up and do what's best for mankind. The guy didn't deserve to walk free."

"And what if he was innocent?"

"You said he raped her. It doesn't sound like you doubt her story."

He thought about it and realized for the first time that he didn't doubt her. "It doesn't make it right, though. You know the road to hell is paved with good intentions."

"Well, now that I'm talking to the cop, I thought I'd let you know she stopped by Ann Wesley's house yesterday."

Will straightened. "Why?"

"She wanted to question Ann about the guy who didn't wake up at the motel. She had the guy's picture."

"Eddie Chavez. Did Ann recognize him?"

Lincoln shook his head. "No, but I did. He showed up at the memorial the other night. No one knew him, so I figured he was crashing. He looked like a scumbag. I asked A. J. and Jeff to escort him out." Lincoln's account matched pretty closely to Leanna's story. Will was thankful that Lincoln had offered the information instead of Will having to force a formal interview.

"Did he say anything to you?"

"I don't pay attention to scum, little brother."

"Did you see him after that?"

"No. In fact, I had no idea he was dead until the pretty Latina stopped by. You have a suspect yet?"

"Possibly. I appreciate the information." He didn't want to tell him about Danny Nunez, especially if he had been trying to help Danny go clean.

Will stared out to the street. He watched a woman in a pickup drive past. She had a cell phone to her ear and almost missed the stop sign.

"Mom told me to invite you to dinner tonight. Think you can make it?"

Will laughed. He knew his mother so well. "A celebration dinner for breaking up with Erika?"

Lincoln shrugged. "I'm not getting between you and mother."

"Tell her I can't make it. I'm on my way over to see Erika now."

"How are things going between you two? Still fighting?"

Will glanced at his watch again. "She won't talk to me. I don't think I can make it work when she keeps so much from me."

Lincoln dropped his cigarette and stepped on it. "I've known Erika a long time, Will. If she's not telling you something, it's only because she doesn't want to hurt you."

Chapter 34

Detective Dade drove Ric back to the motel. Neither spoke. Ric's truck was missing, and the office was locked up tight. If Ric knew his sister, she was following Erika's every move.

He unlocked the office. Dade followed him in.

"Where's Alex?" Dade asked.

"Knowing her, she's probably tailing Erika."

"Is that safe?"

Ric didn't answer.

"Where's the disc?"

"I told you it was destroyed."

Dade walked over to the computer. "You haven't changed that much, not to back up important evidence."

Ric watched as his old partner turned on the computer. "You have a knack for thinking of every possible outcome, Delgado. Always a step ahead, right? But the reason you're always ahead is because you often skip a step." He pointed to the computer. "You want to bring up the file or are you going to make me search the whole computer?"

Moving in front of Detective Dade, Ric opened the file. Dade pulled over the chair as the video started. Ric watched the screen over Dade's shoulder with little interest. The cameras showed nothing except Alex on the phone. Probably with the landscaper again.

"Is she happy here?" Dade asked.

"Of course not. She's not happy anywhere." Ric turned toward the door. "I'm gonna get a soda. You want one?"

Dade didn't answer. When Ric returned from his room, Dade hadn't moved. He sat behind Dade to watch the last day of Eddie Chavez. Ric watched himself enter the screen and walk into the office. He'd already watched the tape three times and knew the schedule.

Dade glanced back at Ric. "You never used to drink soda. Used to complain it was just another drug."

"Caffeine free. No drugs here. Don't tell Alex, but I switched her coffee too."

Dade turned back to the screen and sped through the next several minutes of tape. He resumed normal viewing as the sun faded in the distance.

"Why'd you relocate to hell?" Dade asked.

"It's a dry heat."

Dade laughed. "As if that makes it better."

"You're wasting your time."

Ric watched the tape as Alex started her evening routine. She walked upstairs and emerged fifteen minutes later in her bathing suit and robe.

"Another boring night. Just like the rest. He never came out."

"He may have gone out and been missed by the camera," said Dade. "The blind spot is right in front of his room."

"Unlikely," Ric said. The time on the screen read 7:30 p.m.

Dade leaned back. "Stellar said Eddie died somewhere between three and five." He sped through the next few hours.

"I still don't know how the guy got in the door," said Ric. "Eddie must have let the killer in."

"Erika? A woman would be the perfect bait."

Ric shook his head. "The killer had to be able to overpower this guy. He's not small and he's been in a gang most of his life. He wouldn't be easy to outsmart."

"You don't think Erika's responsible, do you?" Dade looked back at him.

"I never said she was."

"But you just told Stellar…" Dade paused. "Why would you have Alex following her?" Dade didn't wait for a response. Instead, he answered for him. "You wanted her out of the way. And Stellar."

"Someone has to look out for her." Ric kept his eyes on the screen. "Tell me why you said you understood my anger with you, even if it's undeserved."

Dade turned back to the screen. "You know why."

"I wouldn't ask if I knew the answer."

"You're not angry with me. You just need someone to be angry with. You can't blame her for putting a bullet in Davy's head, because you wanted to do the same thing."

"So I blame you?"

"No," Dade said. "You blame yourself for not being there at the bar a year earlier. We both know the case could have waited. You made the call to blow off your sister that night."

"It wasn't my fault."

"I know," Dade said, meeting his eyes. "And so does she." He turned back to the monitor and paused the tape. "Who's that?"

Ric looked at the frozen image of a woman in the office. "Della. She rented a room for the night. She leaves just after two."

"A *prossie?*"

Ric looked away from Dade. He didn't need Dade judging him, too.

"You failed to mention her before. Stellar will need to get her statement."

"She's not a suspect," Ric protested. "Or a witness. She doesn't need to be hassled."

"That's not your call to make, Delgado. She may have evidence."

"I already talked to her. She didn't hear or see anything. She was gone before Eddie was killed."

Dade said nothing. He turned back to the tape and watched it play out in real time. Ric looked at his watch. He would need to check on Alex soon, but he wanted Dade gone before she came back.

"Did you get a look at her date?"

"I didn't get a great look at him. He didn't come inside. You know how nervous johns can be."

"There isn't a clear picture on the monitors, either. He keeps his head down the whole time. And he's wearing a hoodie. Who wears a sweatshirt in this heat? I can't see his face."

Ric watched as Della reappeared in the office and handed him the key. They spoke for a few minutes. Then she walked out. Ric watched her as she left.

"You got a thing for her?" Dade asked.

"Shut up."

Dade rewound to when she first arrived and watched it again. "No car?"

Ric shook his head. "I didn't hear one. Most of the time she has them park behind the wall and walk. It makes them feel more comfortable."

"I was wrong. You have changed."

"People don't change."

"If you believed that you never would have turned your back on the badge."

Ric said nothing. Dade turned back to the screen.

"Why'd you keep the disc from Detective Stellar?" Dade watched the key exchange again. "You didn't want to get her in trouble. You're protecting a hooker. How many times did you watch this?"

Ric didn't answer. He was watching his old partner. He knew his mannerisms, knew his tics. Dade saw something. Ric strained his eyes to see what he was missing. It pissed him off that he hadn't seen it. Dade continued to watch the monitor.

In silence, they both watched until they saw the sun light up the parking lot.

"Her john doesn't leave when she does," Dade said. "In fact, the camera doesn't catch him leaving at all."

"He must have left through the blind spot."

"Which means he passed Eddie Chavez's door. And we can't identify the time."

Dade was right. He had missed it. "I'll get the information, but I may need your help."

Dade turned toward him. "Tell me why you left the force."

"I had no choice. The line between right and wrong got blurry for me."

Ric glanced at his watch. It was almost six. He was running out of time. He needed to rein Alex in. He dialed Stellar's number. Stellar picked up on the first ring.

"I may have something, cowboy. I'd be willing to share, for a favor."

"First, tell me what the something is."

"I may have a witness. She won't talk to a cop, but she may be able to ID Eddie's killer. Can you keep an eye on Alex for me?"

"Where is she?" Stellar asked.

"Wherever Erika is. She's got my truck."

"Already on my way. Call me once you get an ID."

Ric hung up and looked at Dade. "What now?"

"We need to talk to Della."

"She probably won't be on the street for another hour."

"You gonna pick her up?" Dade asked, leaning back in his chair.

Ric thought about this. "She won't come with me."

Dade smiled. "Are you going to have my back?"

"If you can pick her up, I'll question her. She won't talk to you."

Dade paused. After a moment, he asked again, "And you'll have my back?"

"Of course." Ric reached into the cabinet, grabbed his revolver, and relocked the cabinet.

Dade stared at it. "What's the cannon for?"

"Only for looks," Ric said. "This isn't going to be a legal interview."

Chapter 35

Alex was focused on the newspaper parking lot in front of her. She watched as two women walked to the front door. Neither one resembled the blonde Erika Mack. She watched a black Dodge Magnum pull into the lot. The windows were tinted dark. No one got out.

She jumped when her passenger door swung open. Detective Stellar stepped in and sat down. His shades hid his eyes. He wore a blue polo shirt tucked into his jeans. She saw the badge hooked to his waist and the gun strapped next to it.

Holding a bag in one hand, he smiled at her. She didn't smile back.

"Hey, killer," he said. "Can I join you for the stakeout?" He closed the door and made himself comfortable.

She didn't answer.

"Sandwich?" he asked.

She looked at the bag.

"I got steak. It seemed fitting for a stakeout. Get it?"

He laughed to himself and opened the bag. She watched him pull a large sandwich from the bag. She could smell the onions and meat.

"Your loss. I'm starving." He took a bite. "I released your brother," he said through a mouthful.

She turned away to watch the door again. She had no idea why Stellar was here, but she was starting to worry. She sized up the situation. The tight surroundings would make it difficult to fight hand to hand. He also had a gun within quick reach, and just out of reach from her, which played to his advantage. She checked her door to make sure it was still unlocked, in case she had to bolt. The odds were against her coming out on top, but she would never stop fighting.

He continued to eat. "This is a nice truck. I prefer my Escalade, though. More legroom."

Alex raised her right knee, almost touching the keys dangling from the ignition. She turned to watch him. The movement, although slight, made Stellar stop chewing. He glanced at the steering wheel. He smiled again and Alex saw the dimples Ann had referred to. It made him look young and just a bit sneaky. She could see how the girls would fawn over him, but Alex saw it was just a mask. He wore a badge and a gun.

"Can I turn this off?" he asked pointing to the radio. "That bass line's making my head ache." He reached over and turned off the radio.

She froze at the movement. Silence replaced Cypress Hill. She waited for him to take a bite. As he did, she ran her hand slowly down to her knee.

"How'd you get here? You don't have a valid driver's license," he asked.

She grabbed the pocket knife from the keychain. Without a sound, it clicked off the hook and into her palm.

Now she smiled. "I lied."

"You seem to do that a lot. So are you planning on just staking out the *Times* office until you see Erika? Then what? Tail her to her ultra-secret hiding spot so you can catch the killer red-handed?"

"Don't mock me."

"But it's so easy. And kinda fun." He wiped sauce from his chin. "Why are you playing cop?"

"Because I'm better at it than you."

He laughed.

She imagined opening the knife and shoving it in his throat. She just might be able to kill him in one swift move if it became necessary. The best thing about being a woman was that most people had no idea how dangerous she could be. Any delay on his part could cost him his life.

Stellar grabbed the bag of chips from the center console. The bag was already empty. "Look at all these carbs. This will only make you tired." He offered his sandwich again.

"The coffee will keep me awake," she said.

He looked at the coffee and shook his head. "It's ninety degrees in the shade. Have you ever been on a stakeout before?"

"You're kidding, right? And your sandwich is better?"

"Lots of protein. It's healthy. When you do enough of these stakeouts, you just get fat eating that crap."

He lifted his sandwich to take a bite, then stopped. He looked over the rim of his glasses and took a long look at her from head to feet, glaring a bit too long at her legs.

"But don't let me stop you," he added. "You could use the extra weight. You probably don't even weigh a hundred pounds." He took a large bite.

"Prison does that to some people."

He stopped chewing and looked at her. She still couldn't see his eyes, but he knew the humor was gone. She could feel the tension. She wasn't worried about her safety anymore, but she couldn't quite explain the uneasiness in her gut.

"Why are you here?" she asked.

"To stop you from making a fool of yourself. How long have you been waiting?"

Alex checked her watch but didn't answer. It gave her the opportunity to slide the small knife in her pocket. She wouldn't need it just yet.

"Erika didn't kill Chavez," he said.

"She may not have pulled the trigger, but she's guilty."

"And you think I'm a bad cop because I haven't questioned her?"

"No, I think you're a bad cop because you haven't even looked at the evidence. I know she's your girlfriend, but she knows something."

"She's still a reporter at heart. She follows a story."

Alex grabbed her folder from the floor. Stellar's glare followed her every move. She pulled out the picture of Erika searching the Mercedes.

"Tell me why she's so interested in Chavez's car?"

He glanced at the photo but didn't say anything for several moments. "I'll be sure to ask her when she gets here. Got anything else, killer?"

"She knew about the cameras."

"So did your brother," Stellar countered.

Not understanding, Alex just stared at him.

"He switched the discs on you, too, huh?"

"What are you talking about?"

"The morning Eddie was murdered. He took the disc. Probably figured you wouldn't be interested or would want to separate yourself from the murder, but he was wrong, wasn't he? So you spent all your time dissecting a disc from the previous night. That's why you spent so much time focused on Leanna. When did he switch it on you? You were in the office the whole time, weren't you?"

Alex turned away. She thought back to that morning. She had left the office to look at the crime scene. When she returned, Ric was watching a movie. He didn't look the least bit interested in the security discs. It didn't make sense, but she hadn't seen it then.

She tried to picture the recorder. The light hadn't been on when she ejected the disc. It wasn't taping. She had assumed Ric turned it off so she wouldn't be recorded leaving the office. That he had been protecting her. But if he had turned it off, why hadn't he taken a few minutes to look at the disc?

Stellar was right. Ric must have switched the discs. He had left her there all day to scan through a useless disc. She was a day behind Ric.

An old white Toyota Corolla pulled onto the street. Alex straightened and watched the car pull into the parking lot. Stellar paid the car no attention. He was watching her behind his shaded glasses.

"Why are you really here?" she asked.

"Same reason you are. Erika's a pro at keeping things from me, but when it's vital to an investigation, I can push."

"I'd like to be there."

He grinned, flashing the dimples again. "You don't think I can ask the tough questions?"

"I think you're emotionally involved."

"I can care about someone and still do my job. How do you think I could yell at you right after you spilled your guts out about being raped?"

Alex turned away from him. She watched as the Corolla parked.

"Can you tell when she's lying?"

"Of course." He flipped the last bite of the sandwich in his mouth, wiped his hands, and dropped the napkin in the bag.

"You couldn't tell when I was lying to you."

"That's different. I know Erika."

"That's the problem. She knows you, too. You're easy to lie to. You really think you can interrogate your girlfriend?" She turned to look at him. "Prove it."

Alex pointed to Erika walking up toward the office building. Before he could say anything, his watch beeped.

"Right on time." Stellar opened his door. "She's always punctual."

Alex followed.

"Hey, killer, just for the record, she's my ex-girlfriend."

Chapter 36

Alex followed Detective Stellar and waited for him to make the first move. After all, he was in familiar territory. He ignored the receptionist behind the desk and called out to Erika. Feeling awkward, Alex smiled at the blonde wearing a headset. She turned away.

Erika walked up with a smile on her face. Then it disappeared. She looked from Stellar to Alex. Within seconds, she had sized up Stellar's intention, and her back was up.

"You didn't come here to apologize?" she said.

"No, I came to introduce my new partner."

Erika rolled her eyes. "If you're looking for a threesome, I don't have the time."

"Was that an option?" Stellar asked, his brows rising. Alex rolled her eyes.

"Detective, I've got a newspaper to get out. You'll have to make an appointment."

Alex smiled at the formality. She wondered if they were this adversarial in bed.

"I don't think so. You'll make time for me now."

"No," she said. "I don't think I will. I have work to do."

Alex noticed faces popping around the corner. The buzz in the newsroom was picking up. People were waiting for the show.

"Erika, why don't we go to your office," Alex suggested. "Maybe it's a little quieter there."

Erika glared at Alex. Any chance of becoming friends after all of this was probably a long shot.

"You don't want a scene any more than we do," Alex added.

Erika turned, and they followed her into an office. Alex wondered if it was hers. The desk was empty except for a diet soda, a pen and stapler, and an unopened newspaper placed neatly in front of the chair.

Stellar slapped the picture on the desk. "I need answers, Erika. No more stalling."

Erika looked at it. Shock crossed her face. She looked at Alex first.

"What were you looking for?" Stellar asked.

Erika composed herself. "What I'm always looking for, Detective. A story."

"In a dead man's car?"

"If that's where it takes me, yes."

"Damn it, Erika!" He moved fast. Before Alex realized what he was doing, Stellar had grabbed Erika's wrists and handcuffed them in front of her. "Erika Mack, you're under arrest for tampering with evidence in a homicide investigation."

"Stellar!" Alex turned on him. "What the hell are you doing?"

He didn't bother to look at her. Alex watched as the couple stared each other down. Neither one turned away. She sighed and waited for the lover's spat to be over. This was why she was still single.

"You're an asshole, Stellar," Erika said. "You know it won't stick."

"Oh, it'll stick, sweetheart. It'll be interesting to see if I can get the DA to agree to murder one. Now let me read you your rights. I know the part about remaining silent won't be tough for you."

Alex grabbed his arm and pulled him from the office. "Take the cuffs off her."

"I like the good cop, bad cop thing," Stellar said with half a laugh. "Normally, I'm both, but this could work."

"You're not going to get any information from her if you play the cop here. You play cop, she'll play journalist. Journalists go to jail for their stories every day. You won't break her like this. We need her to talk to us. She needs to talk to *you*, her boyfriend."

Stellar looked back at Erika and sighed. "Fine. But for the record, I have no problem interrogating her."

"I believe you," Alex lied.

Alex leaned against the door jam as Stellar took the handcuffs off. Erika looked annoyed but said nothing.

"You have to tell me what's going on, Erika," said Stellar. "Did you kill Eddie Chavez?"

She laughed. "If I did, I wouldn't have told anyone about the cameras."

Alex shifted. "How did you know about the cameras?"

"I'm a journalist. I have my sources."

"Don't screw with me, Erika," Stellar seethed. "What was your relationship to Eddie Chavez?"

Alex cleared her throat. Both looked at her. She flashed a friendly smile. Sitting on the edge of the desk, Stellar picked up the stapler and tried to look relaxed. He looked uncomfortable, maybe a little scared of what he might hear.

"I told you, there was no relationship," Erika said flatly. "I never even spoke to him."

"Where did you first see him?" asked Stellar.

"He showed up at the memorial service for Cole. It was quite a scene." Alex remembered the bar full of mourners as they grieved over that young boy—Cole.

"I already know this." Stellar didn't look at her. He played with the stapler. "Why the special interest in him?"

"Because he knew Cole Wesley."

She waited for Stellar to continue with his questions. His eyes stared through Erika, but nothing came from his mouth. Alex could hear voices in the hallway, but couldn't make out the conversation.

"Tell me what happened at the memorial service," Alex picked up.

Erika stared at the floor. Alex could tell she was stalling.

"I saw Eddie Chavez come into the church. I didn't recognize him, so I watched him. He walked past everyone, right up to Cole's casket. I thought it was strange—he didn't say anything to anyone, but he said something to Lincoln. Lincoln told him to leave. Chavez became mad and started yelling. A. J. and Morgan escorted the man outside before Ann Wesley came in."

Alex could feel Erika's energy, the energy that comes when a story starts to come together. She was starting to see all the pieces.

"What happened then?" Stellar prompted.

"Nothing. I asked Lincoln about the man. He said he was trying to buy drugs or something."

"Why were you looking in Eddie's car?"

"I was interested in his death, like any reporter would be." She looked at Alex. "After I saw the picture you were waving around at O'Sullivan's, I called Leanna to find out what she knew about the man. She said Eddie was crazy. She said he screamed at her about drugs and murder. Cole's murder."

Stellar dropped the stapler. He gritted his teeth, and his face went from pale to bright red. Erika watched him with a mix of sympathy and anger on her face.

"Cole was not murdered," Stellar countered. "He drowned. It was an accident."

Alex stepped forward, picked up the stapler. "What were you looking for in the car?"

"Evidence. I wanted the story. Leanna told me Danny had the car. I paid Danny to look in the car. Eddie Chavez knew Cole and he knew Ann."

"How do you know this?" Stellar asked.

Erika walked around the desk and unlocked the drawer. She pulled out a silver cell phone and laid it on the desk. Alex stared at it as if were a beacon.

"She was the last person he called."

"You took his cell phone?" Stellar exclaimed. "Why didn't you tell me?" He stood and paced for a minute without looking at anyone. Finally, he picked up the cell phone. Alex thought he was going to throw it across the room.

Erika crossed her arms stubbornly. "I have a right to my stories just as you have a right to investigate, Will."

"And it never crossed your mind to hand over vital evidence in a murder investigation? You should have told me. You're wading in pretty deep, Erika. Your prints are on his vehicle, and you've stolen evidence from a crime scene. Do you have any idea what it's going to take for me to fix this?"

"I don't need you to take care of me," Erika shouted back.

"I got it. Obviously, you don't need me. At all. You were pretty damn clear about that this morning. I'm done."

Stellar stormed out of the office. Erika stared after him, not moving. Alex, caught in the middle, wondered if she should chase after Stellar or comfort Erika.

Chapter 37

Alex caught up to Stellar as soon as he walked out into the hot sun. She had to play this just right or she'd be making the drive alone.

"Erika's information is mostly hearsay," she said. "We need to talk to Ann Wesley. We need to know what Chavez told her. Ann can help us figure out who killed Eddie."

"She's left town." Stellar pushed past her, his stride determined.

Blinded by the sun, Alex trailed after him, dodging between parked cars. "She could know more. We need to find her."

Stellar didn't argue.

"I can help," she protested again.

"I'll be doing all the talking. You're only coming because I can keep a better eye on you this way. We're taking my truck, and I'm driving." He spun on her as if he just remembered something. "Give me the knife you pocketed earlier, and you can get in."

Alex knew when to give in and shut up. She handed him the knife.

~~~

Roomy, with climate control and a fancy navigation system. Stellar's Escalade was definitely not a base model. Yet Alex felt completely uncomfortable in the luxury SUV. She flipped off the radio. The country music was giving her a headache.

She looked over at Stellar and realized she had made a rash judgment, and now she was trapped. She was a fighter, but her training had also taught her to think. Still, she had stepped into a car with someone she barely knew, and without a weapon. He was a cop—a good cop, she imagined, but how could she be sure? She realized she had no idea where they were going.

His stern face focused on the road ahead. His hands gripped the steering wheel tightly, his arms still tense. Stellar looked more uncomfortable in the silence than she did in the leather seat. She was surprised when he finally spoke.

"What did you mean when you said I was easy to lie to?"

Alex cranked the seat back, trying to look relaxed, and considered his question. "You make assumptions quickly. If someone tells you something that matches that assumption, you believe it. Even if it's not logical."

His eyes narrowed, but stayed focused on the road. "Explain."

"You drove into the parking lot of the Death Valley Motel and saw one truck in the lot. When Ric told you it was his, you assumed I didn't have a car. It was easy for me to lie about not having a driver's license because you already assumed I didn't have a car. Why would I need a license if I didn't drive, right?"

Stellar remained quiet; his thumb tapped the steering wheel.

"The problem with my statement was that it made no sense. A grown woman without a driver's license? At the least I would have a DMV-issued ID. How else would I write checks, open credit card accounts, own a business? But you stopped at the lie and didn't question it. It helped keep my past hidden a little longer."

Stellar watched the road.

Figuring the conversation was over, Alex leaned her head back and stared into the empty blue sky. He wasn't a threat, she realized.

"Did Erika lie to me?" Stellar finally asked.

Alex didn't look at him. "Yeah. She said she didn't need you."

~~~

Her mind was still racing. The Escalade bucked on the uneven pavement. Alex checked her watch. An hour of silence, and he still wasn't going over the speed limit. This was going to be a long trip.

"Tell me about Cole," she said.

Stellar didn't answer. She wondered if he had even heard her. He stared out at the empty highway, lost in thought.

Alex laid her head back and wondered how Cole had looked.

"Cole drowned. A week ago. He was only eleven."

"Any reason to think it was murder?"

He looked at her. "I did my job. My officers and I scoured the scene. It was clearly an accident. No question. He wandered off in the middle of the night. There's evidence he may have slipped off the pier. It was dark, and he panicked. He drowned. The ME confirmed he had water in his lungs."

"I'm not saying you didn't do your job. I'm asking if there was anything about the scene that bothered you. Maybe it seemed a little odd, looking back on it now?"

"No." He didn't hesitate.

Alex sighed. Stellar was too defensive. She wasn't going to get any information from him. Alex leaned back in the seat. She hoped Ann Wesley could shed more light on her son's death.

The sun warmed her face through the window. She cranked up the air. "I hate this heat."

"It's not so bad. You get used to it."

She stared out at the desert. It was brown everywhere she looked. "What's with the bridges here? You have no water."

"Dry rivers. The bridges have been built over the lower elevations. When the monsoon thunderstorms come, the desert can become raging rivers of mud."

"Monsoons?"

"We get them just about every summer up from the Gulf. It's enough to wet the ground and help with our wildfire risks. Sometimes they cause flash flooding, but after a good hour of rain, the desert floor can be covered with beautiful flowers of every color."

Alex looked out at the brown landscape. Large, puffy clouds loomed in the distance. "Why don't you guys have any birds?"

He looked at her. "What?"

"Birds. You know, warm-blooded vertebrates with beaks and wings. They fly."

"We have plenty of birds."

"I never see any here. It's depressing. I look out every day and expect to see one or hear one, but I never do. It makes this place sad. Lonely."

He looked confused. "Are we still talking about birds?"

"Never mind."

"Los Angeles is full of birds, right, killer? Too many to count. Too many to pay attention to. You probably ignored them most of the time." He shook his head.

She looked back at the ugly desert and tried to picture the array of colorful flowers. "I only need one."

Chapter 38

Ann Wesley looked uncomfortable in the hotel suite. Her clothes were still stuffed in her suitcase as if she might have to leave any minute. The suite was clean and classy, with two rooms, a living area, and a bedroom. She looked completely out of place.

Sitting on the couch and wringing her hands, Ann looked as depressed as she had at the funeral. She wore a black sundress and no shoes.

"I'm sorry to bother you with this, Ann," Stellar said, looking pained to have to question her, "but I need to know if you recognize this man." Stellar handed the old arrest photo of Eddie Chavez to her.

She shook her head. "He doesn't look familiar." She tried to hand the photo back.

"Keep it for a second. He showed up at the memorial. Did he know Cole?" Stellar asked.

"I already told her," she said, pointing to Alex. "I don't know him. I'm sorry."

She looked up at him, so he sat down next to her. He pulled out Eddie's cell phone and scrolled through the outgoing calls.

"What about the name, Eddie Chavez? Have you heard the name before?"

She shook her head. He could tell she wanted to get rid of the picture, but she held it anyway.

"He called you Tuesday night. At your apartment."

She looked confused. "No, I don't know—"

"Was there anyone else at your home?"

She shook her head.

"Try to remember Tuesday evening." He showed her the phone. "You got a call just past seven. It lasted almost eight minutes. Do you remember speaking to someone?"

She stared at the picture now. "This is him?"

Stellar glanced at Alex. She looked annoyed and impatient standing by the door.

"What did he say?"

Ann put the picture on the coffee table and stood. Stellar watched as she walked over to the window. Her face was flushed despite the cool room.

"He didn't tell me who he was. I thought it was a crank call. He said he knew something about Cole. I … I couldn't hang up."

"What exactly did he say, Ann?"

"He rambled." Tears fell. Stellar got up and handed her a tissue. She waved him away. "Some days are harder. I wake up every morning thinking he's going to come running into my room and demand breakfast. He was a good kid." She turned around. "He was just starting to test the boundaries. He would come home late. He lied about where he'd been. I thought he was too young for the teenage antics, so I put my foot down. He threatened to run away. Your brother saved me." She smiled. "He offered a place for him to hang out with his friends while he was being supervised. I didn't have to worry. So I didn't."

"I'm sorry."

She smiled at him.

"You're not at fault. No one is. Lincoln likes to blame himself. He's a good man, but boys will be boys. It just makes me seem foolish to have gotten so wound up when he was a little late coming home."

"Why does Lincoln blame himself?" Alex asked.

Stellar glared at Alex. She had promised to stay quiet. He wished he had left her in the hallway.

"Lincoln had punished him the day before. He wasn't listening to the counselors, and Lincoln was notified. He was rough-housing around the lake, and Lincoln was worried he would hurt someone. He told Cole he wasn't allowed to swim that day with the other kids. He was put on cleaning duty with some of the staff. He was hoping to teach him a lesson about being a better role model for the younger kids. He did the right thing. Lincoln always does. He had no idea that Cole..."

The tears fell harder as her voice gave way.

Stellar nodded and remained silent. There wasn't any comfort he could give her.

Alex broke the silence again. "Ann, we need to know what Eddie said to you on the phone."

"I know. Murder is always more important."

"That's not what I meant."

Stellar glanced at Alex again to try to silence her. "Ann, we need to know if Eddie knew Cole. We need to know why he showed up at the memorial service."

She shook her head. "I don't know, Will. He talked about Cole as if he knew him. He said he didn't deserve to die that way. I told him you said it was an accident. He said you were lying."

"I didn't lie."

"I know. He said you were trying to cover up Cole's murder."

"Did you tell anyone about the call?" Alex asked.

She shook her head. "I don't think so."

"No one? What about Lincoln?"

"I didn't think much of the call. I don't think I mentioned it to Lincoln. Why?"

Alex took a step forward. "Lincoln paid for this hotel room, didn't he? Helped you get out of town and out of the way?"

Stellar glared at Alex.

Alex ignored him and continued. "Someone tells you your son was murdered, and you ignore it?"

"Excuse us," Stellar said, grabbing Alex's arm and pulling her into the bedroom.

She pulled her arm away. "Let go of me." She squared her shoulders, ready for the fight.

Remembering what Dade had told him, Stellar took a step back. "What the hell are you doing, killer?"

"I'm doing what you're too afraid to do."

"You don't have to be mean to get someone to talk. She's grieving."

"I don't do tears."

"Her son is dead."

"And I think she knows who murdered him."

Stellar sighed. "He wasn't murdered."

"How does she know that? She took your word for it? If it was my son, I sure as hell would have made sure you were right. She's hiding something."

"She got a call from a stranger. Despite the fact that I am a trusted, honest detective, the investigation was handled by several people. We all came to the same conclusion—that her son's death was an accident. It's not unbelievable to doubt a strange voice on the phone. This is my investigation, killer. If you want to stay in the loop, I suggest you stay quiet and let me ask the questions." He walked back into the living room to finish the interview.

Ann was still standing by the window, staring out at the Vegas strip below.

"I'm sorry, Ann," Stellar said. "I appreciate you talking with us. I know this is hard."

She wiped her eyes, but the tears kept falling. Stellar heard Alex behind him. He moved closer to Ann and put his arm around her shoulders.

"Can you remember anything else Eddie may have said to you?"

She nodded. "He said I should ask the doctor what happened."

"What doctor?" Alex asked. "The medical examiner?"

Stellar turned toward Alex. "Back off, Alex, or you can wait outside."

"I don't know," Ann answered. "I assumed he meant the doctor at the camp."

"Was that it?" Stellar asked. "How did the conversation end?"

"I told him he was lying and I didn't want to talk to him anymore. He said he was getting evidence and he was going to tell the girl."

"What girl?" Alex interrupted again.

"I don't know. He wasn't making sense." She looked at Stellar. "I hung up on him."

Chapter 39

Ric heard Dade breathing heavily through his earpiece. He couldn't help but remember their years in the field. Ric had enjoyed his years working undercover. He was surprised the instincts were still there. Even years after quitting, Ric was playing through every possibility in his head.

He didn't expect Dade to be in any danger with Della. She was self-employed, so there was no pimp to worry about. She wasn't the violent type, but Dade was putting himself out there for Ric, so Ric would be sure to watch his back every step of the way.

He settled into Buddy's Jeep and watched the street. Out of the corner of his eye, he could see Dade in his hybrid. The front driver's seat had been rigged with a wireless microphone so Ric could hear everything in the car. Dade wore his Bluetooth earpiece, which was currently connected to Ric cell phone.

"Relax, Dade," Ric said into his phone. "She's not dangerous, but she does keep mace in her purse. I've never seen her with anything worse. If you get the chance, separate her from the purse."

Dade continued to breathe loudly.

"You'll do fine. Don't make eye contact with her."

"I haven't done this in a while, but I still remember how to pick up a prostitute, Delgado."

"I didn't ask about your hobbies." Ric smiled and glanced back at Dade's car. Dade was a pro. Dade would be working his story in his head and probably fussing with his wedding ring.

"You could take the ring off if you'll feel more comfortable," Ric offered.

"Alice put the ring on fifteen years ago. It hasn't been off since. It stays."

Ric smiled. "How is Alice?"

"She's good. She misses you." Ric could hear Dade relaxing. He moved deeper in his seat.

"Don't lie, Dade. I know she hates me for quitting."

Dade laughed. "I think she likes you more than she likes me. She hates my new partner."

"She's a good judge of character, so he's probably a moron."

"Where's your girl?"

Ric glanced down the street. "It's still a bit hot out there. Give her time."

Forty minutes later, Ric caught sight of Della walking down the street. An early start meant desperate times. He grabbed his binoculars and watched her walk.

"She's out. Short, blonde, long legs. Gray or navy short-sleeve shirt, black jeans with dark athletic shoes. Drive past her, then circle back."

Ric turned to watch his old partner pull out of the liquor store parking lot and drive down the street.

"I got her."

Dade didn't even slow down as he passed her. Ric lost sight of the car and kept his eyes on Della. She was nervous, glancing at every car. If she kept walking, she would catch sight of Ric.

"Let's go now," Ric urged, "before she attracts any attention."

Ric watched the car pull up beside Della. Della turned and walked toward the open window. Ric frowned. *Too easy.*

Ric heard her voice through the earphones. "Are you lost?"

"Ask her for directions to the motel," Ric instructed.

Dade ignored him. "I was hoping for some company. Are you interested?"

He was going for the direct approach. Ric wasn't sure it would work. Della was too conscious of cops.

"Maybe," she said. Ric watched as she took a step back. She was being cautious.

"I have twenty if you get in now, another twenty if you don't make me beg. Everything else is extra."

Ric cringed. If they were planning on arresting Della, they had just lost their chance.

"You idiot," Ric said through the phone. He watched as Della's shoulders relaxed. She grabbed the money Dade offered and walked around to the passenger seat. She took a good look at the car.

"You a cop?" she asked as she opened the door.

"Nope. No one's getting arrested tonight."

Dade was speaking to him. They were there for information on Della's mystery man, not to book her for prostitution. He heard Dade's lighter flick.

"You from California?" She had noticed the out-of-state plates. *Good girl*, Ric thought.

"Let her tell you where to go," Ric said as he started his car. He hoped she would head to the motel.

"Yeah," Dade said. "Just passing through. This is legal here, right?"

She didn't answer. "Take a left at the light."

Ric followed Dade's car. He hoped since this wasn't a regular john for Della, she would be smart and take him to the motel. A dark street wasn't optimal for her. Or him.

~~~

He didn't want to use his gun. She wasn't really dangerous. He only wanted a few answers. Scaring her wouldn't work. She had been scared when he questioned her before. This time, Ric needed her to trust him.

He parked in the motel parking lot and walked around the dumpster to where he had watched Dade park his car.

Ric jerked the door open, and before Della could react, he reached in and grabbed her right wrist. Surprised, she looked back at Dade and with her left hand reached for her bag.

It was quick, but Dade was quicker. He had his Glock pointed at her face.

"Don't move," Dade shouted. "Police."

Ric cringed. He knew it was habit for Dade, but Ric didn't want this to go bad. Della's hands froze, but she turned away from the gun and looked at Ric. He could see her disappointment. Her trust in him had vanished.

"I'm not saying anything, fo' sure," she said.

"Get out of the car," Ric ordered. He didn't want to pull her, but he would if it became necessary. "I just need to ask you some questions."

She jerked her arm away from his. He let it go, hoping to get something back. Stepping from the car, she rubbed her arms and then turned around and joined her wrists behind her back.

Ric spun her around and stepped close. "I'm not a cop, Della."

"No," she said, pushing him away, "you're worse."

Dade came around the car with her bag in his arms. He dropped it on the trunk and started to dig through it. "Pepper spray and a roach. Oh, we got us a switchblade."

Ric ignored Dade. "I need to know who you were with the night Eddie Chavez died."

She didn't answer. Dade approached with his gun still drawn.

"We can make this difficult for you."

"Put the gun away, Dade," Ric said.

"She hasn't been searched. The gun stays out until you hook her up."

"I'm not handcuffing her. She's not under arrest."

Dade holstered his weapon and then grabbed Della and pushed her away from the car. "Put your hands on the back of your head."

Ric watched as Dade patted her down. Dade had changed in the past ten years as well. He played the bad cop much too well. Della didn't flinch, but kept her eyes on Ric.

"That's enough," Ric said. "Della, you need to tell me who you were with."

"I know my rights."

"I'm trying to help you out. This man is dangerous. If he had something to do with Eddie's murder, he may very well come after you."

She looked to the ground, and Ric guessed he was right. She knew the man was dangerous.

"I can protect you."

She shook her head. "No, you can't. You're nobody. You run a motel. These people are too powerful, fo' sure."

"What people?"

She didn't answer.

"I need a name."

She shook her head. "I'm not an idiot. Eddie challenged them. I'm not going to end up like him."

Dade stepped up. "We're not getting anywhere here. Tell us who was with you at the motel. Otherwise, we'll get Stellar down here."

Ric saw the flitter of fear. He knew her well enough that she wouldn't be scared of getting arrested. In fact, if she was scared of someone coming after her, a jail cell would be a welcome offer.

"You're scared of Stellar?" Ric asked. She jerked her head back to him at the sound of the name. He felt the panic grip at his own throat.

He grabbed her arms and pushed her against the car. "Tell me, Della. My sister is with the detective right now. If he's involved, I need to know."

"The guy's a cop."

He saw her fear, but knew she saw his as well. He pulled out his revolver.

"I didn't ask for his resume. What's the john's name?"

"I don't know his name, fo' sure. I don't know." The tears fell now. Thunder clapped in the distance.

"Does he work with Stellar?"

She didn't answer.

"Have you seen this man before or since that night?" Dade asked, lighting a cigarette. Dade offered the cigarette to her, but she shook her head again. Her eyes focused on the revolver.

Ric gripped harder. He hadn't intended it, but they had officially changed roles. He was now the bad cop.

"Where'd you meet this guy?"

Her answer was barely a whisper. "He was with Lincoln."

"Who the hell is Lincoln?" Dade asked looking at Ric.

Ric released Della. "Lincoln Stellar. He's Detective Stellar's brother."

Chapter 40

W ill Stellar paced outside the truck, cracking his knuckles. The valet had returned his truck and Will had tipped him, but he had refused to get in. Alex stood near the passenger door, waiting. Her calm made him furious. He wanted to rattle her, but he wasn't sure he could handle her if she struck out at him.

"Did Davy Knight have a family?" he finally asked.

Alex rubbed her tired eyes, not answering. "Can we go?"

He shook his head. "Tell me about his family."

She sighed and sat on the curb. He could outwait her. He leaned against the truck and watched the other gamblers returning to their cars.

"It's hot out here." He looked up at the sky and spotted the thick gray clouds moving in. "But humid. We're gonna get some rain tonight."

She sighed, shaded her eyes, and looked up at him.

"His mother was in the courtroom when I gave my plea. I don't think he had anyone else."

He looked at her. "You don't regret what you did at all?"

"No," Alex said, without hesitation. "That's what really bothers you, right? The fact that I feel no remorse."

He didn't answer. He watched a couple walk past him into the casino.

"He never felt any remorse for what he did to me. I did everything I could to make him pay. I gave a perfect description. The police had a picture lineup in front of me within hours of my rescue. I identified him without hesitation. I gave the detective the license plate of his truck and described it perfectly. They picked him up at the exact same bar where he had kidnapped me."

She stood now. "I can never get his face out of my head. I close my eyes, and I see it, but the jury didn't care about that. I had two lousy beers while sitting at that bar. Two beers that could have impaired my judgment enough to name the wrong guy. That's what they focused on. I don't regret what I did. I let the system do its job. It failed."

He waited a bit before giving his response, wanting it to hit home. He got in her face, knowing it was a dangerous move.

"Why the gun?"

"What?"

"You could have killed him with your bare hands, right? It would have felt good, too, taking his life with your hands. Why did you bring the gun?"

As expected, she didn't back down. She pushed closer as her temper rose. He could see it in her eyes, her face, her body.

"You couldn't do it, could you?" he continued. "You didn't want to risk losing control again. You didn't kill him because the justice system failed. You killed him because you have control issues. Obviously, you still do."

Her eyes narrowed on him, but he didn't want anger. He wanted that split second when she let the anger go. He needed to see just how dangerous she was. He felt the valet watching them.

"He took my sense of security and left me helpless," she said, her voice low. "He thought he could control me the rest of my life. He thought it would leave me weak and powerless, but he was wrong."

She stared at him, fists clenched, eyes red. He was close enough to touch her. He realized he wanted to. She was about to fall over the edge. He knew he should grab her. Instead, he pushed.

"There's no way you thought it over and decided prison would make you powerful again. It wasn't the best thing for you. Or your brother. Or for anyone else who cared for you. Davy controlled you for those several hours. You were vulnerable. I understand that, but it wasn't justice that made you pull the trigger. It didn't give you the control you wanted, did it? After you killed him, the state controlled you. For the past ten years of your life, you've had no control over your own life. You still don't. And you don't have the slightest idea how to get it back."

Stellar watched her, waiting for the explosion. He kept his eyes completely focused on hers. If her control snapped, he could end up dead, but if she had anything left, she would see he was right.

He saw the anger peak, and then her face loosened. Her eyes watered, and he heard her breath escape her. He allowed himself to breathe.

"I'm not telling you something you don't already know," he said.

She looked away and rubbed her eyes. She stared at the casino doors as they opened to let someone through. Wind kicked her hair around.

"Tell me why you're so interested in Chavez," he said.

For a long moment, she didn't respond. The wind came in bursts. He leaned against the car, folded his arms, and waited.

"The night I shot Davy, I was sitting at home watching television and the next minute I was standing in my brother's driveway. I went back and calculated I lost five hours. Five hours are blocked from my memory. I don't remember how I got there. I don't know why Davy was there."

"You blacked out?"

"Since the attack I've experience memory lapses. Nothing very long, usually a few minutes here and there. The doctors said it's just leftover from the Taser attack. They promised it would go away with time. It did. Or at least I thought it did until Tuesday."

"Do you remember shooting Davy Knight?"

She smirked. "Yeah, I remember that pretty clearly. I don't remember the details leading up to it."

"And you don't remember this past Tuesday?"

"Wednesday morning, when Ric came in to tell me Eddie was dead, I was sitting at the desk and realized I couldn't remember Tuesday night."

He studied her, realized what she was saying. "You probably shouldn't say any more, or I'm going to have to read you your rights."

"I didn't kill Eddie Chavez. I don't know what happened, but in my heart, I know I didn't do it, but I also didn't stop it."

He studied her. "You can't control every situation. You can't control the actions of other people. If you want to control something, control yourself."

She said nothing.

"Let's get you back home."

"We need to talk to the doctor first. The doctor that Eddie was referring to is our link. He knows something."

"Lincoln always has numerous doctors on hand during camp season. They come in from Vegas and spend a day or so working for free. It'll take too long to interview them all on such a thin link."

"I can help you start narrowing down the list. Or you can continue to waste time by chewing me out." She snatched the keys from his hand. "Let me drive."

He shook his head. "No way. My truck, my investigation, my way."

"*Dios.* Talk about control issues."

He bit his lip to stop the argument. He had gotten what he wanted. "Fine. Try to keep the speed limit in mind."

~~~

The way she drove his truck, it was hard to keep his eyes from the road at first. Eventually the exhaustion crept in, and he felt his eyelids drop and his muscles relax. As the grips of his control lessened, he felt his brain twirl the facts around. It continued to land on Danny.

"I think Leanna is the link to the evidence," Stellar said, his eyes still closed.

"Leanna was raped. The only thing Eddie wanted from Leanna was sex."

He shook his head. "She wasn't raped."

"Why, because she didn't cry?" Alex snapped back.

He opened his eyes and looked at her. "I guess I'm not the only who believes the lies I'm told."

"She didn't lie to me."

"Leanna approached Eddie at O'Sullivan's. She saw him at the memorial service. He made a comment to Lincoln about getting a hit. Drugs. It sparked her interest. She couldn't let it go, so she followed him to O'Sullivan's."

She looked at him. "What are you talking about?"

"Leanna and Danny are common thieves. Danny is mainly a pot dealer. Leanna, she's a con artist. She's great at lying and stealing. She met Eddie, offered him some of Danny's inventory with the intention of robbing him."

"Why did he bring her to the hotel? If he was only interested in drugs, he could have gotten that a number of easier ways. Why drug her and bring her back to your room?"

"I know," Stellar said. "It didn't make sense to me, either. He seemed angry with Leanna for selling drugs and yelled at her for killing people. He believed Cole was murdered, but I don't see how Leanna had anything to do with his death. She leaves upset, and he ends up with a bloody nose. The next day, he stays in. What was he waiting for? Now factor in that Leanna helps out at Camp Courage. She knew Cole. Maybe Eddie thought Leanna could prove the boy had been murdered."

"But it still doesn't answer the real question. Who wanted Eddie Chavez dead? Maybe Leanna knows the doctor."

"I still peg this on Danny. Cole wasn't murdered. Eddie was chasing something, but it wasn't a murderer. He assaults Leanna and pisses off Danny. He's not someone you want to piss off."

"You think Danny would be able to pull this off? The suicide stage?"

He shrugged.

"You got any change?" she said, digging in the center console.

"Why?"

"Guy's on my ass." Alex found some coins and opened the sunroof.

He sat up. "What are you doing?"

She didn't answer. She tossed the coins out the sunroof and smiled.

"Are you insane?" Stellar jerked up. He grabbed the dash and looked in his rearview mirror. The black car had slowed from the shock of the coins hitting the windshield but was now gaining speed. It was getting close to their bumper. Too close.

"Damn it, Alex. You just pissed him off."

She didn't get a chance to answer. The car slammed into the Escalade.

Stellar reached over and turned on his police lights. He turned around and looked through the back window. Through the flashing red and blue, he saw the car falling back.

"I don't think that's going to stop him," Alex said. "This guy wants us off the road."

"Just pull over."

Stellar felt the car slow and glanced at the speedometer. She dropped to fifty-five. Fifty. He grabbed his cell phone and dialed Florio.

He looked back, but the black car wasn't slowing. He was gearing up to hit them again.

"Florio, I need you to run a plate. Nevada. Dodge Charger—"

"Dodge Magnum," Alex corrected. "Hold on."

The Escalade was bigger, and Stellar trusted it to hold. He felt the Escalade slowing more.

"Why are you slowing down now?"

"I'm not all that comfortable driving a huge truck like this. If he hits us again and I lose control, I don't want to be going sixty miles per hour. The embankment's too high."

"Florio, get me a patrol car out here now—"

Stellar didn't finish. The Magnum smashed into the truck, shattering the back windshield. Alex slammed on the brakes.

He saw Alex lose control of the wheel. Stellar reached for it, but he felt the Escalade tip sideways. *Don't roll*, he prayed.

The window on his side shattered as the truck crashed on its side. The airbags deployed. Stellar tried to push his down, but the dust filled his view. His eyes burned. He lost his cell phone.

The door hugged him, shards of glass reached for his face. His seatbelt dug into his chest. His shoulder was crushed between his weight and the gravel road.

The groan of metal grinding and scraping was too loud for him to scream. He held on as the truck continued to skid. Stellar prayed they would stay on the road. If the Escalade fell into the embankment, they would flip completely.

They were struck again. He thought he heard screaming. His head slammed against the door, and everything went black.

Chapter 41

The sun was setting, but the heat seemed to be getting worse. Ric watched as the dark clouds quickly covered the remaining blue sky. He waited near his car, despite the searing heat on his feet, and stared at the gate surrounding the Stellar mansion. At least, he suspected it to be a mansion. He couldn't see far enough through the trees and bushes to glimpse an actual house. The black iron gates stared back at him, along with the security camera. Expensive brand. Probably had full color and sound.

He had tried the buzzer. Some angry woman had told him to go away. She mentioned something about soliciting and hung up. He buzzed again, but she didn't seem interested that he needed to speak with Lincoln.

The gate was too tall to climb. Even if he could find a way around, he had no idea where to go. It wasn't just a mansion behind the line of trees. It was a huge compound, consisting of acres of farmland and the lake the city name referred to. There were cows back there, too. He disliked animals immensely, especially ones with beady, staring eyes. So he needed help. He could admit that to himself. He hadn't worked alone all his life; he just preferred it. If teaming up with someone would help him get ahead, he could do it.

He didn't turn around when he heard the car pull up behind him. The car door slammed, and he wiped the sweat from his forehead. He unwrapped a protein bar as she approached. He smelled her perfume before she spoke.

"I underestimated you," Erika said. "First, you threaten the chief with my past drug charge—"

"You thought that would stay hidden?"

He looked at her now. She was beautiful. Not his type, but he could see why Will Stellar kept coming back to her. Blonde hair, large breasts, and long legs. She knew how to walk in heels.

"I never tried to hide my arrest," she said.

"No, you didn't, but if the drug charge was my weapon, I would have gone after you. Your father broke the rules to get the charges dropped. He's the one I needed to … encourage." He avoided the word *threaten*.

"Then the mayor? I've known her my entire life. She doesn't like me, but she knows I'm no killer."

"I didn't need her to think you were a killer. I only wanted her to think there was a reason to watch over the department. Police misconduct could lose her the election. I have to say, I underestimated you as well. I didn't think my visits would get back to you."

"You basically told my boyfriend I was a killer. He handcuffed me. What was your reasoning there?"

Ric shrugged and tried to imagine Stellar arresting his girlfriend. He wished he had been there. "Call us even. I had to get the cuffs off me somehow. He only focused on the cameras because you made him think it was important."

"And you were sure they weren't. Why?"

He shrugged, looked back at the house. He needed to find a way to see Lincoln. "I moved one of the cameras. It's my fault there was a blind spot. I didn't realize it. But I wanted to make sure I had Alex's room covered."

"So you made him think I was responsible?"

"How did you know there was a camera at all?"

She considered him, as if unsure she could give up her source. Finally, she said, "Bud Schneider likes to flirt, which means he can't keep his mouth shut. He said you were pretty camera savvy. He said you did a great job installing his cameras and was pretty impressed with the cameras you hooked up for the motel."

He smiled. Buddy was a talkative kid. Ric wouldn't admit he was impressed. He disliked journalists. They were too smart.

"So tell me why you called," she said.

"I've read your stories this week. Very closely."

She smiled. "Always nice to meet a fan."

"I didn't say I was a fan."

"Why am I here?"

He noticed silver hearts hanging from her ears. He wondered if they were a gift from Stellar.

"I find it intriguing you've been a step ahead of me regarding Eddie Chavez."

She smiled. "I like to stay ahead."

"Yet you rarely write stories. Too busy with the details of running a paper."

She said nothing.

"This story intrigues you, but I found no connection between you and Eddie Chavez. And I couldn't find a good connection between you and Danny, either. So I had to ask myself why you were so interested in the case. Why are you playing Lois Lane?"

"I'm a journalist at heart."

"And you're a sucker at heart, too." He grinned at her. "Apparently you can't stop talking about that kid, Cole. A poor young boy who accidentally drowned and a stranger assassinated in a motel room. I think you have the connection, but you've failed to write about it. Why is that?"

She shrugged.

"Only two reasons. One, you have the evidence and you know it implicates someone you love."

"Or?" she asked, with a hint of a smile.

"Or you can't find the evidence."

"And your conclusion?"

"You showed up, so I know you're still looking for the evidence. And I think you're too concerned with your image to worry about anyone else."

She said nothing for a minute. "Eddie Chavez told Leanna that Ann Wesley's son was murdered."

"And you believed him over your boyfriend, the officers who found him, and the medical examiner?"

"I doubted it too, just like you are now. Only one thing makes me believe he was telling the truth."

"He was killed."

She nodded.

He considered this. It was a gamble to trust her. He hoped her drive for the truth and the story would overpower her drive to protect Stellar.

"I may be able to help get you evidence," he said, "but I need to see where Cole died."

She looked interested. "I'll show you where if you show me how."

"Lincoln won't allow me access."

She smiled. "I practically grew up at Camp Courage. I worked here every summer as a kid. I know the back way in. Let me grab some sensible shoes."

Chapter 42

Detective Stellar was trapped. He punched on the seatbelt release, but it wouldn't give. The buckle was jammed. Sweat ran down his face. He heard Alex move beside him. The air was hot and stuffy, and he had trouble taking a deep breath.

"Are you okay?" she asked.

He couldn't answer. He heard the voice of his OnStar. He realized how tired he was and closed his eyes.

It was the siren that finally woke him out of his fog. His vision was blurred, despite the fact that the sun was setting. He tried to take a deep breath, but his chest hurt. He lifted his hand to his pounding head.

"Hey, Detective. Glad you're finally awake. You're gonna have to help me get you out of there."

Disoriented, Stellar looked through the broken windshield and realized he was sideways. Hot air was blowing at his face. He glanced to his left. The driver seat was empty. A man was staring at him through the broken window. He was pretty sure he had never seen the man before. Confused, Stellar stared back.

"EMT," the man explained.

Stellar nodded. His head ached with the movement. He probably had a concussion. His ribs hurt, too. As he moved his limbs, he was thankful he hadn't broken a bone. He tried to remember what had happened. He hadn't been driving. Someone had hit them.

He looked back up at the man. His voice seemed raw when he tried to talk. "I'm fine. Where's the woman who was driving?"

"Ms. Delgado is fine. My partner's looking at her now. We need to get you out of here. Can you undo the seatbelt?"

Stellar shook his head and pulled out the pocket knife he'd confiscated from Alex.

"That comes in handy," the paramedic said.

Stellar ignored him as he sliced through the belt. He turned to the back seat and dug through the glass and clutter. He pulled out his emergency bag. Nausea overwhelmed him, and he paused to take a deep breath.

"Looks like you got good mobility," said the EMT. "Do you think you can climb out?"

"I said I'm fine." He leaned over and grabbed his notes on Eddie Chavez and stuffed everything in the bag. He would sort through it later. Tossing the bag up to the paramedic, he slowly climbed out of his destroyed truck.

On solid ground, he flexed every muscle and moved every bone. His shirt was torn, and he saw blood on his shoulder. His ribs ached and his head was throbbing, but he felt surprisingly well.

"Where's Alex?" he asked.

"You need to have one of us check you out."

Stellar shook his head. It made the dizziness worse. He stuffed the knife in the pocket of his jeans. "No time."

Sergeant Morgan stepped from a black-and-white nearby. Will wondered how long he had been unconscious.

"Holy shit," Morgan said. "Are you okay?"

Stellar nodded. He never looked back at the destroyed truck. He spotted Alex sitting on the ground near the road, her legs folded in front of her. A paramedic was examining her.

Alex looked up at him as he approached. "Sorry about your truck," she said.

She was his responsibility, and he knew all of this was his fault.

"It's okay." He looked at the paramedic touching her abdomen. He didn't know why he wanted to push him away. "How is she?"

"I don't see any major issues, other than the cut on her forehead," the paramedic answered, then turned to him. "Let me take a look at you."

"I'm fine."

But the paramedic insisted. He shined a light in his eyes. Stellar allowed it, since it would be faster than stopping him. When he took the light away, the dizziness returned.

Stellar's worry for Alex overwhelmed his own welfare. "How do you feel?" he asked her.

"Nothing broken. Just a little sore," she answered. "I'll probably be worse tomorrow. I hope you have insurance. I really didn't mean to crash—"

"Forget the truck, killer," he snapped at her.

The paramedic touched his ribs. When Stellar flinched, he stopped. "We need to get you to the hospital."

"We're not going to the hospital."

"You've probably broken some ribs. We need to make sure there's no internal bleeding."

"I'm fine. They're just bruised."

"Better than the other guy," Alex said.

"What?"

Alex pointed back at the truck. "Magnum's in the ditch. Driver's dead. He's lucky, because if I'd caught up to him, I would have made him hurt."

Stellar didn't wait for her to finish describing what she would do. He walked back to where Morgan was standing.

"I've contacted Wags," Morgan said. "He's on his way."

Stellar walked down the hill toward the overturned Magnum. He stared at the Nevada plates. "It's probably stolen," he told Morgan, "but run the plates anyway."

He leaned into the car and saw the body on the front seat. Male. He was face down and his head was covered in blood and hair. He had a feeling he recognized the body, but he would have to wait for the medical examiner to get an identification.

He tried to calm the anger building inside him.

He looked down the street. "Indian Springs is just a few miles back. There's a motel there. We'll wait there until Wags gets here. I want to see who that is. Secure the scene and wait for him here. Take what you need from what's left of my truck. I need to clean up."

Stellar walked back to Alex. He brushed the hair out of her face so he could see the cut on her head. It had stopped bleeding, but it looked deep. "I'm sorry," he said. "I shouldn't have let you come."

"So you're assuming he was after you?"

He considered this as he eyed the cut on her head. "Why would someone want to hurt you?"

"The car's been following me the past two days."

"Why the hell didn't you say anything before now?" Stellar felt the anger boil up.

"I didn't know who it was," she said. "I thought it was one of your officers tailing me. I figured you told him to keep an eye on me."

The paramedic said something, but Stellar ignored him. He couldn't take his eyes away from Alex. It was going to take a long time before she finally trusted him, even if her life was in danger.

"We need to hang out here for a little while," he said.

Nodding, she attempted to stand. Stellar reached out to help her and saw her cringe. She muttered something in Spanish that he couldn't translate. Blood trickled down her face.

"Hold still," Stellar said as he looked at the cut that had opened up. The paramedic attempted to clean the cut. He applied the small bandage as Stellar held her steady. He realized she hadn't pulled away from his touch or swatted his hand away. Instead, her hand grabbed hold of his arm. Surprised, he looked down and noticed her thumb was swelling, too.

"Get her an ice pack," he told the paramedic. Concerned, he kept his eyes on hers.

"Thanks," she said.

"I figured you'd tell me it didn't hurt and that you could do it yourself."

"Well, it does hurt. And I'd find you a bit of a jerk if you just held up a mirror and expected me to patch myself up with this bum hand."

He laughed. His ribs hurt, but it somehow felt good. Maybe she was getting closer to trusting him.

~~~

"One room?" Alex asked, standing in the doorway. She still held the ice bag on her hand.

Stellar dropped his bag on the bed. "We're not planning on sleeping here. I'm not paying for two rooms when we're only going to use the bathroom."

An attempt on their life had just been made. Stellar didn't want to tell her, but there was no chance he was letting her out of his sight until he knew what was going on.

"Fine," Alex said. "I guess that's how you got so rich."

"What?"

"By being so frugal."

He looked at her. "Why do you think I'm rich?"

"It's obvious. The shoes you wear, the watch, the expensive glasses. The Escalade."

"I need a big truck."

"And one you had no problem losing. What, you have three more at home?"

"My finances are none of your business," he snapped.

"Ah, grew up rich. You resent it. Wish you didn't have it. People look at you different with all that money. Don't take you serious as a cop."

Why was every woman trying to pick fights with him today? He sighed. "Why don't you take a shower?"

"I wonder if that's why Erika finds it so hard to admit her feelings. Maybe she doesn't want people to think she's after you for your money. Coming from a poor background and all."

"Erika's not poor," he snapped back, feeling the anger in his stomach.

She smiled at him. "But she was. Now she's made something of herself, with the paper. She likes standing on her own two feet. She can't stand the thought of having someone take that confidence away, even you."

He was done with this conversation. His ribs hurt. His head hurt. He wasn't about to let Alex get under his skin. He pulled the stack of notes from the bag and found his cell phone. He dialed the number to the Death Valley Motel and was relieved when there was no answer. He didn't want to tell Ric his sister had almost been killed.

"You should propose to her," Alex said.

Confused, he turned. She was lying on top of the bedspread. Her eyes were closed.

"Erika," Alex explained. "She needs to know you need her. She needs to know you can't live without her. She needs that big gesture to know you can't function without her."

"Yeah, you sure have her pegged. I don't need relationship advice, killer."

She opened one eye. "It's only advice if you really thought there was a future with her. Otherwise, it's just food for thought. From what I hear, you're better off without her. Of course, you haven't realized that yet. Go ahead with the bathroom. I need to rest a few minutes." She put her arm over her eyes.

He wondered what she knew about relationships. He watched her resting for a minute, before deciding he could use a shower.

Chapter 43

The hot water felt strangely refreshing as it burned the small cuts on Stellar's head and washed dried blood from his shoulder. His ribs were sore, but there was still no bruise. He took it as a good sign. He'd been thrown from a few horses and felt worse than he did now.

He toweled off and tried to ignore Alex's words. He was starting to realize she often said things to distract him. It had worked. He pulled on his jeans and bandaged his cut shoulder, then tossed his torn shirt in the trash.

Stellar opened the door to find Alex sitting on the bed. She had kicked her shoes onto the floor and spread his notes out across the bed. She didn't bother to look up at him as she read the reports he had worked so hard on.

He grabbed the page in front of her. "Hey, killer, you were supposed to be sleeping."

She leaned back against the wall and stared at him. "I don't sleep."

The way she said it, Stellar believed her. She looked sad. He watched as her sleepy gaze dropped to his chest.

"We need to find the doctor," she said, almost in a whisper.

He shook his head. "There are too many doctors and I don't see the point."

"You still think Danny killed Eddie Chavez?"

"I think Eddie's death had more to do with drugs than Cole, no matter what Eddie's last words were. And I'm pretty sure that was Danny Nunez back in the Dodge."

"One problem: Danny wasn't in the Magnum when I visited Ann Wesley at her apartment. Ric was watching him across town ditching Eddie's car. Someone else was in the Magnum watching me. Someone else was upset I was asking questions. If that was Danny back there, someone sent him after me. Someone's pulling the strings. We need to find the doctor."

"You don't need to do anything. You're not a cop."

"Who's Sam?" Alex asked, pointing to his arm. "Old flame?"

He didn't look at the tattoo on his arm. Turning, he took a fresh shirt from his bag and pulled it over his head. He hoped he was the only one feeling the tension in the room.

"My brother," he answered.

"You two must be close."

"He died when I was twelve."

"*Lo siento*," she muttered.

He turned back to her now. She looked relaxed yet striking, despite the bandage on her forehead. She had pulled her hair back in a ponytail. Drawn to her large eyes and high cheekbones, he admitted to himself that she was intriguing. He couldn't deny the feeling in his gut. He thought of that Mexican resort vacation again.

"Tell me about your husband," he said.

"Why?"

He shrugged, pulled out the lone chair and placed it at the far end of the room. He needed the distance. "You know too much about me, and I'm tired of thinking of death."

She sighed and folded her arms across her chest. "His name is Nicolas Carson. He's in real estate."

"I got that from talking to him for two seconds. What else?"

"If you're so interested, run a background check." She closed her eyes.

He stared at her for a minute before realizing the closed eyes were not a sign of tiredness. She was trying to end the conversation. She was excellent at drawing the line.

He was done with her evasions. "Tell me something I won't find in a background check. Something personal."

She opened her eyes. He could see the irritation in them. It brought an array of color to her face, so he didn't regret causing it.

"Why do you care?"

"I'm interested in why you married him. Why you divorced."

"Are you interested in him or me?"

He shrugged. "I doubt I'll ever meet him."

"So why do you care about me?"

Good question, Will. He went with the simple answer, which turned out to be completely true. "You interest me."

"As a murderer or a rape victim?"

Stellar shifted in his seat. "I'm sorry. You just seem too young to have been through so much."

She said nothing. He let the silence drag on, not sure what else he should say to get her to open up to him. He was ready to give up and go home when she finally spoke.

"I was ten when my mother died. She was CHP. She made a simple speeding stop, just like millions she had done before, and it ended her life. A drunk driver collided with her and the other vehicle."

Stellar didn't say anything. He was sure she didn't need the pity. She had dealt with the death and moved on.

"My father shut everyone out. My brother was busy making his own name for himself in the narcotics division. I had no one, except Nick. When my father was killed, Nick was still there. He became my family."

"How did your father die?"

"I thought you were tired of thinking about death."

He shrugged. He realized for the first time that he enjoyed her smile. Like anger, it brought life to her face.

"He was the senior narcotics detective. Sergeant, actually." Alex fingered the bruise on her cheek. "Drug bust apparently went bad. He was shot and killed. I don't know much about it. Ric did his best to keep the details from me."

He found it interesting that she had tried to follow her parents' footsteps into law enforcement. He wondered what type of cop she would have been if it hadn't been for one bad night.

"So Nick was your rock?"

She nodded. "Got married right out of high school."

"Why'd it end?"

"When we got married, his father handed the business over to Nick and retired. Nick became owner, CEO, CFO, everything, overnight. He was good at it, too. His company would find these struggling businesses and make them flourish within only a few years. The same with the real estate he bought. It was amazing watching the transitions happen. He loved every second of it, but he would lose interest when the business was doing well, sell it off, and move on.

"The same happened with me. I was a hurt, damaged girl when he met me. We grew apart, went our own ways." She shrugged. "We had different priorities. I wanted to join the academy. He wasn't pleased with the idea."

She didn't look at him now. It made him wonder if she was telling the truth or just what he expected to hear. "And the rape had nothing to do with it?"

She looked down at her hands, and Stellar immediately regretted asking. Death was easy for her to talk about. The rape was not.

"No. We were already separated. Nick rushed to my side, but I didn't need him anymore. I took care of it."

There was a knock on the door. He didn't want the conversation to be over, but he knew she was done talking. Stellar grabbed his gun and went to the door. It was Sergeant Morgan. He looked very uncomfortable as sweat dripped down his face.

"It was Danny," Morgan said.

Stellar ran his fingers through his hair. "Damn it." He looked back at Alex. "Still doubt my theory?"

Alex said nothing. She was watching Morgan with the stare he was just starting to recognize. The stare that told him someone was about to get hurt.

Stellar turned back. Morgan's hand was on the butt of his gun. "Sir, I need to bring you and Ms. Delgado back to the station."

Stellar squared himself in the doorway. "You want to take your hand off your weapon, Sergeant?"

"Don't make this harder than it needs to be, Detective. I'm just doing what I'm told."

Stellar lifted his own gun, but he refused to point it at his officer. He heard Alex shift behind him.

"Take your hand off your gun, Morgan, and tell me what the hell is going on. You know this won't end well for you if you push this."

Morgan's hand dropped to his side. "Sheriff Mack asked me to bring you in. He said they have a witness and he's bringing in the State Police."

State police was a very bad sign. Sheriff Mack wouldn't make that move lightly.

"Did Detective Dade bring in this witness?"

"Yes, sir. Mack's still calling the shots, but he's a wreck. He said he's just trying to contain this."

"Mack isn't worried about me. There's only one person that would make him nervous."

Morgan shuffled his feet. "Lincoln?"

Stellar nodded and glanced back at Alex. The look in her eyes was still there, but he also saw concern. Any trust he had gained with her was probably gone. He turned back to Morgan.

"He's worried he'll have a riot on his hands if he has to pull in Lincoln for questioning," Stellar said. "Give me the keys to the black-and-white. We have to fix this before anyone goes after Lincoln."

Forced to choose between Lincoln and the department, Morgan didn't hesitate. He handed the keys to Stellar.

"What do you need me to do?"

"Don't talk to anyone. Finish up with the scene and go back with Wags. I'll take Alex to the station and meet with Mack myself. Don't tell Lincoln anything."

Morgan hesitated. "I don't think—"

"Yeah, it's better if you don't." He slammed the door and grabbed his cell phone. "You should wash up," he told Alex. "We'll leave in five." He dialed the phone. Dade picked up on the first ring. "Dade, it's Stellar. Who's your witness?"

"I don't think it's appropriate to discuss that with you," Dade said.

Alex sat back on the bed and watched him. There was no emotion on her face. She had closed herself off to him again.

"Shut up, Dade. You know I'm not involved in this."

"Maybe not, but your brother is."

"Lincoln's no killer. Tell me who your witness is and I'll tell you if the information is reliable."

"She's a hooker named Della Brown. She claims a friend of Lincoln's killed Eddie Chavez to keep him quiet."

Stellar cursed. "That doesn't mean Lincoln knows anything. Lincoln can tell us who we're looking for, but we have to do it quietly. No cop cars, no uniforms. He won't want to turn on a friend. And he definitely won't talk to Mack. I can get him to talk."

"Ric's on his way there now. Is Alex still with you?"

"Yes."

"How is she?"

"She's fine. Why?"

"Make sure she stays that way. I'm holding you responsible. Let me talk to her."

Confused, Stellar offered the phone to Alex. He watched as she almost shrank from it. "Dade wants to talk to you."

Stellar considered her reluctance. The color in her face was gone. When she took the phone, she turned her back to him. He started to pack his things when he realized Alex was whispering. He eased closer to listen.

"I'm fine, Dade," Alex said. "I know how to take care of myself." She paused. "You're wrong. Ric's wrong."

She was rubbing her bandage again. Stellar sat back at the desk and watched her. She was defending him this time, which almost made him smile, but her body language was closed off. Her muscles were tight as she tried to regain control. He thought he saw her shiver. *How can such a strong woman fall apart at the sound of a voice?*

"I don't need you to take care of me," she said, her voice rising. She wiped at her face. She closed the phone and handed it back to Stellar.

"He doesn't know you're in love with him, does he?"

Her head snapped up. She didn't speak, only stared at him. He remained silent and watched her struggle to keep her emotions to herself. He wondered what she saw in the straight-edged, married detective. He wished she trusted him enough to tell him.

"You don't know what you're talking about, Stellar."

"In your eyes, I may not be the best detective, but I'm not blind. I'm a bit surprised he is, though. You should tell him, killer. Get things out in the open."

"Since when did you become my therapist?"

"I think he'd understand your desire to stay away from him, if he knew you were just trying to get over him."

She turned away without a word and closed the bathroom door behind her.

Running his fingers through his hair, he wondered why he'd even opened his mouth. He grabbed his bag and started sifting through the notes Alex had spread out. He slipped his interview notes from Ann Wesley in the murder book.

He decided to go through the paperwork back at the office. As he lifted the entire stack and dropped it into the bag, a picture fell from the pile onto the floor. He didn't recognize it. Eddie Chavez was holding his son in front of the Death Valley Motel.

Stellar stared at Ollie's Camp Courage sweatshirt.

He ran to the bathroom and banged on the door. "We need to go. Now."

Chapter 44

Alex stared at the discarded fire hose lying in front of the apartment building. It was wrapped once around the fire hydrant and snaked its way around a For Rent sign and up to a window that had been broken out. Firefighters stepped over it as they walked up to the smoking house.

Stellar was questioning the only man with a police badge. Tired and confused, Alex remained quiet as Stellar explained why he was there.

"Arson?" Stellar asked.

The officer adjusted the dust mask hanging around his neck. "I doubt it. It looks like Ms. Ochoa was trying to figure out how to make meth and didn't realize the dangers."

"Where's the child?"

"She claimed child services took him last night."

"Make sure they did." Stellar glanced at the house. "Anything saved?"

"The front room, kitchen, and her bedroom are pretty much toast."

"Can I go in and check it out?"

"Hazmat's gonna have to clear the kitchen, but you can check out the back." The policeman yelled at a firefighter at the truck. "Grab a hard hat from the truck. You can go through the back door. The floors are okay back there. It's pretty wet, so watch your step."

Alex followed Stellar to the back door and down a short hallway, using his flashlight to illuminate the walkway. The charred walls crackled, and the floor was covered in wet goo. She put a hand over her nose and mouth as she walked to keep the smoke at bay. Water dripped from above them. A firefighter passed, holding broken plaster. He smiled at her but kept going.

"I'm not sure what we're doing here," Alex said. "You said Danny killed Eddie Chavez and now Danny's dead."

They walked into the boy's room. Spared from the water damage, the room smelled like a Vegas casino.

She looked at the boy's unmade bed and hoped he hadn't been here when the house exploded. There was still smoke in the room, and it burned her eyes and lungs, making it hard to take a deep breath. The smell burned her nose.

Stellar pulled a photo from the wall. "This is why."

She looked at the picture, a group shot of several young boys in front of a lake. A sign to the side said, *Camp Courage.*

"I've been trying to figure out how Eddie Chavez knew about Cole's death. He wasn't in town when it happened. He showed up two days later. No one I spoke to seemed to know Chavez, yet he knew Cole."

"His son was at the camp," Alex said. "He knew Cole."

"More than that." Stellar searched the desk. "Ollie Chavez told his father the boy was murdered."

"Now you believe Cole was murdered?"

Stellar stopped and looked at her. "The boy wasn't murdered. I'm positive that child slipped and fell into the lake. All the evidence points to that conclusion. My ME is positive he died from drowning. He's positive the water in his lungs was from the lake. How much clearer can it be?"

Alex stared at the boy in the picture. He had his father's eyes.

"But you still have doubts," she said. "Otherwise, we wouldn't be here trying to find out what Ollie told his father."

Alex handed the picture back to Stellar and looked at the clothes hanging in the closet. She didn't know what she was looking for. She squatted to look at the shoes on the floor. She picked up a pair of Nike shoes. Jordan's. Mud caked the soles. *Nice expensive shoes for a child*, she thought. Especially one living with a single mother.

She dropped the shoes and picked up the basketball.

"You play?" he asked.

She shrugged. "In prison."

He nodded and turned back to his search. She smiled at his uneasiness.

"I remember my last day with my brother, Sam," he said. "We rode the horses in the morning, played basketball after dinner. We were sweating and panting when we came in for bed. The next day, while doing his homework, he collapsed. Never woke up. The doctors said it was a heart attack. At autopsy, they found a birth defect in his heart. It was small, but it was big enough to be a problem."

Stellar continued his search through the desk. Deciding to stay out of his way, Alex stared at the pictures on Ollie's desk, pictures of father and son in a happier time. In one picture, Eddie held onto his son as if he were about to be pulled away. Both were laughing. A baseball bat and glove were at their feet as a black dog bounced behind them. Her heart broke for the boy's loss.

Alex pulled out the medallion Eddie had worn around his neck: the Patron Saint of Lost Causes, and hung it from the picture. Ollie would need it more than she.

"It didn't make sense to me," Stellar continued. "No matter how much they explained it to me. No matter how much I studied the heart, it just never made sense that an eight-year-old boy could die from a heart attack. Not while sitting at the kitchen table doing his math homework."

"Sometimes unexplainable things happen."

He didn't respond. She noticed he covered his sorrow well, but it was still there. She wanted to reach out to him. Instead, she sat on the bed and kept her hands on her lap.

"Something bothered you about Cole's death," she said. "What was it?"

Stellar shook his head. "I never could figure out why Cole wandered out in the middle of the night to the lake."

"Lincoln told Ann he had been punished the day before. He wasn't allowed to swim with the other kids." She grabbed Ollie's backpack and dug through it.

"The punishment wasn't about the lake. It was about being with his friends. Going out to the lake at midnight by himself doesn't make any sense. I think the other kids were supposed to meet him there. Maybe Ollie saw something."

"So maybe Cole was helped into the lake?" Alex pulled a notebook from the backpack and opened it up.

"There wasn't an unexplainable scratch on him. No other prints on the pier or surrounding dirt." He flicked the flashlight toward her. "What's that?"

She shrugged. "Looks like a boy's version of a diary. It's written in Spanish." She flipped through the pages, translating as she went. "Descriptions of the kids at camp."

"Anything on Cole?"

"He's described as cool. Friends with everyone. Oh, this is interesting," she said. "It looks like a few of the older boys snuck off to smoke."

Stellar walked over and sat on the bed next to her. She stopped reading as she realized how close he was sitting. The lingering smoke from the fire was still making it hard for her to breathe normally.

"Boys will be boys," Stellar said. "Does he name names?"

Alex continued reading with the help of the flashlight. "Cole was the ringleader. He had the cigarettes. A few of the others are named, but Ollie refused. A couple of the boys got sick."

"Maybe the cigarettes made him sick enough to have to go see the doctor."

She shook her head. "Cole seemed to have no problem with the cigarettes."

Stellar's shoulders sank. "Anything else that may be useful?"

She could hear the frustration in his voice and continued to skim the page, hoping for anything that could help. Then she found it. "Looks like the boys found something stronger than nicotine."

"Drugs?"

Alex jumped up. "Ric was positive Eddie was killed over drugs. What about the boy's toxicology? Did your ME look for any types of drugs?"

"The boy was twelve, Alex. And we don't normally request a toxicology report on drowning victims."

She smacked his arm, and he winced in pain. "That's where your murder comes into play."

Stellar closed his eyes. "Wags would have taken blood from Cole, but he probably didn't send it in, seeing as we'd already ruled it an accident." He rubbed his eyes. "I'll call Dr. Wags."

"Wait," she said, looking up from the notebook. "What does Dr. Wags look like?"

He opened his cell phone. "What?"

"Ollie calls the doctor *feo*. He repeats it several times. *El doctor feo se lo dio.*"

"Ugly," Stellar said, grabbing the notebook. "The ugly doctor gave it to them. It's not Wags. We need to get back to the station."

Chapter 45

"Watch for rattlesnakes," Erika said, pointing at Ric's bare legs. "The light will be gone soon and they'll be waking. You won't want to startle one." She walked as if the uneven terrain was no problem for her.

He picked up a stick and cringed. "Same to you, Lois Lane. I won't be able to find help without you, so you'll end up dying here." He tripped over a root, but kept walking.

There were too many trees and too much dirt. Branches whipped him, and he stumbled over the rocks. The air reeked of cow manure. He tried to hold one hand over his mouth and nose, hoping to keep the stench from his throat. Nevertheless, he could feel the smell permeating his clothes and his skin. He wanted to vomit but held it down. It would only make the smell worse.

He felt he was starting to suffocate in all this wilderness. He remembered why he preferred the city. Maybe Alex was right. This place sucked. After all of this, he was ready to move home.

"Tell me about Will Stellar. How did you two hook up?"

"We met in elementary school. Been together ever since."

"You don't look like the badge-bunny type. In fact, you look more like Lincoln's type. Success driven. Ruthless and daring."

Erika continued walking without looking back at him. "Lincoln's not the relationship type. Will is my soul mate."

It was a knee-jerk response that made Ric wonder if those were her words or something someone had told her. He'd heard the rumors running around town. He knew enough to not trust her words.

"How many Stellar boys are there?"

"Lincoln's the oldest, so he's the golden child. He was destined to follow in their father's footsteps and run the ranch. Franklin's a year younger. He's off in Houston running big oil. Then there's Will and Sam. They were inseparable until Sam died."

Ric had heard about the young Stellar's death. He considered Will's loss. He had never been very close with his sister, but he had always known she was there. He couldn't imagine losing her. He felt for the loss, but childhood tragedy often led to a troubled future. Maybe Will had survived with the help of his brother and longtime girlfriend. Or maybe he had become a cop so he could be untouchable.

"Will and Sam used to dream of how they could make names for themselves and break away from their father's dreams. If one wanted to be a doctor, then the other wanted to be a doctor. They were a pair, but Sam died, and Will almost followed him. He was devastated. Lincoln saved him."

"What exactly does the Stellar family grow here?" Ric asked. He was thankful Erika liked to talk. It helped him forget about the bugs and varmints surrounding him. He turned on his flashlight and followed Erika, who didn't seem to have a problem with the terrain.

"Some soybeans and barley, but their largest harvest is alfalfa for the livestock. He's got a few thousand head of cattle. Most of their income comes from the livestock."

Ric's anxiety about the cows returned. It must have showed, because Erika stopped.

"They won't hurt you. They're quite gentle."

"I have enough problems with humans. I don't need to befriend any four-legged creatures."

"You don't like animals?"

"Only dead ones, specifically ones right off the grill," he said. "How many people live here?"

"Nobody but family, except when the camp is open. Lincoln only uses locals to harvest and work with the cattle. During the summer, he brings in quite a few people to help out at the camp, and some of the teenagers stay in the bunks with the kids, but everything closed shop when Cole was found."

"And at the main house?"

"At the main house, it's just Lincoln, their mother, and Lucy, the gatekeeper you heard from earlier. His new assistant, A. J., is staying at the guesthouse."

"What does Lucy do other than scare away trespassers?"

"She's the housekeeper and cook. She's been with the family forever. She handles Lincoln's schedule and hires the staff, both in the fields and at the camp, just like she did for their father. She also watches over their mother."

"So what does Lincoln's assistant do?"

Erika shrugged. "Follows him around and does whatever Lincoln tells him to."

"Tell me about Sergeant Morgan. He's a friend of Will's?"

She shook her head. "Not really. He's been friends with Lincoln since high school. They played baseball together. Will has to work with him, but he avoids him on a personal level. Why?"

Before he could deflect the question, she stopped and pointed through a clearing.

"There it is."

Through the darkness, Ric saw the lake ahead. It was larger than he had imagined. The dark blue water sparkled against the brown shore.

"My best guess, Cole fell off the pier," Erika said as she walked toward the lake. She pointed south. "Will found him along the edge, tangled in the brush."

Ric scanned the length of the pier. It was short, but the water was slapping against the stilts only inches from the top of the pier. Ric stared at the cliff in the distance. The water ran straight to the cliff's edge. He estimated fifteen feet. Nowhere to climb out. The current, stronger there, slammed the waves against the rocks. He looked up and noticed a shed perched on the cliff.

"They found footprints all along the pier," Erika added. "He apparently slipped in."

"What's in the shed?"

She shrugged. "Probably farm equipment or feed. Lincoln has sheds spread out across the land."

Ric started walking up toward the cliff.

Erika followed. "You think Cole was up there?"

"The pier is a short fall. If Cole fell in here, he would have recovered enough to climb back up or at least swim close enough to find solid footing below. The current isn't that strong here. A fall from the cliff would have been more likely to kill him. Too far for an adult to swim, way too far for a child. Especially in the dead of night."

He looked up at the cliff and then back to the pier. No way would a child survive. Cole would have drowned before he even realized which way to swim.

Ric found footprints as he rushed up the cliff. "Someone was here recently."

"We had the whole town searching for Cole that morning. These are adult prints."

She was right, but he continued climbing up. He reached the shed and found bags of fertilizer packed along the wall. The shed looked unused from the outside, but as he walked toward the door, his flashlight lit up an electrical box. It shone brand new.

"Why does he keep the fertilizer outside the shed?"

Erika didn't answer. "We're going to get rain."

"Stay out here, at least five feet from the side."

"I'm coming in."

Ric ignored her. He opened the door and shined his flashlight inside. The shed looked as clean as an operating room but resembled a culinary kitchen with clean white countertops. Stainless steel stovetops with huge pots lined an entire wall. Hundreds of jars of fluid were lined up on the counter. Ric knew exactly what they contained. Despite the cleanliness of the room, the toxic smell was still evident to his trained nose. He wished for a gas mask and a hazmat suit.

"What is this?" Erika asked.

"This is what I'd call a bomb in the making. It's a cookhouse. A very sophisticated operation to make methamphetamines on a very large scale. This is why Cole died."

"I'm calling my photographer."

"Outside. One errant spark could light up the entire desert, not to mention blow us to red dust. Keep an eye on the door for me."

Ric was left alone in the meth lab. He wasn't too surprised with Erika's lack of loyalty for the Stellar bunch. Apparently her need for the "big" story outweighed any future she saw with the family.

He turned from the sinks and opened several cabinets containing bags of white powder. These were larger bags than the ones he had found under Danny's bed and were labeled with the same L.I. as the duffel bag.

He smiled as he walked past the cabinets towards the boxes stacked up to the ceiling. After quickly estimating the weight and number of boxes, Ric figured there was at least 10,000 pounds of methamphetamines, street value in the millions. In all the years at LAPD narcotics, he'd never been on a bust this large. The boys in L.A. would be jealous. He wished Dade were with him.

Ric glanced at his watch. He dialed Detective Stellar's phone number.

"Is my sister still with you?" Ric asked when the detective answered.

"Yes. Where are you?"

"Where I always like to be—in the middle of it all. Did Dade tell you about Della?"

"Yes, but just because she claims it's a friend of Lincoln's doesn't mean he's involved. We need to tread lightly."

"Tell me how the boy died. Cole." Ric spotted an open box in the corner.

"Asphyxiation. He drowned. His lungs were filled with lake water. No question."

Ric appreciated the no-nonsense answer. It was straight to the point, but he didn't believe it. "Erika told you the boy was murdered. How come you don't believe her? She's your girlfriend."

"Did you ever trust a journalist over the evidence?"

Stellar was right, but he needed to know how much Stellar knew. "And how did you explain the methamphetamines in his system?"

The detective sighed. "I'm having the ME rush the tox screens, but it doesn't change the original findings. He didn't die of an overdose. He died from drowning."

"Still covering for your brother, huh? Della says the guy had a badge, police identification. A cop wanted to shut up Eddie Chavez."

"The badge was probably a fake. It was just a way to get Eddie to open the door."

"Relax, Stellar. I know you didn't kill Eddie Chavez. Do you know where Sergeant Morgan was at the time of Eddie's death?"

Ric looked past the boxes and saw more bags of fertilizer. He wondered how safe holding a cell phone was in there. He should call the DEA, but he'd always wanted to blow up a place like this. The drugs would be hauled away to some evidence room, where some of it was likely to go missing or be stolen—somehow it would get back into circulation.

"It's not Morgan," said Stellar. "I can guarantee it. I know my men."

"Stop covering for him, cowboy. I'm looking at evidence that your brother and his cop friend are working together on a big project. I think it's impossible for you not to know something was up."

"What evidence?"

Ric opened the box and found bottles and syringes. The bottles had a white liquid. It was ready to be injected. No more lighters and spoons. No more mess. No more waiting for the high. It was as clean and simple as injecting insulin.

"This isn't just your run-of-the-mill crank cookhouse," said Ric. "This is ice." He thought about it. L.I. stood for Lincoln Ice. "This could be close to 100 percent pure methamphetamines, made by a professional hand. This is a serious, sophisticated operation, cowboy. He didn't do this alone. I need to know if you're involved. Did you agree to go in on this with them? Help them cover this up?"

"What operation?"

"I heard ever since your brother Sam died, the two of you have become inseparable. Co-captains on the baseball team. You share tools, swap horses. Even share your girlfriend. I'd call that close."

Stellar didn't respond. He heard the change in breathing on the other end.

"Don't tell me you didn't know Erika was sleeping with Lincoln when you were too busy for her. I won't believe you're the last person in town to find out. She's not that good of a liar."

The silence told Ric what he needed to hear.

"Keep my sister safe, Stellar, or I drag you down with your brother."

In Stellar's silence, Ric heard the movement outside. Erika should have been behind him. The footsteps were louder than a woman's. He switched off his flashlight.

"I've got company." He snapped the phone closed and grabbed a syringe, filling it past the line. For good measure, he grabbed a second one and did the same. He didn't bother with his gun.

He heard Erika cry out, then silence. He didn't hear a gunshot, which meant he had a chance. He stepped behind the door. He calculated Lincoln's size and waited. He reminded himself the man was a criminal, so his actions were justified.

But it wasn't Lincoln who opened the door.

The man was nothing short of hideous to look at. He was taller. His hands were huge. The man's eyes bulged when he spotted Ric.

Ric didn't feel bad as he stabbed the needle into the man's neck. The man jerked back and pulled a gun. Ric plunged the second needle in and squeezed both into the monster's bulging veins.

The man swung out and smashed the gun against Ric's head. He crumpled to the ground in pain and tried to stay conscious.

Chapter 46

Keeping his eyes on the road, Will Stellar closed his phone. Large raindrops slammed onto the windshield. He knew the rain would come hard and fast.

"Who was that?" Alex asked.

"No one." He didn't bother to slow the car. He cranked the car at the first right.

"Where are we going?"

He could hear the concern in her voice. He ignored it. "We're going to see my brother."

He pressed down on the gas, and the car shook as it reached eighty. He flipped on the sirens and took the back way to the family ranch. The rain fell faster now.

It took him thirty minutes to get to the family estate. He said nothing the entire way. He stopped at the gate, turned off the sirens, and punched in a number.

"Stay in the car," he ordered as the gate eased open. He tried to contain himself as he drove past the gate and blocked the exit with the patrol car.

"No way." Alex jumped from the car and rushed up the driveway to the front door. Taking his time, Stellar unsnapped his holster and took in his surroundings, letting the rain drench him with every step. He knew the territory backward and forward, even in the dark with the rain pouring down, but he was walking in with a civilian. He would need to control the scene from the beginning. The house loomed large above him. The windows were dark. His mother was inside. The thought made him stop short.

His phone rang as he stared at the steps of the house. He thought of ignoring it; he needed to focus on what he was doing. Instead, he answered as Alex continued to pound on the door.

"Stellar, it's Florio. We ran the Magnum."

"Yeah, I'm a bit busy right now, Florio. Go ahead and let the owner know we found his vehicle."

"It wasn't reported stolen. The car is registered to A. J. Corredor. He's the son of the Reno doctor who reported the gun stolen, Wayne Corredor. Morgan said he's the new guy with Lincoln. He said you'd want to know right away."

"Did Morgan pull his rap sheet?"

Will eyed the windows as a light flicked on. He heard the door open. Lucy, his mother's housekeeper, opened the door. He couldn't hear what was being said, but Lucy was shaking her head.

"Yeah, he was arrested last year for manufacturing methamphetamines," said Florio. "He skipped out on bail three months ago."

"Tell Morgan to get some officers over to my mother's house right away. I want cars on the Northeast and Southeast to cover the back garage and exit. I want you here at the front gate. No one enters the property until I say." Will closed the phone, his patience completely gone. He took the steps two at a time.

"Where's my mother?"

Lucy's face brightened when she saw him. "Hi, Will. It's late. She's sleeping."

"Where's Lincoln?"

"He's in the guesthouse with his friend. Why? What's going on?"

"Lock the doors and don't let anyone inside until I clear the property."

Fear lit into her face. "Is this about that guy that was trying to talk to Lincoln? He said it was urgent, but I wouldn't let him through the gate."

"I'll take care of it, Lucy. Lock the doors and keep an eye on my mother."

He waited for her to close the door and listened for the lock.

"Is your brother dangerous?" Alex asked.

"He's not the one I'm here for."

Will turned to the side of the house and followed the path to the guesthouse. His brother was the only one who still used the guesthouse. He used the study for his Wednesday evening poker parties. Will knew most of the people who attended and tried to avoid it when he could. Morgan was a regular. So was the mayor.

He also guessed the guest bedroom was now occupied by A. J. Lincoln had never liked bringing strangers into the family home, not since their father had left, but the guesthouse had been their second home as children. Sam had always referred to it as his castle. He would charge fees on rainy days for Lincoln and Will to enter. After Sam had died, Lincoln had taken the house over.

As Will approached the doorway, he was drowned by a flood of memories. He shook them off and let the anger push him forward. Alex stayed at his heels.

"Stay back, killer. I don't know how many people we're going to find in there."

"I can handle myself."

He hesitated a minute, trying to think of any way he could keep

Alex out of there. He guessed it was hopeless, so he opened the door and inspected the entryway. He didn't push away his memories now. He let them come over him. The right led to the small kitchen and dining room. The left hallway led to the only bedroom through a study. They had often played in the study because of its larger size.

Thinking like a cop, and like a brother, he walked toward the study.

"You still haven't considered his involvement?" Alex followed close behind.

"He's not capable of murder." There were lights on in the study. "Stay behind me."

"Everyone's capable of murder. Your brother may be pulling the strings."

"My brother couldn't have killed Eddie Chavez," Will said. "Your brother just proved it. His alibi is my girlfriend."

Before she could ask any more questions, Lincoln emerged from the study. Will stepped back but noticed that Lincoln's eyes were on Alex.

"What the hell is she doing here?" Lincoln demanded.

"Lincoln, I need to talk to your assistant, A. J. Where is he?"

Lincoln looked at Will. "He's busy. What's this about?"

"I'm arresting him for the murder of Eddie Chavez."

Lincoln stared at him. "Are you out of your mind, Will?"

"Does he own a Black Dodge Magnum?"

Lincoln didn't answer. Will could see him trying to figure it out. He saw the guilt in his eyes. Alex was right. His brother knew more.

"Danny just tried to run us off the road with Eddie's car," Will explained. "Now he's dead. My shoulder is cut, my ribs hurt, and I'm hungry and tired. I'm not in the mood to be patient. Get him now."

He ran his fingers through his hair. "Shit."

"Where is he, Lincoln?"

"Will, we need to talk. Without her."

Detective Stellar looked back at Alex. She wasn't paying attention to Lincoln. She was watching the doors. Watching his back. *She would have made a good cop*, he thought.

He smiled as he turned back to his brother. "She stays with me. Tell me where A. J. is, and I won't arrest you for obstruction."

Lincoln's eyes flamed red. "Is that how you treat your brother?"

"A real brother wouldn't sleep with my girlfriend behind my back."

Lincoln ran his fingers through his hair again. "Shit, Will. I wanted to tell you. I did. She didn't want to hurt you."

"Where's A. J.?" Will put his hand on his gun.

Lincoln opened his mouth to say something but thought better of it. He shrugged his shoulders and turned toward the study. "I was just about to call you. He's handling a trespasser for me." He opened the door.

Chapter 47

When the study door opened, Alex saw her brother. He was sitting in a chair, his head down and his right eye bloody and swollen. His arms were pulled behind him.

She screamed his name and rushed in before she noticed the man standing beside him with a gun in his hands.

"Don't move!" he shouted, the gun at his side now pointed at her.

Alex took another step forward before she heard Ric's voice.

"Alex, he's tweaking."

She looked at the man now and knew this was the ugly man Ollie had referred to: the doctor who had killed Cole. His eyes darted around the room. She saw the twitches in his hand as he held the gun. His fingernails were painted black, his arm covered in scratches.

Stellar pulled his own gun and pointed directly at his brother's friend. "A.J., put the gun down."

Lincoln turned and saw the gun in Stellar's hand. "What are you doing, Will? This guy trespassed on my property."

"I understand that, and a cop just walked in. There's no need to point a gun at him. And no reason to point it at her. Let me handle this."

Lincoln looked confused as he stared at Stellar. "He had a gun. He stabbed A. J. with a needle."

Stellar ignored his brother. "A. J., I'm a detective with the Lake City Police. I'm also Lincoln's brother. Lower the gun, now. It's no longer needed."

The gun was lowering an inch with every word Stellar said. Alex looked back at Ric. He slowly shook his head at her.

"*Espera*," he whispered.

She obeyed and waited.

Lincoln walked over to A. J. and took the gun from him.

Stellar's hands relaxed. "I need to speak to A. J. and you about Eddie Chavez."

"I had nothing to do with his murder. I swear."

Stellar looked at A. J. "What about you, A. J.? Are you claiming innocence, too?"

A. J. said nothing, merely darted his eyes from Stellar to Lincoln. Alex was stuck in the middle of the room, watching, unsure what to do. A. J. looked as if he might bolt, but Alex didn't want to move. Not yet.

"Lincoln can't alibi you, A. J. He had his own company Tuesday night. Isn't that right?" Stellar didn't take his eyes off A. J.

"Will—"

"Shut up. I'm talking to A. J. You had to pay for your date, right, A. J.? You took her to the motel. Della's good with faces, especially ones as ugly as yours. I'm sure she could pick you right out of a lineup. And you couldn't resist showing her the forged ID you made, right?"

A. J.'s face straightened and looked at Stellar. Alex saw that Stellar had guessed wrong.

"It wasn't fake," A. J. said.

Lincoln spoke up now. "It was Morgan's. He's always leaving things here. I'm sorry, Will. I swear I didn't know."

Stellar still didn't look at Lincoln. He was focused on A. J. as if he were scared to look at his brother. "Della can place you at the motel the night Eddie was killed. I have trace evidence I'm sure will place you inside his room. And you used your own father's gun. That was pretty stupid. I've got enough to lock you up for a very long time."

Alex noticed Stellar kept his gun trained on A. J., despite the fact that Lincoln held the only other gun in the room. She wondered about his loyalties. What would he do if this all turned bad?

"What's your connection with Danny?" Stellar asked. "Why'd you send him after us?"

Ric answered, "A. J. needed Danny to get rid of Eddie's gun and car. In exchange, A. J. provided him with street ready meth. You had no problem killing Eddie, but you couldn't kill Detective Stellar, could you? Lincoln wouldn't allow it."

Will blinked. Alex saw the surprise in his eyes, but he continued to stare at A. J.

"You told Danny to kill me?" Will asked.

"I told him to get rid of the girl," A. J. screamed. "You weren't supposed to be hurt." He turned to Lincoln. "I swear, Lincoln. He wasn't supposed to be hurt."

The detective refused to acknowledge his brother and kept his focus on the doctor. "We were getting too close. Just like Eddie."

A. J. looked at Lincoln, pleading. "Eddie was going to talk to the reporter. We had no choice."

"He was going to tell everyone about how you gave the boys meth, right?" said Will. "Tell me, did you mean to kill Cole?"

Lincoln turned on A. J. "You gave it to the kids?"

A. J. started to shake. "The kid wanted some. I just gave him a little. I didn't know he was going to go out in the middle of the night to find another hit."

"Oh my God," Lincoln said. "I didn't know…"

Alex waited.

Stellar turned the gun toward Lincoln. "If you expect me to believe that, then you'll have to explain why you employed a scumbag like A. J. Tell me about the meth."

"It's about time we get to the interesting part," Ric muttered. "It's a nice-looking cookhouse you got."

"Shut up, Ric."

Alex heard the detective's irritation but couldn't tell which side he was on. His eyes were now completely focused on his brother.

"I told you I had a plan, Will. It's the next big thing. Mass-produced methamphetamines. It's inexpensive to produce, and the market is huge," Lincoln said proudly. "The mom-and-pop shops are cropping up everywhere, but the amount they produce is nothing to what I can produce. I have the ingredients just lying around here. I have a lab all set up. And I already have the trucks to distribute, since the medicine thing didn't work out."

"It's drugs, Lincoln."

"No, marijuana and cocaine are drugs. Meth is a money-making pharmaceutical. I'm not growing illegal plants to sell to prostitutes and homeless dropouts. I'm putting completely legal substances together to produce a stimulant that helps people cope with this crazy world. Top executives around the country are using it to stay on top. Businesswomen are using it to keep their work and home life balanced. New mothers are using it to lose their baby weight. Even doctors are using it. We can mass produce this stuff and ship it anywhere in the country. We can ship it to people's doorsteps. With your help—"

"A little boy died. Don't make me read you your rights."

"Will, we're family. We can work this out without badges and guns."

"I've wanted to be a cop a long time, Lincoln. I'm not going to let you take everything I worked for away from me. Put the gun down."

Alex saw something flash in Lincoln's eyes. The gun jerked back up, pointed directly at her head. She closed her eyes and waited for the shot.

"Lincoln!" Will shouted. "I will shoot you. If you pull that trigger, I will take you down. You know me as well as I know you. You're not a killer. Put the gun down."

Alex slowly opened her eyes. The gun was back down at Lincoln's side. Stellar still had his gun trained on Lincoln. But it wasn't defeat in Lincoln's eyes. He stood taller, arrogance shining in his eyes.

"Family should always be more important than the badge. A. J.," he called, "bring her here."

Stellar moved the gun and pointed it directly at A. J. "Don't move, A. J."

Alex squared herself, ready for A. J. to approach her, but A. J. ignored her and walked slowly past Ric toward the door. His eyes stayed on Stellar's gun.

Alex turned toward Ric, who kept his eyes locked on Lincoln.

"What are you doing, Lincoln?" Will asked. Alex could hear the hesitation in his voice. She needed to make a decision, and she needed to make it fast.

A. J. entered a minute later with Erika Mack in front of him. Her face was wet with tears, but the crying had stopped. She didn't look at anyone in the room. A large gun was held to her head, and that kept everyone's attention on A. J.

"Lincoln, what the hell are you doing?" Will asked.

"You always said I should have insurance in case my plans fall through." Lincoln put his gun on the table. "You won't shoot anyone now."

Stellar glanced between Erika and Lincoln. He didn't move his gun, but Alex saw the change on his face. The doubt. The anguish.

"Take the gun off of her."

"Now why would I do that?"

Will lowered his own gun. "Because I've loved her longer than I've wanted to be a cop."

Lincoln nodded toward A. J. He saw what Alex saw in Will's face. It was over. The brothers had come to an agreement.

Chapter 48

Will Stellar knew the life he had led up to this point was over. Things would be completely different after tonight.

He had walked into this room remembering the child he had once been and the cop he now was. As a child, they had used the room to build forts, play hide-and-seek and cops and robbers. There were two doors to this room, but only one exit, since one door led to the bedroom that had no escape and the other led to the entryway and out to freedom. The only way to survive was to get to that door—the door he now kept to his back.

As a cop, he had entered eyeing the hiding spots and the possible weapons, but Lincoln had rearranged for his poker party and the room was wide open. No weapons within reach in this room. No places to hide. He felt every eye on him. He couldn't win as a cop in this room.

He lowered his gun and stared at Erika. She was breathing hard now, almost hyperventilating, but she didn't move. He loved her with everything he had. She had cheated on him. Lied to him. And yet the love was still there.

Lincoln walked over and easily took Stellar's gun from him. He took his time pulling out the magazine and the bullet from the chamber and then placed the gun next to his on the table.

Will glanced at Alex, standing in the center of the room. If there hadn't been guns and crying, she would have been the centerpiece—beautiful and confident and poised. She was out of his reach and in the most danger out in the open. He looked at Ric, tied to a dining room chair. His back was against the gas fireplace. His hands were bound behind his back, but his feet were loose. Stellar wondered how much of a reach Ric would have from the chair.

Stellar noticed both looking at him with disappointment in their eyes.

He looked at A. J. with his back to the bedroom. Too close to Erika. He could save her. He had to proceed one step at a time, and Erika was the logical first step. He had to remove the innocent bystanders who could cause his plan to go awry.

"Erika, come here," he said.

She moved slowly, obviously scared of every movement. When she reached him, he pulled her in his arms and held her tightly. He felt his energy draining from him.

"You need to go outside," he instructed her. "Now."

She shook her head.

"You have to go," he begged again. Despite his training, tears sprang to his eyes. Erika sobbed now but wouldn't let go. "I can't think with you in here, sweetheart. You need to go. Please."

Lincoln interrupted, "She stays. You mentioned you were interested in a partnership. I think now's the time to discuss."

Stellar nodded and looked toward Lincoln. "Tell me the plan, Lincoln. How do you get out of this clean?"

Lincoln smiled. "We were always great partners. With my vision and your perseverance, we're going to make a lot of money, the two of us."

"We already have a lot of money, Lincoln. What else you got?"

Will saw Alex move. He turned to her and felt his stomach drop. The disappointment had disappeared. What he saw now was evil.

She turned to Lincoln with a smirk. "Are you really going to trust him?" she asked. "He's a cop. Like he said, he won't break the law with you. If you're looking for a partner, you need a fast mind. You need someone who won't flinch and knows when to pull the trigger. Like me."

Stellar groaned to himself as he felt Lincoln's attention swiped from him. He studied Alex. She stood stone faced. Strong and determined. Dangerous. He tried to take a step toward his brother, but Erika held him tight.

"I can help you with your plan. Better than A. J. and better than your brother."

"Don't listen to her, Lincoln," Will said.

But Lincoln was listening, intently.

"First, you need to get rid of these two," she said. "They'll only bring you down. A cop, seriously? He'll turn on you the second he's out this door. He's already planning your arrest. Family never has your back. They sure talk a big game, but they're always thinking of themselves first."

Stellar cringed. He didn't know how to shut her up. As Erika held onto his arm, he felt powerless to do anything. He had made a mistake. He had chosen Erika to remove from harm's way, and now he realized he should have removed Alex. With Alex in the crosshairs, she had attacked. Hadn't Detective Dade warned him of just that?

"And A. J.?" Alex went on. "You can't think his pea brain can help you with anything. He almost knocked off your brother by mistake. He's a punk kid with no control."

"Shut up, lady!" A. J. yelled. The kid was over-amped. He was jerky and paranoid. If Alex pushed him, he might accidentally pull the trigger.

She looked at A. J., her face emotionless. "Don't make me kill you," she whispered.

Lincoln straightened at the threat. "He's my chemist. I need him."

"He's a user. He'll snort more than he makes for you, and the one time he tries to cook while high, he'll blow your lab to shit." Then she pointed to Stellar. "And then he'll arrest you."

"Let me shoot her, Lincoln," A. J. begged.

The gun was now pointed at her head. Alex was blocking Will's line of sight. He could no longer see Ric, but with a gun pointed at Alex's head, he was sure Ric wasn't going to sit there quietly.

"Hold on, A. J.," said Lincoln. "I want to hear her out. And what do you expect me to do without a chemist?"

"I know how to make ice. It's so easy a child could do it."

"Where did you learn how to make it?"

"Prison."

Realizing his value was diminishing, A. J. waved the gun. "Shut that bitch up. She's nothing but a whore, Lincoln."

"Stop calling her names, tweaker," Ric warned. "Or I'll shove that Colt up your ass."

Stellar held his arm up and pushed Erika behind him. It was about to get messy, and he didn't have a way out of this. If only Alex had kept her mouth closed. He suddenly wished he had told his officers to come to the guesthouse instead of waiting outside the gate.

"Lincoln, tell him to put the gun down," Stellar begged. "We can work something out."

"Shut up, Will," Lincoln shouted. "I'm listening to the lady. I think she may be right."

Lincoln wouldn't give the order to shoot, but it was only a matter of time before A. J. took matters into his own hands.

"Don't worry, Detective," Alex said, as if reading his mind. Her eyes were focused on the gun, shaking in A. J.'s hand. "He can't even decide for himself when to pull the trigger. Besides, the guy couldn't hit me if I was only an inch from him."

Lincoln laughed. "I'm going to bet he's a better shot than that."

"Let me shoot her, Lincoln," A. J. begged. The gun held steady now.

Alex looked back at Lincoln. "He's so high he couldn't piss straight. You a gambling man, Lincoln? Let's make a bet on his aim."

Stellar followed her gaze. She was looking at the table that held the two handguns. She turned back and took a step toward A. J. *Too close,* Stellar thought. A. J. could almost reach out and grab her.

"If he misses, I become your partner, and we can discuss getting rid of A. J. and the cop."

"Alex—"

"And if he hits you?" Lincoln asked, ignoring his brother.

"You can make the deal with your brother and your mistress over there." She glanced at Stellar only for a second, then back to Lincoln.

"Lincoln, you'll want to move at least two steps to your left, or you're gonna get hit by the stray."

Without hesitation, Lincoln took three large steps to his left. Stellar couldn't see Ric's face, but knew Lincoln was within reach. He saw the picture now. He saw Alex's plan, but there was nothing he could do to stop her.

"*Listo?*" she asked, glancing at Will.

No, he definitely was not ready.

Chapter 49

Ric had been brought to the study unconscious. He wasn't sure what lay outside the door he had been dragged through. When he regained consciousness, he was sitting in an uncomfortable chair with his wrists secured tightly behind him.

He realized Dade had been right. He had changed. He still felt he was a cop, still thought like a cop, but somewhere along the line, he had stopped acting like a cop. He never would have walked into that drug lab without backup. He never would have distrusted the police department. And he never would have put other people in danger.

It was time to start acting like a cop, even if he no longer wore a badge. He had woken alone in the room and had plenty of time to search the room for weapons, but he had come up empty. He could see his feet. They were free and strong enough stand up on if necessary. There were only two doors in the pretty much empty room.

The door that had interested him was the one with the two voices fighting behind it. When A. J. and Lincoln had emerged a few minutes later, he could see it was a bedroom behind them. He determined right away that the door was useless as an exit, but he also guessed it was where Erika had been taken.

When Detective Stellar had arrived, Ric had felt surprisingly happy. He didn't enjoy the fact that he had to be saved from such a dire situation, but he couldn't figure any escape that provided saving Erika, too. His joy at seeing Will Stellar soon diminished when he saw how stupid he had been to allow Alex into the room.

Ric had watched the entire scene unfold with some amusement. He kept his good eye on Lincoln's gun on the table. But his focus was on untying his hands behind him. He was a long way from that. As he watched Alex's plan come together, he could have cried or laughed.

She was risking everything on being faster than A. J. She was putting her life on the line to save everyone else. *Does she have a death wish?* he thought.

Detective Stellar was as useless as his gun. His girlfriend's well-being was clouding his judgment. Nevertheless, Alex was still putting some trust in him. Stellar's magazine had been removed from the pistol, and A. J. was holding Ric's Colt Anaconda. That meant the only gun Ric had to worry about was Lincoln's.

As Lincoln took his steps, he didn't realize he was moving away from his gun. He was almost within reach of Ric now. Alex had found a way to neutralize Lincoln's weapon and Lincoln at the same time.

She was almost within striking distance of A. J. One more step, and he would be neutralized. Alex would kill him without hesitating.

Ric smiled as he waited for the signal to take Lincoln down. He watched her face and saw her steady herself for death in case she wasn't fast enough. He reminded himself to talk to her about this after they all walked out of there.

"Do we have a bet, Lincoln?" Alex asked.

The detective moved before the signal. It wasn't his fault; he didn't know the plan. In reality, Ric was the only one who did. He was the only one in the room who knew that the Colt Anaconda, the revolver A. J. was pointing at Alex's head, was empty.

But to compound Stellar's mistake, he rushed toward Alex, instead of going for Lincoln's gun. A. J. jumped and pulled the trigger before Stellar reached her.

Click!

She blinked hard from the sound before Stellar tackled her to the ground.

A. J. continued to pull the trigger, producing the same empty sound. Confused, he looked at the revolver. Alex threw an elbow to the detective's face as she tried to get free of him.

Ric kept his focus on Lincoln. Realizing his assistant was completely useless, Lincoln turned to retrieve his own gun. Knowing his role now, Ric wasted no time. With his hands still bound, he reached out with his legs, grabbed Lincoln's, and pulled. Lincoln fell hard to the carpet.

Ric didn't get a chance to finish Lincoln. A. J. escaped Stellar's reach and ran toward the open door. Releasing Lincoln, Ric stood and smashed the chair he was still tied to against A. J.

A. J. shrieked and dropped like a sack of bricks. Stellar rushed over and handcuffed him. Ric realized he had underestimated Stellar's quickness.

Lincoln rushed from the room.

"Don't worry about him," Stellar said. "He's got nowhere to go."

"Cut me out of this damn chair."

Stellar handed him the pocket knife and retrieved his own gun, taking his time to load and bump check it. He heard Erika wailing and rushed back to her. A. J. was still screaming in the corner.

"Shut up, A. J." Ric said. "There is no need to yell."

Ric watched the couple as he cut the ropes around his wrist. He picked up his Colt Anaconda and looked around the room. "Where the hell is Alex?"

Chapter 50

"He won't hurt her."

Will knew the woods behind the lake well. He had spent too many years as a child chasing Lincoln or Sam. He didn't need light to know his way. A tree branch smacked him in the face.

Of course, he'd been shorter then.

"I'm not worried about her getting hurt," Ric said. "She can kill him with her bare hands."

Stellar heard voices as he wiped the mud from his face. Just as he expected, Lincoln had run toward the lake in hopes of making it to his back exit. He kept two other vehicles in a hidden garage, but Will knew there was no way out. With the downfall of rain, the dirt road would be impassable, even in the new Hummer. Lincoln wouldn't have thought of that.

Ric rushed ahead. "Two o'clock."

Stellar caught up and found Ric stopped in front of a flowing mud river. He pointed. Stellar could barely see Lincoln through the darkness and the pouring rain.

Stellar yelled out, but the rain pounding through the trees was too loud. Lightning flashed. He saw Alex in front of Lincoln. She appeared to be screaming at Lincoln, but Stellar couldn't hear it. Lincoln shook his head and took a step toward Alex.

Will kept his eyes on Alex. She stood still, her body slightly turned away from Lincoln. Nothing happened as the two stared at each other.

Ric said, "We need to get around this."

Stellar stared at the raging muddy river. "You go right, I'll go left. If you find a place safe enough to cross, do it, but be careful."

Ric disappeared into the woods. Stellar turned back to his brother.

Alex moved first. She was fast. She swung out at Lincoln and connected with a punch to Lincoln's jaw. Lincoln's head jerked back. Lincoln threw a wild punch. Alex ducked as Lincoln's fist just missed her head. She countered with another shot to his chin.

Alex slipped another wild punch, then countered with a jab to his side. She shook off the rain from her face. Lincoln swung again. Again, too high.

She danced back, and Will could see she was evaluating the damage she had done. Lincoln was no longer fighting. He knelt down, sucking in air and clutching his stomach. Alex lunged again.

Fear for his brother gripped him. Stellar didn't wait to watch the rest of the fight. He ran up the mud river. As it thinned, he found a rock path and jumped across. He couldn't hear anything but the pounding rain.

He tore through the trees and waded through the rushing mud, then ran past the shed to where he had last seen Alex and Lincoln. As the lightning lit up the sky, Stellar saw Alex still struggling with Lincoln. Lincoln rushed her and grabbed her by the shoulders. Stellar yelled, and he thought he saw Lincoln turn his face before Alex's elbow made contact with it.

She rolled away from Lincoln's grasp. Lincoln tried to stand up but slipped in the mud. He was twice her size, but Alex wasn't even breathing hard. Stellar thought there may have been a grin on her face.

Pulling his gun, Will approached slowly. Alex's shouts grew louder through the rain. She was covered in mud. He yelled again.

Lincoln turned toward him, blood dripping down his face. Taking the opportunity, Alex flicked a roundhouse kick, knocking him face down into the mud. Lincoln tried to crawl away, but the air in his lungs came out in a loud, gut-wrenching cough. The next kick landed, and Lincoln curled into a ball.

"You killed that little boy," Alex screamed.

Lincoln tried to protect himself, but was making no headway. She kicked him in the head, and the fighting finally stopped.

Will yelled out to Alex. He moved closer, hoping she could hear him. She now had Lincoln in the mud, one arm pulled up behind his back. Lincoln didn't move. Stellar thought he heard bones cracking as Alex yanked at his brother.

"You killed Cole," she screamed. "You'll blame your friend back there, and he'll take the fall, but Ann Wesley is going to know you were responsible. You're responsible for Eddie Chavez, too. You took him from his son. You've destroyed two families."

"Alex, let him go," Stellar yelled.

She looked up now, but he couldn't see her eyes. She was like a cornered animal ready to strike. Thunder shook the ground. Lincoln shifted, and Stellar was thankful his brother was still alive. Alex pushed her knee into Lincoln's back, and the movement stopped.

"You're here to help him?" she asked.

He shook his head and wiped the water from his eyes. "I'm here to do my job. You need to let him go."

Lincoln took the chance to struggle. Stellar watched her push down and heard the snap of Lincoln's arm. He shrieked.

"Don't move, Lincoln," Will yelled.

"Yeah, Lincoln. Listen to your brother. He won't let me kill you, but I can still hurt you.

"Alex, you need to let him go."

"Take the gun off me, Detective, and I'll let him go."

"I can't do that."

She didn't move. He knew he was pushing his luck by cornering her, but he had no choice. He hoped she wouldn't strike out at him.

"Trust me, and I'll trust you." Stellar still couldn't read her face, but she was too dangerous to trust.

Blood dripped from the gash on her forehead and into her eyes. She didn't seem to notice. After a minute, she let go of Lincoln's arm. Stellar took a few steps closer, then lowered his weapon to his side.

"Get off him. Move to your left."

She stood and took two steps. "He killed Cole and Eddie."

"Get up and move to your left. Put your hands where I can see them."

"You're not going to arrest him for murder, are you?"

He looked at her, feeling her pain. "It's not my decision, Alex."

Her shoulders dropped. She took a step away from him. She held her hands up in front of her, but there was disappointment in her eyes.

"You're doing the right thing." Stellar holstered his weapon. "We still have the drugs. He's going to prison."

"No," Lincoln yelled. He jumped up and reached for Alex. She saw the move coming and shifted her weight.

Then she slipped in the mud and fell.

Will ran forward but was unable to catch her as she slipped from the cliff. Instead, he collapsed on Lincoln.

He didn't have the energy to handcuff his brother as he stared into the darkness.

"I'm sorry, Will. I'm sorry about Erika."

Stellar ignored him and strained to listen through the pouring rain. Alex had disappeared right in front of him, like a ghost.

"Will?"

He looked down at his broken brother. He was covered in mud and blood, crying. He was sorry about Erika, but not about the rest. Will tried to wipe the mud, but only accomplished smearing it further.

"It's okay, Lincoln."

He heard Ric come up behind him.

"Where's Alex?"

"The lake," Stellar said. The pouring rain whipped at his ears. "She slipped in the mud." He strained to see below, strained to hear the waves. "I can't see her."

"You got a lighter?" Ric asked.

Stellar searched Lincoln and found the lighter he always carried. "I don't think it's going to help. She won't be able to see down there."

Ric turned to run back from where he had come.

Chapter 51

Alex felt as if she had just woken from a long sleep. Disoriented, she opened her eyes but saw only darkness all around. She tried to breathe but inhaled water.

Panic had her kicking her feet for the surface. She came up for air and coughed out water.

She couldn't remember how she got there. It was pitch dark. She couldn't see her hand in front of her face. And she had no idea where she was. She tried desperately to remember how she had ended up in the water. Another blackout and another piercing headache. She remembered the accident in Stellar's truck. She remembered Stellar's betrayal and her brother's face, bloodied and swollen. She remembered staring into the barrel of a gun. Then everything was black.

Raindrops kicked up from the water and splashed into her face.

She was alone. She was always alone. When her mother had died, her father had deserted her. Left her to fend for herself. Her father's death had pushed her brother further away.

Alone.

Even when she married Nick, she had been alone in that house while he traveled from business trip to business trip. She had been left alone in the bar. No one had come for her—except Davy. He had left her alone in a dirty construction site. She had been freezing then, alone and enraged. Yet she fought back. Every time, she had fought back.

Alex kicked her sore legs and tried to get her bearings. The rain was still falling, but she could tell the storm was fading. She hadn't heard the thunder, hadn't seen the lightning.

She tasted the bitter, musty water.

She tasted blood.

Reaching up to her head, she felt the sting as she touched the left side of her face. She had hit her head or someone had hit her. Had she been shot? She took stock of the rest of her body. Her wrist was hurting and her knuckles were sore. Her head continued to throb, but she could breathe.

Still not knowing where she was, she shivered as the water suddenly turned ice-cold. She knew the signs of shock. She needed to remain calm, but panic gripped her throat. She could fight, if given the chance, but who was she fighting against? She couldn't see. She couldn't hear. She was alone in the dark with no one to fight.

Closing her eyes, she prayed for death to take her. She felt herself falling away, sinking in the water. Her head dunked under, and instead of fear, she felt comfort as everything became silent.

She was back in the parking lot with gravel in her face. Alone and in pain, hoping for the blackness to come.

Her muscles relaxed as she fell further. She saw her brother's face. He spoke to her. *We're in this together now.* She tried to shake the image away, but the image changed to Dade. *You don't have to fight alone.*

But they weren't there. She felt the silence engulf her as the water swirled around her.

Then she heard Stellar's words. *If you want to control something, control yourself.*

Pain gnawed at her chest.

She opened her eyes and felt the burn in her chest as she charged up for life. She surfaced and felt the warm air on her face. She coughed up water. Her chest stung as she inhaled.

It was too dark to see, and she heard nothing but rain smacking the water. Listening more closely, she heard the waves crashing against the rocks. She knew she was in the lake, but on the map the lake had seemed large. She looked up into the darkness. She couldn't see the top of the cliff and knew if she was going to survive, she had to swim.

She kept the crashing waves to her left and swam parallel to the cliff. At some point, she would find a shore without the rocky cliff. She just had to keep swimming and hope she found it before her body gave out.

Her head throbbed. Her wrist hurt with every stroke. She kicked at the waves.

Every so often, she stopped and listened. The rain slowed, making it easier to hear. She thought she heard voices, and she screamed. Only the waves replied.

Feeling as if she were going insane, she continued to swim. Her arms burned, but she pushed on. She couldn't control the water or the rain. She couldn't control her sight, but she could control her muscles. So she forced them on.

She saw the flash of light first then jerked up at the sound of an explosion. She squinted as her eyes adjusted to the light. A huge fireball jumped into the sky above her, and she saw the cliff and the outline of the lake. Her ears were ringing and her head was aching, but she tried to focus. Taking the time to catch her breath, she looked back at the direction she was swimming and saw the pier. She could smell the smoke now and thought of her brother. Ric had always wanted to blow something up.

Alex called out, but she couldn't hear her own voice. She screamed again, calling out for help. She was about to give up and start swimming toward the pier when she felt two large arms encircling her. She attempted to fight them off, but then she saw Stellar's face.

"I got you," he said.

Then everything went black.

Chapter 52

Alex couldn't sleep. After three hot showers, she still couldn't fight off the cold that grasped at her throat. She dressed in her warmest sweats and drowned herself in blankets. Several shots of tequila held the chills at bay.

Her answering machine held several messages from Detective Stellar and Sheriff Mack, another message from Liam, the bartender, and one from Detective Ryan Dade. She didn't return any of the calls.

Exhaustion consumed her, but she still couldn't sleep. When she closed her eyes, the darkness threatened to engulf her.

As she watched the sun creep into her room, she kicked off the covers and pulled herself out of bed. Her reflection in the mirror showed a purple bruise surrounding the cut on her forehead and large bags under her eyes. She dragged a hand through her hair. She took another hot shower, pulled on the sweats again, and walked downstairs to relieve Ric.

Ric didn't comment on her appearance. He switched off his movie and walked out without a word. He was mad at her for putting her life at risk, but the argument would come later. He enjoyed stewing about it, so she let him go.

She glanced in the reservation book. They were expecting a guest later in the day. A woman. She glanced at the landscape estimates but gave up on making a decision. Grabbing her sunglasses, she walked out to sit near the pool.

She pulled on her sweater and listened to the desert surrounding her. She watched the sunrise. She couldn't remember the last time she had been able to do that. The clouds were gone, and only a brisk breeze remained from the storm the night before. She wondered what the weather was like in Los Angeles.

She couldn't help but think about Ryan Dade. He had surprised her with his visit and torn open old wounds. Then he had returned to Los Angeles without saying anything about her decision to stay.

She wanted to try to build a new life. Going back to Los Angeles wasn't an option. She no longer felt alone in the desert, but she wasn't ready to call the place home.

A bird landed beside her. Alex stared at the sky-blue plumage, entranced by its purity.

"Aren't you beautiful?" she whispered.

The bird watched her as it walked around the pool's edge. Every two steps, it stopped to look at her, cocked its head, and moved on. Alex smiled as it moved closer to her. She remained motionless, hoping the bird would inch even closer. It flapped a wing, as if waving hello.

It continued around the lip of the pool and then back toward her. Then it stopped and took a few steps back. It tilted its head again, looking past her.

"It's the mountain bluebird. Males have all the color."

Alex turned to see Detective Stellar standing outside the pool gate. His arms rested on the gate as he stared at her with his deep blue eyes. She hadn't heard his car approach. She felt a chill run through her and pulled the sweater more tightly around her waist.

"We get a lot of them in the summer months," he said. "Especially after a good rain. They kill the annoying insects. Some say the bird comes straight from heaven. The blue comes from the clearest Nevada summer sky." He paused. "I'm rambling," he muttered, then shrugged. "That's what my father used to say."

She didn't know what to say.

He smirked at her obvious uneasiness. "Nice sweater."

She looked at the parking lot.

"Nice truck," she said finally, eyeing the red Escalade. It looked similar to the one she had destroyed only a day earlier.

He didn't look back. Just smiled and shrugged again. "I have another at home just like it."

He opened the gate and walked toward her. She didn't move. He squatted and grabbed her chin, turning her face to get a better view. "How are you?"

"I'm fine." She pulled her head back, breaking his touch. She didn't want him inspecting her bruises.

He stood but kept his eyes on her. "Where's Ric?"

"Sleeping. How's Erika?"

She saw the hesitation in his eyes. He was just as uncomfortable as she was. He looked away, squinting at the rising sun. He rubbed his hand. "Same as you, pretending to be fine. I'm heading over to see her in a little bit. Detective Dade?"

"Back in L.A."

He turned to watch the bird. She felt the silent awkwardness but said nothing. She waited for him to say what he had come to say.

"I wanted to give you an update on Lincoln."

"Don't tell me you released him because you couldn't get a positive ID."

He shook his head and looked back at her, revealing a hint of a smile. He slipped on his sunglasses.

"Despite losing the drug lab, both he and A. J. will be spending some time in prison. Both signed written confessions last night. State police are taking over the case. They'll want to talk to you and Ric today."

Alex nodded.

"I'm meeting with the DA this afternoon; she'll probably go light on Lincoln."

She noticed he wasn't wearing his badge. Or his gun.

"Are you okay with that?"

He shrugged. "It's my job to arrest them and step back. Even if it's family. I was up all night battling between him and my mother."

"So you didn't sleep?"

He shook his head. "You neither?"

She shrugged.

"He's not a bad person, my brother. He just has different priorities. He truly thought he would be helping people. A. J. made him believe he would be doing good."

"I'm not sorry for breaking his arm."

"I didn't think you would be. Do you remember attacking him?"

She shook her head. They fell silent for a moment.

"Is that it?" she said. "Just here to pass on the update?"

He didn't answer for a minute. She searched his face but couldn't read it. She wondered if that was the reason for the sunglasses.

He reached into his pocket and pulled out a piece of paper. "I just wanted to drop this off."

She took it without touching his hand. An address. "What's this?"

"Davy Knight's mother. I've already talked to your parole officer. He agrees it would be a good idea."

She looked at him. "Why?"

"It'll help you sleep."

She didn't know what to say.

"Welcome to Lake City, Alex."

She watched him glide across the sun-baked lot back to his truck. She looked toward the pool, but the bluebird had flown away.

Breinigsville, PA USA
02 August 2010
242897BV00002B/12/P